KENTUCKY FLAME

BLUEGRASS REUNION SERIES -
BOOK 4

JAN SCARBROUGH

SADDLE HORSE PRESS

Copyright © 2018 Jan Scarbrough
Scarbrough, Jan
Kentucky Flame
Media > Books > Fiction > Romance Novels
Category/Tags: American Saddlebred, World Champion Horse
Show, flame of love, horse trainer, secret daughter, adoption

Print ISBN: 978-0-9992474-1-9
1st Digital Release: September, 2018
1st Print Release October, 2018

Edited by Karen Block
Cover Design by The Killion Group Inc.

This edition is published by agreement with Saddle Horse Press, PO Box 221543, Louisville, KY 40252.

Dedication

For Cindy, Sharon, and Sarah, who taught me how to ride American Saddlebreds. The loving came naturally.

And for the American Saddlebred horses I have owned: Mr. Too Little, Royal Tierra, and Starhart's Heritage

Chapter One

Royalty Farm
Near Simpsonville, Kentucky
Saturday afternoon

A cold, black dread gripped Melody O'Shea. Hands tight on the steering wheel, she scarcely breathed. In the distance, a thin plume of smoke floated from a window of Royalty Farm's main show barn.

Fire was a horseman's worst nightmare.

Her Jeep Cherokee slammed to a complete stop in the parking lot. Mel flung open the door and sprinted toward the barn. "Fire!"

A wiry groom poked his head out of the tack room, bridle in hand, shock in his eyes. "Mel, is that you? What's going on?"

"Fire!" she shouted over sounds of panicked horses. "Dave, call 911!"

Lifting the water hose off a nearby rack, Mel raised the pump handle and hoisted the heavy rolls of tubing on to her shoulder. The watering system was used for filling water buckets, not for fighting fires. Jerking the clumsy hose down the hazy aisle of the training barn, Mel settled her intent gaze on the end stall where flames traced their liquid fingers along the sides of the wall.

Trapped horses snorted and circled in their stalls, rearing to get out of the smoke only to stick their heads into the thickest part of the fumes. She heard the sharp complaint of a hoof striking a wooden wall. Another primal scream echoed her fears of the deadly smoke and flames.

Already her nostrils stung from the acrid smoke. What if she couldn't put out the fire?

She had to. There was too much at stake.

1

"Okay. Easy, easy," Mel said to herself, knowing it wasn't okay.

Her words were as worthless as the thin stream of water she shot at the flames. The noxious, gut-wrenching heat was intense. It radiated from a fire she couldn't control. Mel's arms throbbed. Her eyes burned. This was unreal. It wasn't happening. It happened on television or in books where heroic cowboys rescued horses from flaming barns. Other barns burned. Not Royalty Farm's prime training barn.

The old groom's fingers were steel on her arm. "Mel, we can't save it."

"No!"

"C'mon, there's not much time. We need to get the horses out!"

God help them. Dave was right.

"Okay!"

Dave thrust a lead into her hand, and Mel threw down the hose. Coughing, her eyes tearing from the smoke, she took the stall nearest the flames. *Dreamcatcher.* Pop had pegged the stallion his next World's Grand Champion.

Fortunately, the horse wore a halter. Mel snapped the lead to it. Then she stripped off her polo shirt and tied it around Dreamcatcher's eyes. Grasping the lead with sweaty palms, she pulled and coaxed the frightened horse from the stall, down the long aisle into the waiting daylight and fresh air. Outside, she led the stallion to an empty paddock, where she stripped the shirt from his head, let him go, and firmly shut the gate.

Gulping in fresh air, her lungs stinging, Mel turned back to the barn. Other farm workers had joined the struggle—dark, silent forms silhouetted against the blazing inferno. Flying brands made a bizarre sparkler affect in the cloudless sky.

"Oh, my God," she gasped.

Black shapes ran in and out of the barn, calling out in panic, their strident voices heard above the death screams of the horses.

"Don't just stand there. Move your sorry ass!" a voice roared at Mel from behind.

"What?"

"Help, for God's sake. The whole thing's going up!"

Anger held her immobile for a split second as she glared at the back of the nasty-tongued man who disappeared into the barn. She took a gulp of air, determination steeling her heart. The barn *was* going fast.

Running back into the nightmare, Mel ducked the smoke rushing to meet her. The odor of smoldering wood and electric wires and the stench of burning horseflesh engulfed her. At the far end, the barn was now being consumed. Fierce flames licked the aisle. She ran to the first occupied stall and tried to avoid the heavy smoke overhead.

A big gelding flailed wildly in his stall, the whites of his eyes rolling. Mortally afraid, he screamed as she approached. Mel grabbed the bolt on the door, threw it back, and shoved it open.

"Easy. Easy, boy."

The horse wore no halter. With no choice, Mel shooed him from the stall, running after him toward the wide open door nearby. The horse turned and tried to return to what he perceived as the safety of his stall. Mel raised her arms, waving the lead line and her shirt. She shouted until her throat hurt. The gelding veered and bolted through the opening into freedom.

In the next stall, another horse stomped and trumpeted, his chestnut head thrown high in fright, his delicate nostrils flaring. The animal refused to come out. Mel dodged his flying hooves to chase him out of the stall. Once in the aisle, she smacked his rump, hoping he'd make it to the door.

Then she turned toward the tunnel of fire that was swallowing the old wooden structure. She moved in a trance. Overhead, the rafters raged. In only minutes, the yellow fire would take the whole barn.

The angry-voiced man jogged past leading two horses. "Get the hell out!"

Not yet. No. Mel ground her teeth together. Pop had worked too hard for this place. She had to save one more.

Stooping low, she staggered across the smoke-clogged aisle to the stall where Royalty's Dreamer stood.

"Royalty!"

The black mare snorted at the sound of her name.

Thank God she wore a halter. Mel buckled on the lead and draped the shirt over the mare's face. Clutching the leather, she hauled the horse from the stall. Royalty tossed her head, wrenching Mel's shoulder and pulling the lead through her hands. Mel grabbed it and held on.

"No! You can't go back to the stall!"

Tears blurred her eyes. Her lungs complained against the dense smoke. The open end of the barn seemed so far away.

"Give me that damn horse and get out." The rude stranger grabbed the lead from her hand and shoved her toward the door. Mel blinked and stumbled. He caught her elbow and steadied her.

Jake?

4

Something about the way his fingers grasped her bare flesh, the way her body fit by his side, made her think of the man she once wanted to marry.

They made it to the door just as the hayloft collapsed behind them.

"I'll take the mare." Her father's calm, familiar voice was a welcome haven.

"Here you go, Pop." Jake thrust the lead into Pop's outstretched hands and turned back to the barn.

Mel stared after him. Then wracked by a cough, she bent double, and grasping her knees with aching hands, forced clean air into her lungs.

"You okay, darlin'?"

"You shouldn't be here, Pop," she said between gasps.

"Ain't in my grave yet."

Still doubled over, Mel lifted her head in time to see her father guide the spooked mare away. His words were brave, but she knew the old trainer's heart must be breaking. Forty years of work at Royalty Farm was going up in flames. It may have been Bert Noble's farm, but Pop's knowledge and ability had built it into the greatest American Saddlebred show stable in the country. What waste. What heartache. She fought a sick feeling in the pit of her stomach.

Long moments later, Mel stood up and reluctantly turned to look at the chaos around the burning barn. As she watched, flames blasted from the walls like a blowtorch. *Oh, God!*

She shivered. Overhead, a blistering summer sun glinted like a horrible specter, but she was cold, colder than she'd ever been in her life. She staggered because of the smell of smoke and death. In the distance, a fire siren screamed.

Slow tears trailed down her cheeks. Mel swiped the back of her gritty hand across her eyes. Shouts from the frantic men obscured the sickening silence of doomed horses. Had they saved them all? How had this happened?

"Bring that hose over here, Sam!"

"You can't go in there, Jake! It's too late!"

It *was* Jake Hendricks.

Mel swallowed the knot that rose in her throat. Her breath came unevenly. Dazed and shaken by the irony that she'd come home at the same time as Jake, Mel tried to pull herself together.

She'd fallen off many horses in her twenty-eight years. When that happened, she always gathered her courage and climbed back on. Now, she fought for the same control, raising her chin and reining in her sudden panic.

If Jake was at the farm, how long would it be before he learned about Cory?

* * *

An hour later the shell that had once been the training barn smoldered. The stench of scorched wood and charred horseflesh lingered along with a dreadful silence. Firefighters still labored, turning streams of water on hot spots. Feeling like a wet rag wrung out and tossed aside, Mel trembled from loss of adrenalin. She'd hardly had the strength to find a clean shirt in the suitcase in the trunk of her car and put it on.

Dave came up from behind her and patted her shoulder. "Damn sorry sight to see."

She turned to the former thoroughbred jockey who had been Pop's groom for twenty years. "Horrible." Her voice rasped from the smoke.

"Are you okay, Mel?"

6

"Sure, but what a fine homecoming." She shrugged at the sarcasm in her voice.

"Pop wasn't expecting you home until later tonight," Dave volunteered. "I'm glad you showed up when you did."

Mel glanced at him. His face was smudged from the smoke. She guessed hers looked the same. With his gray head and crinkled features, he seemed much older than his sixty-five years. Maybe that was the nature of the job. Caring for horses was hard work and a twenty-four-hour responsibility. Losing them must be even harder.

She changed the subject. "What's Jake Hendricks doing here?"

Dave refused to meet her questioning look. "I suppose Pop didn't want to tell you until you got here."

"Tell me what?"

"Jake's our new trainer." The ex-jockey let his hand drop.

"Why do we need a new trainer?"

"Pop's heart attack." Dave shrugged. "I told Pop you wouldn't be happy about it."

Mel fought to remove the shock from her face. "Why shouldn't I be happy?"

Dave shuffled his feet, looking down at the dirt. "You two were an item back when he was here last."

"That was over and done with a long, long time ago," Mel said, trying to hide the sudden tension she felt. She glanced at the smoking rubble. "So, Jake's dream has finally come true. He always wanted to train at Royalty Farm. I must congratulate him."

"You may get the chance." Dave nodded at the lone figure walking toward them. "Here he comes."

7

A man had separated himself from the milling firefighters and walked across the gravel parking lot holding a leather lead shank in his hands. Mel had trouble breathing, and it wasn't from the smoke. She crossed her stomach with her arms. At thirty-one, Jake looked the same—tall and boyishly good-looking, even though his features were splotched with grime and his clothes covered with soot and sweat. As his crystal blue gaze raked over her, disturbing her, Mel wished she had a towel to wipe her face, knowing it must be dirty and streaked with tears. She wouldn't dare cry in front of this old "flame" of hers.

"Damn it, man," Jake said to Dave, "what in the world happened here?"

The rich timbre of Jake's voice caused waves of remembered longing to surge through Mel's body. His dimples, one in its proper place beside the right corner of his mouth and the other one placed high on his cheek under his left eye, were a reminder of other days. Once she had kissed those dimples, calling them gifts from angels. Once she had run her fingers through his sandy blond hair.

Mel drew a quick breath. God help her. She had thought her attraction to him all in the past. But he stood in front of her, bigger than life, and she was very much aware how mistaken she had been.

Jake had been the love of her life, and the feeling hadn't died.

"If I had my guess, I'd say spontaneous combustion." Dave shook his head. "The weather's been in the nineties for weeks and not a drop of rain."

Watching Mel, but not seeming to recognize her, Jake scraped a hand through his hair. "But how could it happen so fast? Why didn't anyone see it?"

"Mel saw it."

A slow glow of recollection lit Jake's eyes. "Mel? Is that really you? I didn't recognize you in all the commotion."

"Hello, Jake." Mel kept her reply steady.

"I thought you were living in Missouri."

His blunt statement rubbed Mel raw. When had he ever cared where she lived? He'd never come looking for her.

"I've come home." She lifted her chin and firmed her jaw. "I'm divorced finally."

"You are?" Jake seemed bewildered, his eyes softly unfocused. Then they hardened as he leveled a sharp gaze at her. "Was that you in the barn?"

"Yes."

"You could have gotten yourself killed!"

"Same for you."

"I had to do what I could do to save the horses." Jake slapped his leg with the leather lead.

Mel curled her fingers by her side. "Those horses are Pop's life. Did you expect me not to try to get them out?"

"No, it's where I think you'd be, but it was a damn fool thing to do," Jake acknowledged. "The paramedics treated me with oxygen. Did they treat you?"

"Yes."

Dave nodded at Mel. "She hurt her hands. Wouldn't let the medical guys see them."

Mel grimaced at Dave and then sighed. "They're okay. Just rope burns."

"Let me see." Jake tucked the lead line under his arm and reached for her closed fist.

Mel sucked in a breath. His fingers branded her wrist worse than any rope burn. She stared at the top of his blackened hands and found herself wanting to rub the back of his knuckles like she used to do.

"C'mon, let me see."

"Better get 'em tended to, Mel," Dave spoke up. "You were never one to complain."

Complain. No, Mel O'Shea had never been a complainer. She buckled down, accepted whatever came, and made the best of it. Now she tried to make the best of this awkward situation. Jake, his labored breathing betraying his own uneasiness, towered over her, but his touch was gentle. Too gentle. These were the same hands that, with the slightest pressure, could guide a thousand-pound horse or make love to a woman. Images of Jake and their first and only time together clouded her vision. They had been in the hay loft that April day. They had been young and in love and stupid, but it had been thrilling and beautiful just the same.

Mel relaxed. One by one, Jake uncurled her fingers until the palm of her hand lay open for his inspection.

"You need to have these treated."

Unbidden, other memories flashed in her mind. Like the flames that had once raged in the distance, her thoughts blazed clearly as she recalled how comfortable things used to be between them—before the hurt feelings and disappointments. Before he left Kentucky.

Mel jerked her hand out of his grasp.

"I'm sorry I yelled at you in there." Jake stepped back, putting space between them. "I didn't recognize you."

"That's okay. I wasn't expected this early."

"Frankly, Pop didn't tell me you were coming," Jake said with a shake of his head as if Pop had pulled a fast one. He turned to look back to the barn. "I've got Sam and some other men rounding up the horses we were lucky enough to turn loose. Dave, how many do you think we got out."

"How many did you save, Mel?" Dave asked.

"Four." It didn't seem enough.

Dave ticked off the numbers on his fingers. "I got out five and Sam two. What about you, Jake?"

"Five, I think."

"Sixteen." Dave's voice was grim as he made the final tally.

"Damn." Jake shoved his hand through his hair again. "Weren't twenty-four stalls occupied?"

"Yeah, sure were," Dave mumbled as if he didn't want to say it.

"We lost eight. Better start figuring out which ones, so we can tell Vanessa." Jake's tone was bitter. He slapped the lead shank hard against his leg again. "I sure hate telling my boss this on my second day on the job. And I don't buy this spontaneous combustion theory. Damn."

A sudden gnawing in her stomach made Mel nauseous. Something was wrong. Pop had always been careful to keep his barn clean. Even in hot weather, properly stored hay didn't ignite.

"What about Royalty's Reverie?" Mel asked, breaking the silence. She was afraid to hear the answer. The horse was a two-time Five-Gaited World's Grand Champion and the farm's breeding stallion.

"Yes, what about Reverie?" Jake aimed a hard look at the small groom. "He's out in the far pasture, isn't he?"

Dave scuffed the toe of his boot in the gravel. "I put him in the barn this morning. The farrier was coming out after lunch."

"Did we get him out?"

"I don't think so, but I'm not sure."

"Son of a bitch! Was he in there?" Jake pivoted and darted toward the barn.

"What's he going to do?" Dave muttered. "Raise the damn horse from ashes?"

Mel heard the guilt and anger in Dave's voice. She touched his arm. "Don't blame yourself."

It wasn't Dave's fault. No one was to blame. Yet, a cold, dead feeling settled around Mel's heart. How would her father take the news? The old stallion had been Pop's pride and joy. How would Jake cope with the loss of so many show horses and the famous stud? How would this tragedy affect Cory and her future?

Mel watched as two firemen wrestled Jake away from the smoking remains of the building, shoving him hard against a paddock fence.

"Fool youngster," Dave muttered beneath his breath as he left Mel's side. "There's nothing left in there."

But it was so like Jake. Impulsive. Headstrong. There was an animal quality about him like a wild stallion. Jake had become a man who liked to control his own fate. Mel had welcomed the raw, sexual power she felt radiating from him as he stood beside her only minutes earlier. What she resented was her reaction to his maleness. The fact that her attraction to him wasn't over.

Mel shivered and turned her back on the ravaged barn. Fate had taken charge of Jake's life, all their lives. Fate had destroyed something fine and beautiful—Reverie, the legacy that was

Royalty Farm. Her morbid thoughts obscured her vision. Or was it the tears pooling in her eyes?

Why did Mel have the uncomfortable feeling that destiny had, for some cruel reason, thrown her and Jake Hendricks together again?

Chapter Two

Had destiny brought Mel back to Royalty Farm?

Jake gazed out the library window toward the smoking shell that yesterday had been the farm's training barn. His mouth tasted like ashes and his head pounded. The fierce summer heat shining through the window pummeled his skin. Numb and exhausted, he shut his eyes against the sight. When he opened them, the barn was still a burned-out skeleton smoldering in the distance.

Mel. He hadn't recognized her at first. If he had, he would never have ordered her back into that burning barn. In the fleeting glance he'd given her, he thought she was another groom.

Later seeing her near the burning barn, her face covered with soot and smudged with tears, guilt and shock had punched his gut. What if she'd been hurt? He would never have forgiven himself.

Why had she come home? Because she was divorced?

Interesting. It must have happened recently, because he didn't know about it when he'd given up a good job in San Diego and taken the position here. Training at Royalty Farm had been his lifelong dream. He'd never thought of any place else as home.

Apparently, destiny hadn't brought Mel and him together again. It had probably been Pop O'Shea.

Vanessa Noble came up behind him, jerking him out of his daze. "How many horses did you say we lost, Jake?"

He directed a wary look at his boss. "Eight. Reverie was one of them."

The lines of her angular face stretched tight and her thin lips pursed with worry. She flicked a black strand of hair from her green catlike eyes. "I'm glad my father isn't alive to see this."

Shifting uneasily, Jake raked his fingers through his hair. "We did what we could."

"I know. I'm not blaming you." Vanessa shook her head. "Excuse me, will you? I need to phone the sheriff before Mel and Pop get here. I'll use my cell in the living room."

Vanessa might not blame him, Jake mused as she left the room, but he blamed himself. Surely, he could have done something more. All through a sleepless night he had relived the nightmare of the fire—the screams of frantic men and dying horses, the horrible stench of burning flesh. He had experienced over and over the nausea and numbness of destruction.

Leaving the window, Jake paced the confines of the library. This was still Bert Noble's room. It reflected his masculine presence even though the man had been dead for two years. His eldest daughter hadn't changed a thing.

Oversized, brown leather chairs dominated the decor, along with a massive walnut desk. Bookshelves, crammed with tarnished silver trophies and books on horse breeding lined two walls. Above the fireplace mantel hung an oil painting of Royalty's Reverie with a younger Pop O'Shea in the saddle. Horse and rider were making a victory pass at the World's Grand Championship at the Kentucky State Fair. The artist had painted the stallion's eyes gleaming with the look of eagles as Pop proudly presented the horse with the winning tri-colored ribbon in his brow band.

Jake gazed raptly at the painting. The stallion had been the prime example of an American Saddlebred. Pioneers had called them "Kentucky Saddlers." These splendid animals had helped settle the early American frontier. They had carried soldiers into battle during the Civil War. Today they were show horses, pleasure mounts, and sport horses.

Jake loved the breed as much as he had once loved Mel.

The errant thought drew him up sharply. He forced himself to focus on the picture. Reverie had been a once-in-a-lifetime show horse, but now the old stallion was dead. It didn't seem possible.

"Hello again, Jake."

Jake turned, and his verbal response died on his lips. Mel had paused at the threshold as if she was afraid to enter the room with him standing there alone. Something tightened in his chest. He gritted his teeth. She didn't look like the hired help he'd assumed her to be in the barn yesterday at the height of the fire. She was beautiful. More beautiful than he remembered.

In the shafts of late morning light flooding from the picture window, her cascade of dark auburn hair gleamed with red highlights, creating a dramatic frame for her fair oval face. Her hazel eyes sparkled under curling black lashes. Caution was written in her expression, and as she tilted her chin upward, a look of wariness shadowed her eyes. She was petite and dainty still, with an air of quiet dignity and reserve about her. Wearing her Kentucky jodhpurs as if she had been born in them, she seemed molded inside the gray riding pants that clung to her hips and knees, tapering down her legs, and flaring around black, ankle-high riding boots like sixties bellbottoms.

For a moment, tension shimmered between them.

Mel drew herself up, tossed her hair out of her eyes, and walked into the room with an air of confidence. Jake extended his hand to greet her. This was ridiculous. He was acting as if they had never meant anything to each other, never been lovers. Realizing his palm was damp, Jake wiped it on the leg of his jodhpurs before he again put out his hand.

Mel's eyes were unreadable. Their gazes connected just as their hands touched.

Her palm was covered with a white bandage.

He slowly turned it over. "Mel? I thought your hands were okay."

"They're fine," Mel deliberately pulled her hand from his grasp and walked away. "But Pop insisted on bandaging them." She paused and turned back to him. "I'm surprised to see you back in Kentucky. I assumed you liked California," she said with a trace of sarcasm in her voice. Something akin to anger flickered into her eyes.

Yes, that old battle was still there. Not that he wasn't surprised. After all, he'd never asked her to marry him and instead left Kentucky for a job in California. But that was ten years ago. Surely there'd been time for old wounds to heal.

"I couldn't pass up this opportunity." He met her challenge with a slight smile. "I said I'd be back someday."

"Yes you did."

She turned abruptly and crossed to an empty chair. Seating herself, she crossed her right leg over her left knee. The tip of her booted foot jutted from beneath her jodhpurs, and she raised her eyes to survey him from beneath her black lashes.

He'd been right not to marry her back then. She'd been too young. So had he. Although they'd never communicated after his move west, Jake knew about Mel's four-year equestrian degree from William Woods College in Missouri. He'd read about her career many times in the various horse-show publications, and her fine wins at big shows in Kansas City and Louisville were legendary.

"Jake!" Pop shuffled into the library, breaking the uneasy silence.

"Pop." Jake stepped forward, hand outstretched. The old man's fingers gripped his like the talons of a great bird.

"I'm glad you're here," the old trainer said.

Jake was touched. "I'm sorry I couldn't do more yesterday."

Pop settled down in one of the chairs facing Vanessa's desk and cleared his throat. "The horse business is tough."

"As we all know," Jake said with a wry smile. He moved toward an empty chair as Vanessa came into the room.

"I could use a stiff drink." His new boss walked to the window and glanced at the charred ruins of the barn. "The state police think it was arson."

Jake sat down with a whoof. A knife-like pain shot through him, and he gripped the arms of the chair.

"Who'd do such a thing?" Mel's question met a painful silence.

After a long pause, Vanessa turned to face them and shook her head. "They haven't a clue."

"Could be those scalawags at Neely Hills," Pop spoke up. "They were always jealous of us. Tried to cheat me out of a decent mare last year."

Vanessa's expression was forlorn. "I really don't think Jim Neely would be involved in something so heinous."

"Maybe it's those real estate developers you told me about, Pop," Jake suggested.

Mel sat forward in her chair. "What do you mean?"

"Land's valuable. Even out here in Simpsonville." Pop shrugged his shoulders. "Seen all them fancy subdivisions out there just past Middletown? The city of Louisville is a comin' this way. Development. Progress. Damn shame."

"Are you saying developers want to buy Royalty Farm?"

"Yes, they've offered," Vanessa said, "but let's not speculate about how this happened. It won't do us any good until we learn more from the police."

"Damn right," Pop agreed. "Thing is, we gotta go on. What ya' gonna do now, boy?" He turned to Jake with a lift of a busy eyebrow. "Got any plans?"

"Winning this year's World's Grand Championship. That's what I was brought here to do."

Pop grinned and slapped his hand on his knee. "Damn me, boy. I knew you were a man right after my own heart."

Vanessa shook her head. "I see no way we can even go to Lexington tomorrow like we planned."

"Harrumph." Pop blew out a breath of air. "What do you do when you fall off a horse, honey?"

"You get right back on," Mel offered softly before Vanessa answered.

Pop nodded his head, his white hair as short and as blunt as his words. "Yes, damn me. You get right back on, pick up the reins, and go on with the show."

"But, Pop," Vanessa interrupted. "Jake told me all our tack was destroyed. Where will we get saddles and bridles? I don't have enough ready cash right now to replenish our equipment."

Pop turned to look with sympathy at his employer. "I know you don't, honey, but we've got friends. The Saddlebred community will come through for us. Our friends will loan us the tack we need."

They sat quietly a moment digesting Pop's words. A niggling bit of optimism seeped into Jake's heart. The Junior League Horse Show in Lexington was a major event. They needed to be there.

"Which horses do we take, Pop?" Jake asked. "I just got here, remember? You know 'em better than I do."

"Got the horse for ya'," Pop said with another nod. "A big bay son-of-a-gun we call Dreamcatcher."

"Out of Reverie's last good crop of foals, by a Supreme Halo mare," Mel stated quietly.

Jake cocked his head toward her. She smiled at him a little too sweetly. By that look she was letting him know she'd kept up with Pop's operation even if he hadn't.

Vanessa scanned the list of deceased horses. "We saved him?"

Pop puffed up like a proud peacock. "Mel did."

Jake tossed Mel another glance, and she returned it with that same look of annoyance. What was wrong with her? This wasn't a competition.

"He trots like a dream," Pop said, "and his slow gait is perfection. He's comin' on well and should be ready in time for Louisville."

Jake hesitated, absorbing Pop's information. "So we go to Lexington on Sunday?"

"Damn right. Lexington and then Shelbyville. Those two shows should set us up right for the championship in August." When no one spoke up, Pop cleared his throat again. "With all respect to you, Vanessa." He nodded his head in her direction. "I know it's tough for you right now, moneywise. And this fire is gonna set you back even more."

Vanessa nodded, agreeing. "I *have* been stressed financially. I expect insurance will pay for the barn, but you know I couldn't afford to insure the young horses." She circled the desk to come closer to them. Sitting against its edge, she rested her hands on the polished wood. "Do you have a suggestion?"

"The Five-Gaited World's Grand Championship is the key," Pop told them. "We gotta win it. If Dreamcatcher does it, his stud career is assured. We'll have customers knocking at our door for his services. With Jake here takin' my place and Mel here to help him, we can start bringin' in payin' clients."

Vanessa looked intrigued. "You mean train other people's horses?"

"Yep. An' they'll pay handsomely for it too."

"But, Pop, Royalty Farm has always been private," Mel protested.

Jake was surprised too. Pop O'Shea was talking about transforming Bert Noble's farm into a commercial operation. Nevertheless, Jake liked what the canny old trainer said because he was used to training horses for wealthy clients.

"Times are changin', darlin'. Folks gotta diversify to survive. Might have had a chance if it wasn't for losing so many horses. Money don't come easy around here anymore." Pop glanced at Vanessa for confirmation.

"Pop, you are astute," she said with affection.

"Don't know about that." Pop shrugged off the compliment. "I do know we can't be countin' on just one horse. Gotta double our chances."

Vanessa leaned forward. "What do you mean?"

"Gotta have another horse ready for the championship." Pop's look was shrewd. "Royalty's Dreamer. That little black mare is fine as crystal. We'll show her in the open classes, and if she wins or places well in the qualifier, we'll show her in the Saturday night stake with Dreamcatcher. We'll have two horses in the World's Grand Championship and a better chance to win."

Jake didn't like the swerve his stomach took. "Open classes?"

"Yep. Mel will ride the mare. She's got mighty fine credentials, don't ya' know? Did a bang-up job for Mrs. Pepperdine in Missouri, until she decided to come home to take care of her old man. Damn glad she did too." Pop nodded his head and patted Mel's hand.

Could Vanessa afford to hire two trainers at Royalty Farm? But, Jake had to admit to himself his sudden fear was more than concern for Vanessa's finances. Could he handle seeing Mel each day, working with her as if there had never been anything between them?

"Finally got rid of that scoundrel she was married to," Pop went on when Jake and Vanessa didn't speak up. "Never did like that guy."

Mel frowned at her father. "Pop."

He waved Mel's objection off with a flick of his hand. "Hold your horses. I told you not to marry that guy, but you got a mind of your own. Now seein' that Jake here is gonna be in charge, now that I'll be put out to pasture so to speak, the boy here can use another pair of hands."

Mel sought confirmation from the farm's new trainer. "I don't believe Jake has any plans to ask for my help."

Jake's lips tightened. The old man was putting him in an awkward position, and what aggravated him worse was Pop knew what he was doing. He could very well use another trainer, but to ask Mel, who sat with her jodhpur-clad legs crossed revealing a delicious expanse of taut thigh beneath the stretchy fabric, was asking for trouble. He swallowed hard and glanced around him, his gaze finally coming to rest on Mel again. Her eyes were narrowed, daring him.

There'd been bad blood between them when he didn't ask her to marry him after they made love in the hayloft that sunny day ten years ago. It had been her first time and he imagined he had set up a certain expectation. Could he risk taking her on with so much at stake for the farm? He didn't need a disgruntled old flame to deal with when he had so much responsibility on his hands.

"I'll have to defer to Vanessa, Pop. With the fire, I don't know if we can afford more help," he said.

Rubbing his chin, Pop glanced sideways at his daughter and back at the farm's owner. "Don't know. Seems to me two chances to win the big one would be better for the farm than one. Won't have to be for long. Couple of months."

Mel stood up. "Jake has made up his mind."

"Now don't go cutting out on me, Mel," Pop complained, placing a hand on her wrist and forcing her to sit down. "The boy needs more hands and legs for what he wants to do if he's gonna rebuild this place into the best damn show barn in the country."

"But it already is the best show barn in the country," Mel argued.

"Hasn't been in years. Just wouldn't admit it," Pop went on, looking from Mel to Jake. "You need a good trainer, boy, and Mel's the girl for you. Looks like a marriage made in heaven."

The words that slipped so easily from Pop's mouth shocked even Jake. The old guy always ran at the mouth a bit, but now he'd really put his foot in it. Jake felt sorry for him, because Pop realized his mistake and appeared embarrassed. Mel had gone pale. Her teeth gnawed the corner of her lower lip. She took a deep breath and stood again, drawing herself up to her full, though diminutive, height. Resentment filled the gaze she cast at him.

"Look, I came home to do what I could to help my father and this farm. I didn't know you had hired Jake. If I'm not wanted here, I can certainly find a job elsewhere." Mel circled the chair to put it between her and the others. She clutched its back as if to keep from fleeing the room.

Dismayed, Jake drummed his fingers on the arms of his chair.

"Well," Vanessa drawled. She circled the desk and sat behind it.

For once, Pop held his peace. No one seemed to know what to say. Silence settled intensely around them.

"I think Pop may be right," Vanessa finally said. She tapped her fingertips on the desktop. "For the time being, that is."

Jake inhaled deeply. His gaze shifted among the three of them. He wasn't a quitter. They had a slim chance to rebuild from the ashes of total ruin. Did he take it? With Mel? She had become a fractious filly. He liked the change. Maybe he shouldn't quit on Mel either. A gush of excitement shot through Jake's veins as his competitive spirit burst into life.

"Okay, Pop. Let's go for it."

"That's my boy!" Pop said with a smile.

"I don't have a say in this?" Mel asked in an indignant tone.

Pop brushed aside her objection. "Got any better plans for your future?"

25

"Pop!" Vanessa scolded. "Whatever you may think, Mel is not a child. She can decide for herself what she wants to do, but I'll be glad to have her on our team if she wants to stay."

Jake found himself holding his breath. What would Mel do?

* * *

The library door burst open and a white and black dog bounded through it. A dirty little girl with sandy blond hair and big blue eyes closely followed the English setter into the room.

Mel's heart twisted, and she gripped the back of the chair even tighter. She'd always worried about Cory finding out the truth about her real mother. How that would affect Cory? Now being here with Jake, having a conversation as if they had no past and no history, was tough enough. Seeing Cory in the same room with him was a nightmare. Mel had known coming home would be no picnic.

"Pop!" The child, all legs and arms, threw herself into Pop's lap and hugged his grizzled neck.

"Hold your horses, darlin'. You're like a runaway filly." The old man tried to sound tough, but Mel saw his eyes soften and his arms creep around the bundle of energy.

Fighting the emotion that threatened to give herself away, she ignored Jake's speculative glance.

"Cory, don't jump on Pop like that," Vanessa chided. "Remember he's been in the hospital."

Cory's dimpled and adoring smile beamed at the gruff trainer. "Oh, sis, he don't mind."

"*Doesn't* mind," Vanessa corrected. "And take those boots off right now. There's horse manure all over them!"

Pop wagged his finger. "You act like a mother hen to this child, Vanessa."

26

"Well, I don't want Cory growing up like a wild street urchin. She's my responsibility now that our parents are gone."

Cory spotted Mel. Disregarding the talk around her, she jumped out of Pop's lap, dirty boots and all, and planted herself right in front of Mel's chair, looking up at her with keen eyes that mirrored Mel's own. "Hi ya', Mel. Pop said you're home to stay. Can you give me a riding lesson today?"

"I don't know about being home to stay, but I certainly can give you a lesson. Not today, though. Soon." Mel had always cherished these riding lessons. They gave her a chance to spend quality time with her child even though the danger of Cory learning the truth was always in the back of Mel's mind.

"Great! You sure were brave yesterday. Thanks for savin' the horses." She quickly turned her attention to Jake. "You're Jake Hendricks. I'm Corrine Noble. I'm adopted. Vanessa's my big sister. I know all about you."

"You do?"

Mel's fingers stiffened when Jake turned his dimpled smile toward the little girl. His blue eyes gleamed with amusement.

"Yeah, an' I know you're here to take Pop's place, an' I know you trained Stone Davidson's horses out there in Hollywood."

Stone Davidson happened to be the most popular rock star for young preteens. That he rode and showed American Saddlebreds doubly endeared him to Cory.

"You're right on all accounts, Miss Noble." Jake gave her a formal nod.

"Hey, you're cute too. Pop didn't tell me that."

"Not somethin' I'd think to tell a nine-year-old, now is it, darlin'?" The old trainer clambered to his feet. "You come along out of here, will ya', youngster? Your sister don't want a mess in

27

the house. I've told you time an' again to wipe your feet before you come inside. And take Major with you." He pointed at the dog then extended his hand to the child.

She clasped Pop's hand and together they left, the dog romping at their heels.

"What a pair." Vanessa sighed. "Pop accuses me of spoiling Cory, but he's no better."

"They've gotten really close," Mel mused. Vanessa Noble had been Mel's first playmate. They'd grown up together on the farm. The owner's daughter and the daughter of the horse trainer had learned to ride on the same old spotted pony.

"Yes, especially after my father died." Vanessa said. "I thought Cory took my mother's death hard but not as hard as my dad's. Pop sort of stepped in to fill his shoes."

Jake came to his feet. "I've never seen that side of Pop."

Vanessa glanced up at Mel. "Isn't that strange? He never was one to show his softer emotions, even to you, Mel. It's almost as if he has a special bond with that child."

Vanessa was right, but she didn't know it. Neither did Pop. He was unaware of the truly special bond he had with Cory. A knot of fear wrenched Mel's stomach. Her fingers bit deeper into the fabric of the chair as she took a quick look at Jake. He was watching her through half-closed eyes, measuring her.

"What are you staring at?"

A crooked, teasing smile spread across his face, his dimples blatant. He took a step toward her. "I was wondering if you were going to work with me."

Trying to act nonchalant, Mel shrugged. "I haven't made up my mind."

28

"Fair enough," Vanessa cut in. "Remember, Mel, I'll be glad to have you help as long as you can. After the championship, I'll understand if you make other plans."

"Thanks, Vanessa. I'll let you know what I decide."

Turning on her heel, Mel left the library and the big house. Outside, the morning heat and humidity sucked the breath from her. She paused to adjust to it.

Jake came up beside her. "I'm glad you waited for me."

"You assume a lot. I was just catching my breath." Mel started down the gravel driveway.

Jake lengthened his strides to catch her. "Once you would have waited for me."

"That was a long time ago."

"I have a long memory."

Mel tried to ignore him and his very real presence beside her. The atmosphere grew even hotter. She had a good memory too. She remembered spending lazy summer days watching Pop's new assistant trainer exercise horses. One day from astride a young mare, he had looked down at her. His shirt deliciously open at the neck and his sleeves rolled up revealing the muscles of his arms, the sun glinting behind him, Jake had smiled at her. His dimples had dazzled her, his smile had enthralled her, and the approval in his eyes had swept her away. At eighteen, she had fallen head over heels in love.

Six months later Jake had left for a job in California, telling her they were too young to get married—telling her this was a great opportunity for him—telling her to go to college like her father had planned for her to do.

That was so long ago.

"Wait, Mel. We were too young." Jake caught her arm and swung her around to face him. "Don't let what happened between us years ago affect your decision today."

Mel tossed off his hand. "I think I'm mature enough now not to let that happen."

When he didn't say anything, just watched her, Mel tried to apologize for her curtness. "I came home to help my dad. I've just gotten divorced. My emotions are on edge. This fire and talk about arson have me on edge as well."

Jake backed away. "You're right. I have no business hassling you."

"No, you don't." She turned and strode away.

"I'm sorry it didn't work out," he called after her.

Mel paused. Her eyes suddenly stung with unshed tears. "I'm sure things worked out for the best," she said.

Keeping her back to him, she walked away.

Chapter Three

Why had she let Jake get to her like that? Why had she acted like a hurt child? With angry strokes, Mel moved the rubber currycomb around and around Dreamcatcher's brown coat. The circular motion cast up dirt and dander, bringing it to the surface. Her thoughts moved in the same manner, around and around, casting up irate epithets. She wanted to kick herself.

Mel tossed the currycomb into the grooming box outside the stall door and snatched up the hard brush. With firm, quick strokes, she raked the dirt and loose hair off the horse. She had promised herself she wouldn't do anything foolish where Jake was concerned. Never again. Never. And then look what *had* happened yesterday. She'd reacted impulsively to his hesitancy, his lack of desire to hire her as a trainer. She had taken it personally, just like ten years ago.

Well, it was personal. She still wasn't good enough. Ten years ago, he didn't want her to be his wife. Today he had the nerve to apologize for it, humiliating her and raking up all that old hurt.

Mel moved the brush down the horse's rump with one swift stroke. Dreamcatcher snorted in response.

"Shut up, you." Even a horse gave her no respect.

"Ain't you finished with that stallion yet?" Pop stuck his head inside the open door of the stall. "You're gonna rub the hide off that animal."

Mel dropped the hard brush and picked up the soft one. "Oh, hold your horses, Pop. I'm almost finished."

Pop stood his ground and glared at her. "You took off your bandages."

"Can't work with them on."

The old man hesitated, not speaking, but letting his opinion of her actions be known by his silence.

31

"What?" she asked defensively. "I'm okay."

Pop huffed. "Well, Jake's done with the first horse. Hurry it along."

Familiar with her father's gruffness, Mel completed the final brushing and then toweled out the animal's nose and ears. What had gotten into Pop? He certainly was a contradiction. She had thought for sure the loss of Royalty's Reverie and the seven other horses he had bred and trained would have left him dejected and demoralized. Instead, her father seemed to have a new lease on life—as if he was on some holy crusade, which, unfortunately, included Jake and her.

Dreamcatcher was secured to the walls of the stall by two chains that fastened to either side of his halter. Mel ducked under one of them and picked up the hoof pick. Turning her back to the door, she touched the massive stallion's left leg and stooped down to catch his hoof as he lifted it. She rested the horse's leg against hers and bending low began scraping out the caked dirt, cleaning out around the "v" of the frog.

A wolf whistle punctured the silence.

Dreamcatcher snorted and shied. Trying to avoid being stepped on, Mel jerked upward and bumped her head against a crosstie. Flustered, she turned to see Jake standing in the doorway, his saddle in his hands.

"Hey, you startled the horse!"

"Sorry, just a natural reaction when I see such a magnificent creature." The sparkle in Jake's eyes were irrepressible. "Need any help?"

She wasn't fooled by his lame explanation. He'd always enjoyed teasing her. "No thanks. I'm almost done here."

"Good. I'll just set my saddle down outside the stall." With a wink, he turned away.

Mel watched him walk back to join Pop. She must not let him upset her or it would be a long summer. Bending back to her task, a stab of embarrassment tightened Mel's chest when she realized she had unknowingly presented Jake with an excellent view of her upturned backside.

Whoa! No telling what the man had thought, seeing her rump stuck up like some provocative flag. Mel hated to be at a disadvantage. She wasn't a slim schoolgirl anymore.

Finishing the fourth hoof, Mel stood up and threw the metal pick into the box. She wiped her hands on the fabric of her denim riding jeans and stepped outside the stall. Pop and Jake were in front of Royal Tiara, the equitation horse he had just ridden.

Jake was no longer a slim teen either. Dressed in black Kentucky jodhpurs that cupped his trim hips and caressed his muscular thighs, the young trainer was a picture of a mature, athletic male. Mel caught her breath, unable to calm the sharp pang of nerves that churned in her belly. His long-sleeve shirt failed to mask the taut muscles of his arms and shoulders. He stood with his legs slightly spread, his riding crop slapping the side of his booted leg. She sensed Jake's impatience, even from this distance. He was like a horse chomping at its bit, impatient, but he was totally absorbed in his task, his concentration on whatever Pop was saying.

Jake's cutback saddle rested upright with its pommel in the dirt floor. It had been in his truck during the fire and had not been destroyed. Mel hefted the English saddle into her arms, smelling its leather. Jake took good care of his equipment, just like he took good care of his body. Why that thought? Why was she obsessing about Jake Hendricks's physique? With a huff, she made herself attend to the task.

After placing the saddle carefully on Dreamcatcher's back, she fitted the cutout portion around the horse's prominent withers. Mel ran her hand over the flat saddle until her fingers touched the brass nameplate on the back of the cantle. Her fingertips traced his name. *Jake Hendricks.*

The irony of the situation weighted her soul—Jake Hendricks, trainer at Royalty Farm; Pop O'Shea retired because of a bad heart; and Melody O'Shea, the once up-and-coming female trainer, now a groom.

Sure, she could be assistant trainer here if she wanted it. But did she? Mel wasn't sure. She had promised herself when Jake walked out on her that she wouldn't look back. She hadn't been consumed with becoming as famous as her father in the Saddlebred world. Not like Jake. A career hadn't been everything to her. She just wanted to make her living as a trainer, a woman in a man's profession, and she wanted to be respected for her talent.

At first, it had been hard holding on to her dream. Getting pregnant at eighteen hadn't helped. When Jake had announced he was heading to California to pursue his career, she had not told him her problem. If he thought they were too young to get married, then she knew he would think they were too young to be parents.

Desperate and strapped for money, she had turned to Bert Noble. He had paid her medical bills and had given her spending money. Thank goodness, she had been able to use the excuse of college to prevent Pop from finding out. When Bert and his wife adopted Cory at three days old, it had been heartbreakingly hard. In retrospect, Mel knew she had done her best for her little girl.

Her secret went to the Nobles' graves with them. She was the only one now alive who knew the truth.

With a heavy sigh, she lifted the saddle flap and tightened the girth. Mel wished she had done the best for herself during that time.

She'd married Lenny Stephenson in good faith, but it hadn't turned out well. A businessman with a passion for Saddlebred horses, he had been ten years her senior. He'd seemed safe, a shelter from the storm that had been her life after Cory's birth and subsequent adoption. She'd never really loved him. She knew that now.

Mel scrubbed a hand over her face. What a mistake. She had realized it four years into the marriage after Lenny had refused to start a family. Had she been trying to make up for losing Cory by having a child with him? Not sure her motives for marrying him were pure, she had, however, tried to make the best of the unhappy situation.

Until the rumors had started. Until Lenny's veterinarian had been caught in a horse insurance scam and her husband had been implicated. Nothing had been proven against him, but Mel had never felt right about him after that. And then she had discovered Lenny's gambling debts.

Thank heavens that part of her life was over and done with. Not like the weird instant replay going on right now between her and the man she should have married instead.

Circling the horse to the opposite side, she pulled the girth underneath Dreamcatcher's barrel and lifted the other flap.

"Maybe the girth will slip and then he'll fall off and break his stupid neck," Mel muttered as she gave an extra tug to the leather and buckled it on the snuggest notch.

"What'd you say?" Dave asked.

Face suddenly hot, Mel looked up to see the ex-jockey behind her. "Nothing," she said. "Just talking to myself."

"Need any help?"

"I can tack a horse, thank you." Her reply was too curt.

Dave shrugged and left her alone. "Sure. No one said you couldn't."

What was wrong with her? Dave didn't deserve to be the butt of her anger. He'd done nothing to her. She was furious with herself and her reaction to Jake.

For once in his stubborn life, Dreamcatcher let her put the bit in his mouth. She had worked with the colt during the holidays last winter and knew what a pain he could be. *Like some men she knew.* She tightened the cheek strap and adjusted the curb chain.

"C'mon, big boy." She led the stallion out of the stall.

"It's about time," Pop grumbled.

Mel forced back the retort she normally would have snapped at her father. She'd learned early on how to give as good as she got with him. But all too aware of Jake's compelling presence, she refused to be drawn again into a compromising position. Instead, she ordered Dreamcatcher to stand still.

She nudged the horse's front left hoof with her boot, and the stallion obediently stretched out so that his weight was equally distributed on all four legs.

Jake flashed an irritating grin and lifted the saddle flap to check the girth.

"It's tight enough," Mel said in a strained voice, frustrated he would check her work.

"Force of habit." Jake held out his hand.

Mel transferred the reins into Jake's gloved hand. Like yesterday, his touch sliced sensual sensations along her spine. She was quick to drop her gaze.

"Thank you."

"No problem."

Jake drew the reins over Dreamcatcher's head and gathered them in his left hand. "Hold him for me, will you, Pop?"

Making soothing noises in his throat, Pop stepped in front of the impatient stallion.

"Want me to hold your stirrup?" Mel asked to be courteous.

Catching the veiled look of amusement in his eyes, she stiffened. Did he know how much it cost her to ask? When Jake nodded his head in assent, Mel grasped the right stirrup iron and held it to keep the saddle steady as he mounted. When his right leg swung over the back of the horse, Mel jumped away. He settled into the saddle.

Pop held onto the bridle. "Horse's got a mind of his own. Takes the bit well. Canter's a little rough though."

Jake acknowledged Pop's remarks with another tip of his head, collected his reins, and stretched his legs down in the stirrups. The old trainer stepped back, and Jake pressed his calves slightly into Dreamcatcher's side, moving away. Pop followed.

"A mind of his own," Mel mumbled. "Just like his rider."

"What'd ya' say?" Dave asked from Royal Tiara's stall.

"Nothing."

"Gotta stop this talking to yourself, Mel." Dave scraped sweat off the hot horse. "Might get to be a bad habit."

Good ol' Dave. He was kidding her. She could always count on him to call her to account. But was her grumpiness that obvious? She shook herself mentally and stepped into Tiara's stall.

"Need any help?"

"I know how to put a horse away," he replied in teasing echo of her own words.

"Okay. Point taken." Mel rubbed sweat off her brow. "Are we done yet?"

It was hot. The horses didn't need to be worked long, but Jake had insisted on trying out each one before they left tomorrow for Lexington. As if there wasn't enough work to do to get ready. True to his word, Pop had procured the extra saddles and bridles and bits from friends, but the equipment had to be packed in ugly wooden boxes instead of the purple and gold Royalty Farm tack trunks that had been destroyed in the fire. Well, at least they were going to the show—only three days after the worst stable fire the Saddlebred community had seen in years.

"Only one more to go," Dave said. "Get Royalty's Dreamer ready and take her on up to the arena. Pop said to come along as quick as you can."

"Right."

Mel groomed the black mare. Brushing the calm and obedient horse soothed Mel's nerves. If Jake wasn't going to get to her, she had to stop feeling defensive. She had to mask her vulnerability. A best defense was always a good offence. Mel's resolve strengthened as she slipped the bit into Royalty's mouth and adjusted the straps on the bridle.

For ten years, even during her difficult marriage, she'd struggled to become the woman she'd become. Now seeing Jake again had thrown her into the past, back to the immature eighteen-year-old who'd been so in love. She felt out of control, not herself, and she didn't like that feeling. Mumbling to avoid Dave overhearing, Mel vowed to do better. She would not slip again.

Leading Royalty out of the barn, she walked the horse the short distance to the training arena. It wasn't far but having to leave the lower barn where the remaining show horses were now stabled to go outside was annoying. She dreaded what it would be like in the cold Kentucky winter.

Be positive. Be thankful the firemen were able to save the arena.

A delicate spiral of smoke drifted out of the ashes that had been the training barn. The mare snorted and shied when they neared the ruins. Yellow police tape blocked it off. Arson investigators still poked around the wreckage to discover the cause of the fire. Mel firmed her hold on the lead. Another wave of anger washed over her. Who had done this? Someone needed to pay for the carnage.

Royalty's Dreamer danced sideways. Knowing the horse was afraid of the smoldering rubble, Mel hustled the mare out of the sunlight and into the dim arena.

Inside Dreamcatcher made a pass at the slow gait—a four-beat gait that left only one of the horse's hooves on the ground at a time. It was not a gait natural to most horses, but some Saddlebreds were trained to do it. This big stallion performed the gait to perfection.

Her eyes adjusting to the dimness, Mel took in more of the action. Her father stood in the center of the arena and barked out orders. Circling her father, Jake sat motionless on the back of the horse, his shoulders erect and head high.

Lifting her free hand to her lips, Mel felt blown away. She had forgotten the absolute magnetism of this man in the saddle.

She had to remind herself of her new resolution to mask her caring with indifference. Coming to a halt in front of her, Jake shifted in the saddle and observed her with a hooded gaze. Dreamcatcher was hardly winded, but Mel was. She forced the air into her chest, unable to catch her breath or speak.

Jake took his reins in one hand and stretched his other hand back to the horse's rump for an affectionate pat. "What did you think?"

"Do you really want to know?"

"Sure." Leaning back and relaxed in the saddle, Jake presented a quiet and confident image. Only his eyes moved, watching her, assessing her, and giving her an unwelcome jolt.

She reined in her galloping pulse and returned his look with what she hoped was a nonchalant one. "Why?"

Jake raised a reflective eyebrow. "Maybe because I care about your opinion."

Surprised, Mel didn't know what to say.

Pop was not at loss for words. "Damn good job, boy." He came up from behind, nodding his head and chuckling. "Do we have a surprise for those folks who are countin' us out because of the fire. Won't it be grand?"

Jake dismounted and began to unbuckle his saddle. "Think he stands a chance this week, Pop?"

"Damn right. This stallion will blow 'em away." Pop took Dreamcatcher's reins.

"Don't you want me to lead him back?" Mel asked.

"No. He's a handful. I'll take 'im back. You stay with Jake."

It was just like Pop to set her up. "But Pop, I can handle Dreamcatcher," she said.

"You just do what I told you to, darlin'." Pop led the big horse away without a backward glance.

With a soft shake of his head, Jake settled his saddle onto Royalty's back and tightened the girth. Gathering up the reins, he swung into the saddle without asking for help.

Mel didn't like the way Jake rode Royalty. He was too rough, demanding, forcing her into the gaits. From riding the mare last winter, Mel knew enough to know this horse wasn't like Dreamcatcher. She needed to be asked gently, and then the mare would do it willingly. Jake's method was sure to sour her.

"I'll tell you what I think now," Mel called out, forcing him to notice her.

Jake reined to a stop in front of her. "Please? I didn't hear you."

"You said you cared about my opinion. I'm ready to give it to you now."

Jake waited, gazing back at her mildly. "Oh?"

"You'll ruin Royalty riding her like that," Mel said, challenging him.

A muscle moved in his jaw. "And how's that?"

"You've got to ask it of her." Mel's hands curled at her side. "You can't push Royalty into the gaits. She's agreeable if you ask her gently."

"So, she's temperamental—like most females," Jake said with an infuriating grin.

Angry heat flushed Mel's cheeks. This wasn't something to joke about. "I don't believe the horse's sex has anything to do with it. It's simply her personality."

"I see. And you know this, how?"

41

"From observation *and* experience. The same way you know how to train a horse, or, let's say, *should* know if you were more flexible in your training methods."

In the murky light, Jake's eyes were thoughtful. He dismounted and led Royalty toward Mel. "Ah, there's the rub. You disapprove of my training methods."

She took a deep breath then countered, "Where Royalty's concerned. You don't know how to handle her."

"And you're going to teach me?"

He was too alarmingly close. Mel backed a step. Words died in her throat. She'd forgotten how overwhelming the man could be with his blatantly sexy eyes, hard muscled body, and infectious grin. The lopsided dimple under his eye gave his face a boyish quality, a quality she recalled so well from the past.

"You've piqued my curiosity," he said. "Here." He offered her the horse's reins.

She shook her head. "No thanks."

"What's the matter? Afraid?"

He was annoying her. "I'm afraid of nothing." Mel snatched the reins from his hands. "I proved that yesterday."

"Let me give you a leg up."

"No way." Mel turned her back on him, gathered the reins in her left hand, and grabbed the cantle with her right one.

"Oh, Mel, lighten up. I don't bite." With that, Jake laid possessive hands on her backside and tossed her into the saddle.

Chapter Four

Mel's pulse pounded like the beat of a trotting horse as she felt herself being lifted into the air and thrown aboard the saddle.

"I said I didn't need a leg up."

His eyes twinkled with mischief. "I was just trying to be helpful."

"Helpful? I don't trust your motives."

Jake raised an exasperating eyebrow. "And exactly what are my motives?"

"Oh!" How could she admit she thought Jake was trying to mess with her? Mel turned her head away from his evident amusement and urged Royalty toward the rail.

The horse settled into an easy trot that propelled Mel out of the saddle in a rhythmic, up-and-down post. Using the curb rein, she positioned the mare's head into the familiar neck-bending curve of a Saddlebred and then raised Royalty's head with the snaffle rein. This gave the mare a springier, higher trot that made the horse look regal, like a classical Greek statue. Lifting her chin, Mel squared her shoulders and stared between the horse's ears as they circled and circled the arena.

Riding Royalty's Dreamer was spine-tingling. Mel focused her total attention on the mare, quickly forgetting her conflict with Jake. At the slow gait, she relaxed and held the reins firmly at waist level, spaced almost shoulder-width apart. Her knees pressed into the saddle with her lower legs swung away and heels down. The horse was game and eager to please. She couldn't help her happiness. A smile spread across Mel's face when she reversed and urged the mare again into a fast trot.

* * *

The horse and rider burst down the straightaway. Damn! The mare's show trot was finer and more animated than the one

Jake had been able to achieve. Mel's signals were subtle—a slight press of her calves against Royalty's side, a negligible squeeze of the reins.

Jake switched his leg with his crop and turned in a circle to visually follow the pair around the arena. The old trainer was right about Royalty and Mel. The two were a great combination, a winning duo. Was Pop also right about Mel? Would she come around and help the farm? She had to. Jake now wanted more time with her, more time to make up for breaking her heart.

Mel cut the corner and angled into the center of the arena, stopping in front of him. She laughed down at him, her eyes wide, her face flushed.

"She's wonderful, Jake. I just love her."

Jake took Royalty's reins and urged the horse to stand quietly. Then he came around the left side. Mel wore her thick hair pulled back, away from her face. She was sweaty and hot, but remained dainty and feminine, very much a lady.

"You did a wonderful job. Better than I could do." His voice was thick with an unexplained emotion.

Her eyes glowed. "It's Royalty. She makes it easy."

Swinging her right leg over the cantle, Mel started to dismount. Facing the horse, she placed her hands flat on the seat while she kicked her left foot free of the stirrup iron and then slipped to the ground...right into Jake's open arms.

He tightened his arms slightly around her and bent his head so he could see her exquisite profile. His chest constricted at the familiar feel of her. "You have such a lovely smile, Mel."

A lovely and inviting smile. She didn't smile enough. Feeling his body temperature rise, Jake couldn't stop himself. When she turned around, he bent forward and touched his lips to hers.

She smelled of perspiration and lavender perfume. She tasted like salt—earthy and basic. Her lips were warm and yielding, tempting him to ask for more. A wave of desire rolled through his body. He lowered his lashes caught up in a primitive longing.

After a moment of clear surrender, Mel sucked in her breath and drew back. Jake's eyes opened in time to see Mel's raised hand.

"How dare you!"

The sound of the slap resounded through the cavernous arena. Mel shouldered past him, grabbed Royalty's reins, and stalked toward the door of the arena with the horse in tow.

Surprised, but fascinated, Jake touched his cheek. Damn! He ran to catch up, falling into step at Mel's side.

He hoped to defuse her anger by apologizing. "I'm sorry. I don't know what came over me." No reaction. Maybe he should try changing the subject. "Now tell me you want to show this mare."

Mel didn't respond. The air between them reverberated with tension.

He tried another tactic. "Pop was right, Mel. We do need a safety valve. The farm needs two chances at the World's Grand Championship."

"Pop isn't always right."

"He is when it comes to horseflesh," Jake pointed out. "He wants you to show Royalty, and after seeing you ride, I agree with him. You two are naturals. A great team."

"Flattery, Mr. Hendricks, will get you absolutely nowhere."

The hot sunshine scalded as hot as Mel's ire. Her jaw set, she walked swiftly toward the lower barn. He quickened his step to keep up.

"Vanessa doesn't have much money. Mel, if we don't do well in August, she may be forced to sell some part or all of the farm. Pop said you might not understand how desperate things are. Those real estate agents are persistent."

"I do understand. Pop told me."

"Someone may be threatening Royalty Farm. We can't rebuild it into a powerhouse operation without you. Vanessa wants your help. *I* want your help."

She stopped and stared at her boots, chewing her lower lip.

Jake remembered now how stubborn she could be. "Mel, will you show the horse for Vanessa?"

"No. I will not show the horse."

"You won't? Give me a good reason."

They walked on in silence, finally reaching the barn. Mel took the horse into her stall. "I don't have to explain myself to you," she said.

With quick efficiency, Mel stripped the mare of her bridle. Draping it over her shoulder, she slipped the halter on Royalty and tied the horse to the sides of the stall. Jake went into the stall and removed the saddle. He set it on the saddle rack outside the stall.

"All you need to know is that I don't like to be used," she said without looking at him.

"Used? Who's using you?"

"You."

"Oh, come on, Mel. I'm asking this for Vanessa and Pop."

"And *your* fine career. That always come first with you."

Mel maneuvered out of the stall and picked up the sweat scraper from the groom box. Back inside, she raked it over Royalty's wet coat with strong strokes.

"Sounds as if you're confusing today with the past." Jake's voice was firm. "That part of my life is over and done with."

"Yeah, really?" She elbowed around him to pick up a towel. "Move. You're in my way."

Jake jumped aside. *So, that's the way it is?* He leaned nonchalantly at the edge of the door. As Mel worked, her fury was evident in every quick motion. She was beautiful when she was angry—like a spirited filly.

"You're upset because I kissed you," he stated the obvious.

She tossed a sharp glance his way. "What made you think I'd welcome your advances?"

Mel had always been so much fun to tease. She took things so seriously and looked so pretty when she was mad that he couldn't help baiting her, just like he used to do when they were kids. However, the Mel he remembered would have never stood up for herself so directly. She would have ducked her head and pouted, unable to communicate her anger. He liked the new woman she'd become.

"Oh, I didn't expect my advances to be welcome." He lifted an indifferent shoulder. "Your beauty just overwhelmed me, and I got carried away."

"Don't mock me, Jake Hendricks," she spat. "I don't have to put up with your boorish male behavior."

"Whew!" He shook his hand as if he had been stung.

47

"Grow up! I've dealt with a man much more adept in harassing women than you and survived. Your idea of a joke is simply annoying."

She shoved past him again, grabbed the cooler, and threw it over the back of the horse. Jake didn't have a retort. She was right. He had acted like a lout. Times had changed. A man couldn't get away with what once passed as flirting. Women today considered it harassment.

Her comment also made him wonder what had happened to Mel during these last years. What had occurred between Mel and her ex-husband?

Leaving Royalty to stand in the cross-ties while she cooled, Mel stamped out of the stall, picked up the saddle, and strode down the aisle. Jake followed, getting a good view of her full, swinging hips. It didn't hurt to simply look.

In the tack room, she struggled to lift his saddle onto the highest rack. Coming up from behind, he took it from her outstretched hands, and put it easily on the top bar.

She swung away from him in a huff. "I don't need your help."

"But I need yours," he said, following her again into the aisle. He wasn't willing to let the subject drop. "Stop, Mel. Wait a minute."

She stopped and fell into a hostile silence.

"You'll only have to put up with me for two months."

"Right. Then what?" Her eyes were wary.

"Then what? I don't know. It depends on what happens at Louisville. If one of us wins, this farm will continue to need two trainers. If neither of us wins…" Jake shrugged his shoulders as he let the implication hang in the air. Without a win, the farm had to change dramatically. "There are no guarantees in this business."

"You're just finding that out?"

He took a breath, not wishing to continue the argument. "What about it, huh?" he begged.

"No."

Damn, she was stubborn. "Then why did you come home, Mel?" His voice was filled with annoyance. "Why did you come back to Kentucky?"

"I came home to take care of Pop after his heart attack." She almost added something else but stopped herself.

"If you care about your father's physical condition, why don't you care about his dream?"

Mel stiffened and scowled at him. "What do you mean?"

"The World's Grand Championship. Your father knows he may not be around next year. He wants to win it now. One more time. For Vanessa and the farm and for his legacy."

"Why do *you* care so much?"

She'd turned the tables on him. He was quick with his answer. "This place is in my blood. My years in California taught me that. And the Nobles were always good to me. I think I've always loved Pop." *And you too*, he thought as he watched emotions play havoc with her face.

Mel turned from him, standing with her back toward him in the hot and dusky aisle. The horse behind her moved and snorted in his stall. She bowed her head. It was as if the weight of the world pressed on her shoulders.

"C'mon, Mel. Make an old man's dream come true."

"That's just it, dreams don't come true." She sounded as if she had voiced an inner conviction.

"Sure, they do, Mel. If you make them come true."

He offered a sad smile in response to her pain. She sounded so pessimistic. Would she deny him again? But what more could he say? He didn't like the sorrow he'd seen in her eyes.

Turning back to face him, a resigned look in her eyes, Mel surprised him. "I'll go with you to the show in Lexington. I'll give you my time through the show in Louisville. I'll try to win the championship on Royalty. After that, who knows?"

What made her change her mind? He didn't know but he wanted to hug her. Instead, he grinned like a little boy caught with his hand in a cookie jar.

"You won't regret this, Mel, not at all! We'll *win* the Five-Gaited World's Grand Championship."

* * *

Would she regret her decision? Tomorrow, when they left for the show in Lexington, Mel and Jake would be thrown together for a long, hard week. Could she survive it?

There was no choice. She had to endure it for the sake of her father. And her daughter.

Mel renewed her determination that night. Pop's shaky movements, as he shoved himself away from the kitchen table and stood up, fortified her resolve. Her father was once a tall man, but the recent heart attack had stooped his shoulders and slowed his actions.

"It's a good thing I came home, Pop. You need someone to

As soon as she said the words, Mel regretted them. A look of anger shadowed Pop's eyes.

"Humph. Don't need no help. Been takin' care of myself for most of my seventy-five years, and no need to go an' change that now."

Her father shuffled to the counter where he popped a pod into the coffeemaker and pushed the button for a single, steamy cup. Swallowing hard, she remembered other days, happy, childhood days, when Pop and her mother had laughed together during the nightly ritual of hot tea or coffee and toast. Back then, the piercing whistle of the hot kettle had announced the boiling of water. Now Pop used his newfangled machine. Somehow it wasn't the same.

She chewed her lower lip as Pop made another mug of coffee and brought both mugs and spoons back to the table.

"Still fill yours with milk and sugar?"

"Yes."

"Sissy way to drink coffee."

Stirring sugar into her coffee, Mel watched Pop's slow and careful movements. He shuffled to the refrigerator and retrieved a plastic jug of milk. After pouring milk into her mug, Pop returned the jug to the counter and then set a plateful of crusty, half-burnt toast on the table. The jam was store bought now, not her mother's familiar homemade strawberry preserves. The butter was corn oil margarine and came in a tub. But the hot toasted bread smelled the same—warm and comforting. Some things had not changed.

But Pop had changed. It was more than his physical limitations. Pop's eyes were sad. Was he thinking about her mother too? Sarah O'Shea had died thirteen years earlier of a heart attack that hot August after Pop won the World's Grand Championship for the last time. Life had been different for Mel after that, like a raw wound, always open and festering.

Then Jake Hendricks had come to Royalty Farm and taken her mind off her grief.

When they finished eating, Pop cleared the table before Mel could offer. It was if he tried to prove himself still capable.

"Well, at least the boy won't let this place become a subdivision," Pop muttered.

"Who are you talking about?"

Pop grunted. "Jake Hendricks, the boy you're so mad at me about."

Her father called every younger male "boy," but for all his boyish qualities, it was hard thinking of Jake like that—not after seeing the strong, assured man he'd become. Not after he'd kissed her.

Mel was horrified by the implication of Pop's remark. "Oh, surely turning the farm into a subdivision isn't an option."

With his back to her as he washed the dishes, her father shrugged his stooped shoulders. "Never know."

"Vanessa wouldn't destroy her father's dream." No more than Mel could destroy her father's dream.

"Maybe she wouldn't want to, but if times got bad, she might not have a choice." Pop shook his head. "Those real estate developers have pestered the hell out of her lately."

Mel pushed back from the table. "Well, we won't let that happen, will we?"

"Not likely. Night, darlin'. Sleep tight. Don't let the bedbugs bite."

"Night, Pop."

Mel climbed the narrow wooden steps to her attic bedroom. Pop was allowed the use of a small two-bedroom frame house on the farm property. Mel had grown up there. It was home.

Pausing at the threshold of her room, memories overwhelmed her. Mel missed her mother. Her mother would have understood her ambivalence about Jake. She would have understood why Mel had given up Cory. Maybe if her mother had lived, Mel wouldn't have made as many mistakes—or gotten pregnant in the first place because she wouldn't have been searching so hard for someone to love.

Mel flicked the light switch revealing her tiny room. A jumble of stuffed animals waited for her on the patchwork quilt covering her Jenny Lind bed. A battered chest of drawers stood sentry in one corner next to a plain, straight-back chair. The braided, multicolored throw rug added a meager touch of warmth to the worn wooden floor.

What delighted Mel most were her ribbons. They hung on sagging strings tacked to the yellowed white walls—faded blues, reds, whites, yellows, pinks, greens, and even purples. They were all there, crowded together, from her first blue ribbon as a four-year-old in the lead line classes to the ribbon won as a catch rider in the World's Championship Five-Gaited Pony Stake.

She gazed at her little-girl room, feeling a bit unnerved because it was the same as when she'd left. She wasn't the same girl. She'd grown up. Fast. She'd had to.

Immense sorrow swelled in Mel's heart. She sat down on the bed and surveyed the wall covered with ribbons. Why did she feel like a child hiding her head in her mother's skirts?

For twenty-eight years, Pop had always brushed away her busted knees or bruises. He'd told her scrapes and falls made her tough. She had experienced plenty of them over the years—physical as well as emotional ones.

Trouble was, she didn't feel tough. Not now. Not since she'd finally signed the divorce papers and headed home. Pop needed her after his heart attack, sure, but she had other reasons for returning home. Reasons that had everything to do with her own past mistakes. She wondered if she could ever make amends. To Pop, to Cory…and to herself.

Mel roused herself from her reflections and went to the bedroom window, placing her clenched fists on the wooden sill. Those fleeting wisps of memory were cunning. For years, she'd promised herself not to think about Jake, to relegate the unhappy memory of their separation to her past—to forget.

But in the end, she'd never been able to forget.

She shuddered as she remembered their argument before he left Kentucky. He wouldn't marry her, he'd told her. All she heard was that he didn't want her, so she hadn't told him the truth.

It had been selfish and cowardly of her, but in the end, she'd been glad to leave Royalty Farm before her pregnancy became obvious. Pop believed she was in college in Missouri, and she had been going to classes before Cory was born, so technically, that wasn't a lie.

The Nobles had been kind to her. How easy they'd made it for her to hide her pregnancy from her father. Cory's birth had not taken much time. It had been over and done with so quickly. *So simply.* The Nobles had taken Cory away, bringing a new adopted baby home to Kentucky, and Mel had continued her college education.

Mel was sorry she'd made such a mess of her life. Had that hard-headed trainer thought more about her and not his stupid career, they might have been a family now. The three of them. Nonetheless, Cory was happy and healthy, and that's what mattered. Unaware of her birth parents, she had grown up the pampered child of Mary and Bert Noble. She had been given the monetary advantages Mel had lacked as a child and, so far, Cory had turned out just fine. Mel was proud of her little daughter and the girl's love of horses, for Cory was as horse crazy as Mel had been at that age and rode just as well.

She must force herself not to look back—not to regret the choices she'd made.

In the distant darkness, the black shell of the training barn haunted the land. For as long as she remembered, the O'Shea family had lived near the big barn at Royalty Farm. It had always been there—familiar and imposing—Mel's touch with childhood. The present destruction filled her soul with a cold ache. The barn symbolized her life—ashes, burnt wood, rubble, and failure.

But the barn and Royalty Farm could be rebuilt. Just like her life.

"Jake may be right," she whispered.

Maybe she did have the power to make her dreams come true now that her horrible marriage was behind her. Maybe now she could start again. Maybe she could assure Cory's future would be bright.

Mel relaxed her grip and opened her palms. Her hands might be small, but in them there was strength. She could use these hands to control a thousand-pound horse. Jake had held her hands in his larger ones. He had smiled at her, teased her, and kissed her. Jake would be with her. They could rebuild Royalty Farm together.

Would he also play a part in her life when she took it into her own hands again?

Chapter Five

Sunday evening
American Saddlebred Museum
Lexington, Kentucky

A bronze statue of the famous Saddlebred stallion Supreme Sultan dominated the parking lot in front of the museum. Jake barely glanced at it because his eyes were focused on Mel. She looked so totally different from yesterday, lovely in her backless, black sheath dress and stilettos. Her calves, muscled from so much time in the saddle, gave her legs a sexy shapeliness. The sway in her walk tantalized him. That he was here in Kentucky with Mel amazed Jake—a dream come true.

Mel ignored him, acting as if he was not there. The schoolkid in him was determined to correct that. In the past, he could always tease her out of her bad humor. He might as well give it another shot. Putting two fingers to his lips, Jake blew a long, wolf whistle.

Mel halted abruptly and turned around. "Did you whistle at me?"

"Guilty as charged.

"You whistled at me yesterday."

"And I kissed you too."

She tossed her dark auburn hair away from her eyes. "Don't look at me like that."

"Like what?"

"Like a bratty little boy," Mel shot back. She turned away and walked ahead of him toward the museum.

"That's a mighty good view," Jake called, ribbing her again.

She stopped with her hands on her hips. "Can't you keep a civil tongue in your head?"

57

"Just the facts, ma'am."

"Look, I didn't want to go to this charity thing," Mel said, irritated. "You can at least be civil."

"What's the matter? Nerves?"

She turned away once more. "Well, yes."

This was a surprise. "Wait a minute. You said you feared nothing." He caught her arm. "I'm sorry I teased you. You're not afraid of a silly cocktail party, are you?"

Color crept into her cheeks. "My customers were horse-crazy girls and their mothers. I never had to attend fancy functions."

"You have nothing to worry about." He tried to encourage her. "You look lovely. Just pick up a drink. That gives you something to hold. And stick near me. I'll protect you."

"You are such a comfort." Mel whipped around again and stalked away.

Jake watched her leave, regret settling in his gut. He'd meant to make her feel better, not rouse her anger. The way he was going he was no better than Pop, always putting his foot in his mouth. He supposed she didn't want his protection. Well, he'd change her opinion somehow. He hurried to catch up.

* * *

Mel's heel caught on the curb, and as she tripped, the steadying hand of her tormentor grasped her elbow.

"Thanks."

Jake's work-calloused thumb stroked her skin. "Don't mention it. I said I'd protect you."

Mel slowed her pace, allowing him to walk by her side, his hand on her arm. She remembered tripping the day of the fire.

She remembered the sparks and the low, acrid smoke. Jake had supported her then as he did now.

"I'm not an invalid. I can take care of myself."

"I know you can." His whispered words were hot on her bare shoulders.

Jake was too close. His attention too intimate. After all, they were just co-workers dedicated to saving Royalty Farm. There was nothing left between them. This party was a merely a professional function, something she had to tolerate.

So why was she kidding herself? She didn't feel a bit professional.

They reached the door, and a group of partygoers swept them up, separating Jake's grip on her arm. Mel let it happen, glad for the respite. With Jake so near, she felt flustered. First, she'd practically begged for his help, admitting formal assemblies frightened her, and then she'd asserted her ability to take care of herself. He must think her crazy.

Accepting a long-stemmed glass of red wine from a white-coated waiter, Mel escaped into the museum itself and wandered anonymously among the crowded exhibits. Her thoughts pounded in her head like a trotting horse. Jake believed she worked for Vanessa solely out of loyalty to Pop, to make her father's dream come true. But she had a more elemental reason for trying to restore the fortunes of Royalty Farm. *Cory*. Her daughter. Royalty Farm was Corrine Noble's heritage too.

She spied Jake at the other end of the room surrounded by other trainers. He looked so handsome in a tuxedo. Her skin prickled as she remembered how his fingertips felt on her bare arm. When his gaze caught hers through the crowd, she glanced away, turning her attention to contemplate a nineteenth century painting of a chestnut mare. The colors blurred before her eyes.

An ever-familiar sense of guilt flushed her cheeks. Sometimes she regretted not telling Jake about his daughter. She touched the glass to the side of her face.

"You look quite becoming, Melody, darling," a recognizable voice said behind her.

Blood surged in her ears. A horrible pain shot through her stomach. When Pop called her *darling*, it was a term of affection. This version sounded sneering, as if the speaker didn't believe what he said. And she knew he didn't. Swift, wild resentment overpowered her.

"Aren't you going to say hello?"

Mel turned slowly. "What are you doing here, Lenny?"

His expression coolly neutral, her ex-husband gave a polite nod. "I believe I'm attending a charity party."

A shudder coursed through Mel's body. Why had she once thought this man attractive? His salt and pepper hair now seemed dull and dingy gray and his brown eyes sardonic. He was a tall man, powerful—much like Pop had been in his prime. Somehow this very power only suggested dominance, not strength and security. His very presence reminded her of the years of manipulation and hurt.

"Why are you here?"

He appraised her though half-closed eyes. "I'm doing my part for charity."

Mel felt her face grow hotter. Surrounded by so many people, she felt trapped. She looked for a place to set her wine glass, feeling as if she might break the crystal between her fingertips if she held it a minute longer.

"Allow me." Lenny removed the goblet from her hands, his fingers skimming hers, and placed it on the glass-covered exhibition case of old bridles and bits. She shivered involuntarily.

Mel tried to regain control of her emotions. "You never could keep away from these functions."

"Yes, I find them stimulating. I am surprised to see you here though."

"It's part of my new job." Mel lifted her chin. She hadn't owed him that much explanation, but old habits die hard.

"Royalty Farm. I heard." Lenny's expression was cold. "It didn't take you long to find a prestigious job once you left me."

Mel bristled. Her ex-husband knew Royalty Farm was her home. "Look, Lenny, I don't know what you want. Please excuse me."

He blocked her path. "Melody, Melody, your feelings would have been hurt if I hadn't spoken to you."

"Don't delude yourself. We're divorced."

"Okay, okay. I'll be nice." He smiled now, very full of his own importance. "Tell me, have you seen any good horses since you've been here? I'm thinking of going to the auction this week."

"Can you afford it?" She gazed at him incredulously. "What happened to the thirteen thousand you owed that bookie in Vegas?"

"That's history, Melody, darling."

"Well, if you can afford to buy another show horse, you can certainly pay me what you owe me. I'll let my lawyer know you've somehow come into money." She refused to stand there with Lenny any longer, and skirting him, slipped away.

He dogged her as she weaved in and out among the partygoers. The noise was excruciating and so was the heat. Mel struggled to reach the door to the lobby, Lenny right behind her.

"Who was that man hanging all over you?"

Even the lobby was crowded. Panicked, Mel pushed her way out the front door. "What man? What are you talking about?"

"The tall, blond man. You came in with him."

Knowing Lenny had been watching them made her panic even more. "That's my boss. He took Pop's place at the farm."

"What's his name?"

Mel spun around to avoid him. The statue of Supreme Sultan was at her back. "What's it to you? You're no longer my husband."

Lenny somehow managed to look innocent, but Mel knew it was an act. He never indulged in idle curiosity. He always had reasons for his questions and those reasons usually boded ill for her.

"I just wondered," he said with a self-indulgent laugh.

"Keep wondering!"

"I thought perhaps it was Jake Hendricks."

"What do you want?" She shouldn't have let him drive her outside alone. Now fearful, she saw her mistake.

"Ah, so it *is* the famous Jake Hendricks." His gaze settled back on her like a heavy cloak. "Will you have dinner with me this week?"

The evening heat suffocated her. Moisture glossed her upper lip. "Lenny, let me remind you again that we're divorced. Even if that doesn't mean anything to you, it means something to me."

"I have a business proposition to discuss with you."

Mel drew a deep breath and expelled it slowly to prevent herself from screaming. "I have no desire to discuss anything with you."

She shoved past her ex and stalked toward the safety of the building and the crowd inside.

Just then, Jake came out of the museum. "There you are, Mel." He held the door open. "We got separated."

Mel slipped past him into the building. "I know."

Jake followed her inside. "Who were you talking to?"

Mel took an uneven breath before she answered. "Nobody. Nobody at all."

* * *

On Monday morning, Mel led Dreamcatcher from the barn, hitched him to the two-wheeled jog cart, and led him to the outdoor practice arena. Dawn had broken quietly over Lexington's Red Mile. Part of the famous harness horse track had been transformed into an elegant show ring for the Junior League Horse Show. With the first class only hours away, caretakers and trainers were already at work, and the barn area reflected the hectic activity.

Nerves jangled in Mel's stomach as she climbed aboard the jog cart. Like a harness horse driver in a racing sulky, she sat with her boots lifted near the shafts of the cart, her butt tucked low in the seat. Picking up the reins, she clucked to the big stallion and started a slow, warm-up jog. She was glad to be away from the chaotic barn.

Lenny's appearance the night before had spooked her. A ghost from a not-so-distant past, her ex-husband's specter hung over her today. What did he want? What was he doing in

Lexington? Old emotions of inadequacy and frustration surfaced, twisting her gut.

As horse and jog cart picked up speed, wheeling around the sharp turn of the race track, Mel welcomed the morning breeze after so much heat and humidity of the previous day. Down the hard-packed straightaway, Dreamcatcher held his head high, stepping out proudly, his tail whipping in her face. She welcomed the sting of the horse's tail because it was something real and vital, not the phantom fear of her ex-husband.

Suddenly, with a wrenching snap, the jog cart tilted perilously to the left. She fought to pull the stallion to a halt. Dreamcatcher neighed shrilly and jerked to one side. The cart toppled over, slamming her to the ground beneath it.

"Oof." Mel bounced roughly through the dirt. Still clutching the lines, she heard the staccato of the stallion's hooves strike the surface of the track. Pain shot through her ankle, and she fought to keep her face up and out of harm.

"Mel!" Jake's voice echoed from somewhere far, far away. "Whoa, there, boy. Whoa!"

Dreamcatcher reared, his sharp hooves striking out. Coming back down, he shied to the right, dragging Mel and the cart along with him.

"Easy now. Whoa there."

When the cart came to rest, she was face down in the dirt.

"Mel! Are you okay?"

"I'm fine." Mel sputtered out dirt with her words. What had happened to the cart? "Can you get this thing off me?"

"I can't just yet. Dreamcatcher is too nervous, but here comes Dave."

The groom approached cautiously, making soothing sounds. He grabbed Dreamcatcher's halter and stroked the stallion's nose, leaving Jake to untangle the twisted leather lines and traces.

Sweat trickled between Mel's breasts. She shut her eyes and pressed her cheek flat against the rough track.

"Mel, I've got the lines untangled. Give me a minute and I'll have the cart off you."

"Okay."

When Dreamcatcher was unbuckled, Dave led him safely out of the shafts. Jake lifted the cart from her then hoisted Mel up with his strong hands.

Standing her upright, he held her at arm's length searching her face. "You're sure you're not hurt?"

Mel nodded then put all of her weight on her left foot, and pain shot through it. She stumbled forward. "Ouch!"

Jake caught her, his warm and sturdy arms surrounding her. He was so big and safe, his heart beating close to hers, his musky smell comforting. In an instinctive act, Mel relaxed for a moment. Jake's breath was warm on the top of her hair.

Regretting her weakness, Mel pulled away. She balanced awkwardly on her foot. Her ankle throbbed, but not as much as her heart. Jake held her steady, his fingers burning like brands into the flesh of her upper arms. She was all too aware of their contact.

"Well, I was a bit premature. My ankle hurts." She fought to keep her expression remote. She didn't want his help, not if it created within her such a strong response.

"You'll have to get a doctor to look at it, or you may not be able to ride tonight."

The frailty Mel had tried to suppress bubbled into anger. She had no business responding to Jake as if she was a silly school girl. Although he talked of helping Vanessa and the farm, Jake hadn't changed. He didn't care about her injury, just winning the horse show to further his stupid career. It had been like that when they were kids.

She shook herself free from his grasp and hobbled away. "Thanks for your concern. I'll find a doctor."

"Oh, Mel, don't be so stubborn. Let me help you." Jake caught her arm to steady her.

"I don't need your help."

Jake released her. "Yes, I know, but you've got it anyway."

Before Mel could reply, Pop shuffled up. "What in the hell's goin' on here?"

"Mel got a face full of dirt when the jog cart broke."

"I can see that for myself. Damn me, darlin', your face looks like a cat mauled it."

Mel reached for her face and touched the skin on her cheek. Her father was right. The scratches were tender.

"How'd Dreamcatcher do?" Pop's attention shifted to the horse. Dave held the horse's bridle as the stallion circled, snorted, and tossed his head.

"I've already given him the once-over," Dave spoke up. "He's okay. Just full of himself, as usual."

"Won't hurt to go over him again." Seeming satisfied, Pop turned back to his daughter. "Now, how'd this happen, darlin'?"

"I don't know. One minute we were going down the straightaway, and the next I was upside down in the dirt."

With one wheel gone, the cart rested at an awkward angle. Pop knelt beside it.

"Can't tell exactly what happened. Nut and bolt are gone though." He struggled to his feet. His voice was irritated. "Guess that's what ya' get with old equipment."

Their newest jog cart had been burned in the fire. This one was old, but until now, serviceable. Mel hobbled unbalanced on her foot, drawing everyone's attention.

"Now what's happened to you, darlin'?" Pop asked.

"Nothing. Just twisted my ankle or something."

"Makes ya' tough," her father said with a shrug of a shoulder. "But ya' need to get off your feet and have that looked after."

"My sentiments exactly." Before Mel had time to blink, Jake swept her up into his arms.

"Put me down!"

Jake strode toward the barn. "Hush, you stubborn, pigheaded woman."

Mel squirmed in his arms, humiliated beyond belief. Other trainers in the practice area turned to watch. She thought she heard Pop chuckle.

"Why are you doing this to me?"

"Because this is the fastest way to get you to the barn." His shameless grin deepened the furrows of his cheeks.

Mel fought her sensual awareness of his lean, hard body. Her breath came in gulps, as if she were the one walking. She was too intensely conscious of his strong, musky aftershave and the steady beat of his heart. His beard-roughened cheek chafed her own. Why was she so attracted to him after their history?

"I can walk." Mel's protest sounded weak even to her ears.

"Sure, you can, but we've got to get you ready to ride."

What had made her think he was concerned about her?

"Don't worry," she said with as much dignity as she could muster. "I'll ride tonight, and I'll win that damn class."

* * *

"Does it hurt much?" Seeming subdued by the accident and Mel's injury, Cory stood beside Mel's chair in the hallway of the stable.

"Not much." Mel propped her leg up on another chair, an ice bag covering her bare foot.

"How are you gonna put a boot on?"

Mel marveled that Cory understood her problem. The doctor had proclaimed it only a mild sprain, even though her swollen left ankle was painful.

Glancing at Cory, Mel smiled, "Verrry carefully."

Cory giggled. "Silly, I know that."

"Seriously, Vanessa brought me her riding boots. I'll wear them." She held up the borrowed boot for Cory's inspection. "See how they lace up, so the left one will fit over my swollen foot. I won't have to pull it on." Mel bent over her leg to wrap her injured ankle.

Cory stood over her, watching intently. "I still don't know how you're gonna ride."

Mel wondered herself, but she wasn't going to let on. She was determined to ride, just as she was resolved not to complain.

"It won't hurt that much to ride."

Mel relished the child's presence and her real concern. That she cared for other people was a good sign. That she cared for the woman, who she didn't know was her mother, made Mel warm with pride and gratitude. Cory's curiosity and gumption also pleased her. Once again, she was thankful that her decision years ago had paid off. Cory had turned into a bright, happy, little girl.

Jake walked down the shed row toward them. "Need any help?"

Mel didn't say anything. The memory of being carried in his arms was too fresh, her emotions too raw. She slanted a hard look at him.

He winked impudently. Mel's cheeks grew hot, an all too common habit around Jake.

"Still going through with this?" he asked, his husky voice making her lightheaded. "You don't have to, you know."

"What do you think?"

Jake let out a resigned sigh. "At least, let me help you with the bandage." Before she could protest, he knelt and took the bandage from her hands. "You are sure making a mess of this."

Mel was unable to speak. With his shoulders stooped and his head bent, Jake looked strangely vulnerable as he knelt before her. She longed to reach out and touch his bowed head, to tangle her fingers in his hair. She longed to kiss his misplaced dimple.

The feel of his powerful hands on her bare foot sent a wave of desire surging through her. She fought these sensations as he placed the end of the bandage on her instep and rolled it three times around her foot. Already churning because of preshow nerves, her stomach now roiled. Slowly, Jake moved the bandage around the ankle and downward across the front of the foot in a figure eight pattern. Mel watched his experienced hands. Her eyelashes drifted across her eyes as her imagination caused other violent waves of desire to track through her body. He touched her instep once more, and she drew in a sharp intake of breath.

"Did I hurt you?"

Mel's eyes flew open. Jake's gaze was level with hers, his expression unreadable.

"No, no. I'm fine." She could barely talk.

Jake lowered his head and continued with his task. She had to handle the way she felt about him. She realized she couldn't react so physically toward him or she'd never be able to work with him until the Louisville show. She had to toughen up. Try to avoid him and curb her unbridled responses to him.

"I think I can put on my own boot." Mel snatched Vanessa's boot from his hand and shoved it over the bandage.

"Sure thing." Jake stood up and backed away.

Mel didn't miss the wink he directed at Cory. The little girl's face beamed as if she had witnessed a wonderful secret. Mel wondered what she had failed to see, or was it that Cory had sensed her response to Jake?

When she finished lacing both boots, she straightened and placed her hands on the arms of the chair. Mel pushed herself out of the chair and tested her foot on the ground. It didn't hurt too much. Not any more than her heart.

Dave led Royalty's Dreamer up and made him stretch out.

Cory handed her a black, wool hat. "Here's your derby, Mel."

Mel settled it on her head and then pulled on black leather gloves.

"I think you've forgotten something else, madam."

Jake held a red rose in one hand and a long pin in another.

Her eyebrow arched. "What now?"

"I know you've about had all the help from me you can stomach, but I think this time it's a must." Jake said. "That is, if

70

you want your boutonniere pinned on your lapel. Cory's so small, she'd pin it to your knee."

"I would not!" Cory protested, kicking dirt at Jake.

Mel thrust out her chin and took a steadying breath. Then she averted her eyes. "Hurry up."

Jake stepped forward. He touched the lapel of her coat, overwhelming her with his nearness. As he pinned on the red rose, she stood motionless, feeling his warmth and hearing the rhythm of his breath.

"See, that wasn't so bad." Jake's voice had changed, lowering an octave.

His eyes glowed for a moment, and then raw sexual attraction vibrated once more between them. Her throat dry, Mel ogled him.

"I'll give you a leg up," he offered, his voice thick with emotion.

"No, you won't. Dave can do it," Mel said. Why did the old groom looked so pleased?

Chapter Six

The next afternoon, Jake relaxed in a director's chair near their rented stalls. Resting his hands behind his head, his long legs stretched out in front of him, he had a good view of the woman who caused intense tremors to race through his body. True to her word, Mel won the ladies' five-gaited class on Royalty's Dreamer. Phase one of winning the World's Grand Championship had begun as planned.

Dressed as she was in a formal white shirt with sleeves rolled up to the elbow and wool Kentucky jods, Mel had to be hot. Perspiration beaded her upper lip. Her glorious auburn hair was severely pulled back into a bun at the nape of her neck, emphasizing her high cheekbones and firm jawline. Stubborn jawline, he amended as his thoughts drifted.

Her distracted gaze caught his and held until he winked. She stiffened, and he acknowledged her uneasiness with a nod. She presented him with her back, continuing to help Cory dress for her afternoon equitation class.

Talk about mother hens. Jake had never seen so many at one time. Pop, Mel, and Vanessa crowded around the little girl, all of them getting into each other's way. He had never taught youngsters, so this whole process held his undivided attention.

"Quit wiggling," Vanessa scolded, her mouth full of bobby pins. She was trying to capture Cory's a hair into a bun similar to Mel's. That hairstyle and traditional attire—black paddock boots, wool jodhpurs, matching saddle coat, vest, conservative tie, black gloves, and a derby hat—were requirements in the horse show ring. However, Cory's sandy hair was finer than Mel's and not a bit cooperative.

"Hold yer horses, darlin'," Pop joined in. "Yer almost done."

Mel sprayed the child's hair. A hiss of spray plastered every strand in place. Vanessa held out a hairnet.

"Shoo. That stinks," Cory complained about the spray but held unmoving until Mel and Vanessa finished putting the hairnet over the bun and adjusting her derby.

The three "mother hens" had slowly transformed the rambunctious nine-year-old into a carbon copy of an adult rider. Mel pinned a fresh red rose on Cory's lapel, much as he had done for Mel the night before. His eyes narrowed. Why did a knot suddenly form in his stomach? Except for their coloring, Cory and Mel were mirror images standing side-by-side.

Cory came up to Jake and stood for inspection. He lowered his hands and sat up straight, feeling a sudden twist of nerves in the pit of his stomach, something at odds with his nonchalant manner.

"Looking good," he drawled. "Question is—can you ride that horse?"

"Damn straight!" Cory responded, her chin high, a gleam of resolve in her eyes.

"Cory!" Vanessa, Pop, and Mel chided simultaneously.

Jake laughed. "You guys are insufferable. You'll make this child a bundle of nerves. C'mon Cory, let's go find your ride."

Jake captured the little girl's hand and then swung her onto his shoulders. The echo of her laughter sounded down the quiet barn shed row.

* * *

Vanessa and Pop followed Jake and Cory. Mel tagged along in the rear. Her ankle wasn't so painful that she needed to lag behind, but her awkward limp gave her an excuse to dawdle. Seeing Jake and Cory together tugged at her heart. Had she been

74

wrong to separate them? For once, she felt regret, not just guilt. Had the decision she'd made alone as a frightened teenage girl been the right one?

Mel reached the make-up area in time to see Jake warm up Cory's horse. Five minutes before the call to the class, Dave held the gelding's head while Jake lifted Cory into the saddle. The little nine-year-old looked so grown up and beautiful. Having a hard time swallowing, Mel watched from a distance.

"Chin up!" Jake called to Cory. "Look between your horse's ears."

"Get those heels down, child," Pop ordered.

"Hands up!" Vanessa added her instruction.

This was a beginner walk and trot class for Cory's age group. However, the way the adults acted, it might as well have been the World's Grand Championship. The class was called. Cory asked the horse to pick up a trot, got her diagonal correct, and rode into the arena. Mel followed everyone, and as the gate was shut, shimmied in on the rail for a good view.

Jake joined her. "You're mighty quiet."

Mel shrugged. "Not much to say."

"Just nerves. Like me. I know how it is." Cory passed by their spot on the rail. "You're off. Change diagonals!" Jake shouted. "Now show that horse!" To Mel, he said, "She's doing great. I don't think the judge saw her mistake."

Mel poked him in the ribs. "Not until you yelled at her, he didn't!" Literally sick with nerves, Mel clutched the wooden rail. She didn't watch the whole class, only one horse and one small rider.

She'd taught youngsters all during her career. She'd worked at horse shows with many little girls and anxious mothers. This one was different. This time, Mel was the nervous mother, and it was a new and petrifying experience.

As the thought crossed her mind, Mel noticed Jake studying the riders intently. He was as nervous as she.

Suddenly, she felt very sad. They could have been a family. Her shoulders sagged, and she fought back tears.

When Cory won her first blue ribbon, everyone thought the tears she shed were tears of happiness.

* * *

Mel couldn't sleep. Pop's snoring was one reason. To save money, they shared a motel room at the hotel near the horse show facilities. Yet, the second more pressing reason for her wakefulness had to do with Jake and Cory and the mess Mel realized she'd made of her life.

We could have been a family.

Her mind replayed those words like a child repeated a favorite song.

Wearing a T-shirt, shorts, and sandals, Mel picked up the door key and slipped out of the sonorous confines of her room. The long hallways were dim and quiet. With only a slight limp, she padded down her hall and turned the corner, the lobby a bright beacon in the distance.

"Mel!"

"Hi, Vanessa. What are you doing out here?" Vanessa linked arms with her and they continued toward the lobby.

"I just got Cory to sleep. Now I can get that drink I need," Vanessa said. "Join me?"

"Sure. Pop's snoring keeps me awake."

Vanessa cast a sympathetic look her way. "Wondered what you were doing out so late. You and Pop keep early hours." They went into the bar. "We need to celebrate anyway. Cory's blue ribbon thrilled me to death."

Mel climbed onto the bar stool. "She did a great job."

The bartender came up to them. "What will it be, ladies?"

"Give me a Maker's and water." Vanessa said. She turned to Mel. A diamond ring on her finger sparkled in the garish light of the bar. "This is on me."

"Just a Coke, please."

"Be right up."

"Cory was so excited," Vanessa explained, her voice chatty like a proud mother.

If it hadn't been for the heaviness of her heart, Mel would have been excited too. Her daughter had ridden almost perfectly. Cory had talent. It ran in the family, it seemed. But she couldn't acknowledge her pride, not in the way she wanted.

"She made me put the ribbon on the pillow beside her head or she wouldn't go to sleep."

The waiter brought their drinks. Removing the paper from the straw, Mel toyed with it a moment before putting the straw into the glass.

I should have been the one to put Cory's ribbon on her pillow. I'm her mother.

Mel lowered her head and sipped the cold, effervescent liquid.

Vanessa picked up her drink. "Remember your first blue ribbon?"

"Yes," Mel murmured, squeezing her eyes shut. "I was mighty young."

She briefly considered her childhood, but her thoughts returned like a boomerang to her later screw-ups.

We could have been a family.

Opening her eyes, she saw her soft drink glass, wet with condensation, and trailed her fingertip along a droplet of water.

Vanessa spoke again, catching Mel's attention. "I was so upset when my mother and father adopted Cory." She glanced at Mel. "You know how it is, being an only child too. I had been the center of their lives for so long." Mel heard a trace of self-deprecating amusement in Vanessa's voice. "You get used to being spoiled."

"Mmm, I know," Mel mumbled.

"But Cory bought my parents so much joy. She's comforted me too, filling a void after my parents' deaths." Vanessa sipped her drink again.

The fuzziness in Mel's brain focused. She straightened up and drew a deep breath, realizing she had never come to terms with giving up Cory. *Never.* There had been a void in her life too, and it had nothing to do with her failed marriage or disappointment in love. It was an emptiness only a mother who had lost a child could know.

Oh, dear God. She wanted Cory back.

Hardly breathing, Mel felt the texture of her skin prickle with a strange heat. She felt her face flush. Why now? She'd never wanted her daughter back before. It had been so tough carrying a child for nine months, loving her even before she was born, dreaming of holding her in her arms, and all those years so filled with guilt that she had given her baby away. She'd told herself she'd dealt with her emotions after the adoption, but here they were, bubbling up into her present.

What had changed? *She had changed.* She'd finally got up enough gumption to divorce Lenny. Then Pop had scared her with his heart attack. It frightened her to think she might lose him. Finally, Jake Hendricks had slithered back into her life like some insidious serpent.

Jake—with his burning blue eyes and appealing dimple. Jake—exasperating but exciting, a splendid figure on the back of Dreamcatcher, athletic and sexy. Warmth suffused her whole being with a curious glow. She remembered the roughened palms of his hands and the rhythmic rise and fall of his chest as he carried her. She longed for him as a wife should long for her husband.

The thought stopped Mel's breath. She confronted the idea of Jake as a husband, and her breathing started again, coming in slow, strained jerks.

"Why, how do you do, Miss Noble?" A jarring voice snapped Mel back to the reality of the crowded bar.

She turned to find a large man with a ponderous belly hovering by Vanessa's side.

Vanessa acknowledged the man with a polite nod. "Mr. Bishop."

"May I sit down?"

Vanessa nodded her head again, and the man collapsed onto an empty bar stool. Mel noticed Vanessa's fingers tighten on her glass.

"Mr. Bishop," Vanessa said. "May I introduce Melody O'Shea. Mel, this is Kyle Bishop, owner of Bishopgate Realty."

"Melody O'Shea? Any relation to the famous horse trainer?"

"Yes," Mel replied. "My father."

79

"Mel works for me now. She's one of my best trainers and a most valued employee. She saved many of our horses from the fire."

"Ah, yes. I heard about that. I'm so sorry," Bishop murmured his condolences and then turned to the bartender to order a Bud Lite.

"Mel, Mr. Bishop has offered me a considerable sum of money for Royalty Farm," Vanessa remarked dryly. She then lifted her glass to her lips as if to wash away her words.

Mel glanced at her employer. She felt an odd tension between the two. This must be the realtor Jake and Pop worried about, the guy with his sights set on building a subdivision on Royalty Farm property.

"I didn't think the farm was for sale," Mel remarked.

"Ah, that's what Miss Noble tells me." Bishop looked down at them. "I can't convince her running a horse farm alone is not the job for a beautiful woman."

"Well, what kind of job is a *beautiful woman* supposed to have?" Vanessa asked with a quick, disgusted snort.

Mel tried to hide her smile. Vanessa was on the warpath, and she silently cheered her on. The man's comment was certainly not politically correct.

Bishop must have realized his error. "Any job a beautiful woman wants," he agreed but without conviction.

Fortunately, fate saved Bishop when his dinner companions arrived. "Ah, my drink is here, and there are my friends." With a nod to the waiter to keep the change, he collared up his bottle and climbed to his feet. "Do we still have an appointment next Thursday, Miss Noble?"

"Yes, but it's a waste of your time, Mr. Bishop."

"Ah, we shall see, now won't we?" He tilted his head away and rolled his eyes with skepticism. "Just give me a chance to explain my proposition," Bishop said and turned to Mel. "Nice to meet you *Miss* O'Shea, or is it *Miz?*"

"It's simply Mel."

"Then good night to you, Mel, and Miss Noble." He flashed a cold smile and departed.

Mel let out a huge breath of relief. "What a weasel. He makes my skin crawl."

"Mine too. Kyle Bishop doesn't know what century he's living in." Vanessa shook her head in apparent disbelief. Her short laugh had an edge to it.

"That's for sure. You're not thinking of selling Royalty Farm, are you?"

"No."

Vanessa's reaction was a little too quick and sharp for Mel's comfort. They remained quiet for a time while Mel toyed with her straw.

Vanessa swirled the ice in her glass. "Had you heard that Jake worked at a farm in Altadena when that training barn burned?"

"If memory serves, Jake's first job in California was in Altadena. That was ten years ago. What does that have to do with the fire at Royalty Farm?"

Vanessa leaned forward, nodding slowly. "Just curious. A few owners were talking about it last night at the show. I overheard them."

"What are you suggesting?" Mel studied the gleam of Vanessa's diamond ring. She was unable to look Vanessa in the eyes. "Do you believe Jake had something to do with our barn fire?"

"I think it's interesting Jake was at another farm that had a barn fire."

"Jake didn't have anything to do with the fire." Mel tried to suppress the sinking feeling in her stomach. "What would his motive be?"

"To make himself look good by winning the World's Grand Championship."

"What? No way!" Mel slanted her body away from her friend. "Competing in the championship was Pop's idea. The thought never crossed Jake's mind."

Vanessa toyed with her drink. "You sound as if you're privy to his thinking."

"No." Mel shook her head. "I simply made that assumption from the way he behaved afterwards."

"You know what they say about people who assume?"

Mel caught the mean implication and pressed her lips together in a slight grimace. She was reminded of their childhood. Once when she and Vanessa had played together too long, they had gotten tired and started throwing their toys at each other. That's when their mothers had stepped in and separated them, saying they behaved like sisters.

Not having a mother to do the honors, Mel pushed her glass back and stood. "Sorry. I don't think your speculations are worthy of my comment," she said. "Unless you have firm facts, you shouldn't gossip about your own trainer. For one thing, it's bad for business. For another, that's not Jake. Thanks for the drink, but I need to get some sleep."

She'd never talked to Vanessa that way. It was scary but felt really good. Letting out the anger instead of allowing it to simmer was something she'd learned to do only recently. Chin jutted forward, shoulders back, she stalked through the bar and sought sanctuary in the darkness beside the hotel swimming pool.

The night air was close and damp, and heat sucked the breath from her lungs. Mel welcomed it after the coldness in the bar. Collapsing in a lounge chair, she stretched out her legs. In the distance, thunder grumbled. Lightening flickered all around—sharp sparks darting here and there.

Really, Vanessa was amazing. Did she really think Jake could be involved in setting the barn fire after all he'd done to save those horses? Vanessa hadn't been there. She hadn't seen his horrified eyes or felt his strong hand that had propelled her out of the inferno.

"It's going to rain."

Mel wrenched into a sitting position when she heard Jake's voice. As he sat beside her in the neighboring lounge chair, Mel slumped back into hers and said, "It doesn't take a brain surgeon to figure that one out."

"Testy tonight, aren't we?" Jake stretched out and put his hands behind his head. "What are you doing here?"

"Trying to find a little peace and quiet."

"With a thunderstorm coming? You have a strange sense of peace and quiet."

"And you have a strange sense of what it means to mind your own business."

Jake chuckled staring up at the sky. His amusement angered Mel even more. Thankfully, he had the grace to remain silent.

83

The only noise was the distant thunder and the remote sound of music and laughter from the bar. Overhead, the erratic natural light show played its frenzied game.

"I can't seem to get that fire out of my mind," Jake said after a while. "Who thought we'd make it to Lexington after what happened?"

"We've got Pop to thank for that."

"You've got to admit, Pop's a cagey old cuss." Jake dropped his hands and folded his arms over his chest.

Mel fought her physical awareness of the man by her side. She glanced his way, envisioning the times they had stretched out together in the hay loft, talking, touching, and kissing. She frowned at her line of thinking and at the overt response of her body. It was easier to allow her anger flow—less threatening, easier to contend with than emotions and desire she had no business feeling.

Their gazes connected for one intense moment. "I still can't believe someone deliberately set that fire."

Mel had trouble turning her head away. "The police are trying to find out who did it."

"The police," Jake growled. "Just a bunch of country bumpkins, if you ask me."

"Now look who's testy tonight."

For a moment, Jake avoided direct eye contact. "Besides destroying some fine horses, the fire has devastated Vanessa financially and Pop emotionally, not to mention almost ruining my career."

"Ah, the sacred career." Mel's words were heavy with scorn. "I forgot about it for a moment."

Jake scowled, a tightness in his expression. "My career is my life. It's who I am and what I do. You never understood that about me."

"But I *have* understood that about you. All too well."

The direction of this conversation made Mel uneasy for it hit too close to home. It had been at the core of her disagreement with Jake ten years earlier, a disagreement that caused her to give up Cory and lose the family she now so desperately wanted. Jake had refused to marry her. Not that she'd told him the most pressing reason why they needed to marry. She had wanted to be wanted for herself. To be loved for herself. But Jake had said they were too young. He had a great career opportunity in California. He was going to take it. He didn't need a wife tagging along.

"Well, if you've understood that about me, you also know I take responsibility for everything that happens when I'm in charge. Therefore, it's my duty to salvage something from the barn fire."

"Yeah, I know. For Pop's dream."

"What's so wrong with having a dream? What's eating at you anyway, Mel?"

"Oh, don't act so high and mighty with me, not after I just defended you to Vanessa."

Jake sat up and shifted his legs to sit on the side of the lounge chair, his eyes wary. "Defended me? What for?"

"Our boss has heard rumors *you* set the fire."

"What?"

"Apparently, it's the gossip of the show. Jake Hendricks, arsonist personified," she said, derision in her voice.

Jake leaned forward and grasped Mel's chin in his fingertips. She couldn't turn away. She swallowed, her throat suddenly dry.

His eyes glittering and dangerous, Jake asked, "What do *you* think?"

"I told you I defended you," Mel said in a bare whisper.

"But do you believe it of me?"

Something important rode on her answer. Something like trust, which she wasn't sure she had where Jake was concerned. She felt her pulse quicken as he watched her intently.

"I don't think you'd deliberately start a fire that would kill horses." Mel took a steadying breath. She had defended Jake to Vanessa, because bottom line, she did trust him. Suddenly making up her mind, she threw up her hands. "No, you didn't do it."

"Good." He released her. Coming to his feet, he walked to the edge of the pool. Backlit against the stormy night, he stood with hands on his hips.

Mel was fascinated by his broad shoulders, trim hips, and long, muscular legs. Absently, she rubbed her jaw. Had she really said she trusted him?

Turning around, Jake came back to her. "You know what's ironic?" When Mel didn't answer, he went on, "I've been thinking Vanessa has a pretty good motive herself for wanting to burn down the barn."

"What?" It was Mel's turn to scoff in disbelief. "Why would Vanessa do that?"

"Money."

"Money?"

"Yes. Insurance money," Jake said. "And if she sells the farm without rebuilding the barn, she'll have more of it."

"Jake, that's ridiculous." Mel stared up at him, her breath catching in her chest.

He took a step closer. "What's ridiculous about it? People do crazy things for money."

"But Vanessa has plenty. Why should she want more? Why would she destroy her father's farm?"

Their conversation was only secondary. They communicated with their eyes, bright and glossy with unspoken emotion. Mel's face felt flush, not just with heat, but with emotion that permeated through her motionless body.

"Vanessa doesn't have all the money you think she does. Her father had debts," Jake said, his voice suddenly hushed. "Vanessa has added her own debt."

He moved closer and pulled her to his feet and into his arms. Mel's heart now galloped in her chest, just as thunder shattered the stillness. Warmth radiating from his skin. His work-roughened fingers chafed the soft flesh of her upper arms. He held her tenderly, reverently.

She searched his face then shuddered with desire. She leaned toward him, almost begging, almost pleading.

Jake's kiss was like soft raindrops. He showered her mouth, her chin, her closed eyelids, and her mouth again with tiny offerings. She returned his kisses, finally securing his mouth. Desire pulsed through her body. Then his tongue tested the softness between her lips. Mel responded, leaning into him, aching for him.

As the first raindrops began to fall, he broke off and held her away from him. "Nothing like a shower of reason to cool us off." His voice was thick with passion. "This is stupid for us to do."

Mel couldn't respond. She opened her eyes, wanting to scream at him that it wasn't stupid. That it was right. Perfect. Beautiful. But she couldn't speak.

Jake left her standing in a shower of rain with no more adequate explanation than when he had left ten years earlier—left her wanting more, wanting him.

Chapter Seven

The next day, Jake stood in the middle of the make-up area while Mel warmed up Royalty. Damn! He'd been stupid. He should have known kissing her would lead to his craving more. Jake had wanted Mel so much last night he'd forced himself to walk away. It had been the hardest thing he'd ever done.

No. Leaving Mel ten years ago had been the hardest.

Jake beat a riding crop against his leg. What he had done those years ago—he'd been right to leave her. If he hadn't, Mel would have skipped college and not gotten a degree as Pop had planned.

He hadn't figured on her getting married. That hadn't been part of *his* plan. He'd intended to marry her after she received that degree, after they'd both grown up a bit. But it wasn't meant to be.

Jake cracked the crop even harder against his leg, almost relishing the sting as Pop gave Mel last minute instructions, and Sam the assistant groom checked her girth.

Last night he'd felt Mel's response to his kiss, and it had only quickened his own desire. Even remembering it, he grew uncomfortable. He recalled the honey flavor of her lips and the aroma of her perfume.

Jake shifted his stance. He couldn't go on like this. The championship in Louisville seemed a lifetime away. He would be a walking maniac if he didn't get some relief before then.

But it was more than his physical reaction to the woman who now sat calmly on the back of the black mare. His leaving Kentucky had left a big emptiness in his life. He'd filled that hole with hard work. He was older now. Wiser. And Mel was wrong. He wanted more from life than simply a great career. If he succeeded at Louisville, if his career at Royalty Farm took off, he wanted someone to share it with. The thought of being alone for the rest of his life made him miserable.

Unfortunately, his stupid scheme to have Mel react to his male charm had backfired big time. Except for her obvious sexual reaction to him, Mel had not shown any inclination to consider him anything more than a bothersome jerk. Another dumb male, like her ex-husband.

Jake's jaw tightened. What if they lost at Louisville? What if Mel left the farm? He had to think about how he would cope if she vanished from his life again.

He must be realistic. He'd hurt her once. From the things she'd let slip, her marriage had hurt her badly as well. Why would she want to trust another man? Why would she trust him?

The announcer called the class. Jake pulled himself out of his musings.

"Mel!" He walked to where she sat astride the horse.

She glanced at him, warily but didn't speak.

"Here's your crop," he said, handing it to her.

She took the end, and for a moment, they were connected by the leather stick. What was she thinking?

Mel nodded to him. "Thanks."

Jake stepped back. Sadness settled inside him. Jake hated that her conversation was always guarded and awkward, that Mel could no longer be free with him like she'd been as a teenager.

She straightened in the saddle, stretching down her heels and squaring her shoulders. She lifted her chin as if to gain confidence. Shortening her reins, she nudged the horse slightly with her legs and said "Trot." Royalty's Dreamer responded like a finely-tuned car. The horse picked up the trot and carried Mel into the competition.

Up to the rail, Jake put his hands on the rough wood. Once, just once, he and Mel had consummated the love they had shared. Granted, it had been a puppy love, a young love, but he'd found over the years that nothing else had equaled it.

Back then, his cooler head had prevailed. He'd done the noble thing, only to have fortune intervene when Mel married another man. He'd been a fool never to speak up and tell her his plans. Now that she was divorced and he had another chance, would some other cruel fate keep them apart?

Jake took a long breath, turning his mind to the business at hand. Quickly assessing the circling horses and riders, he decided Mel was definitely wining the ladies' five-gaited championship. She had Royalty set up nicely, going down the straightaway at a fast, five-beat rack. One judge marked his score card as she passed.

Mel rounded the sharp corner, handling it perfectly. That's when it happened—quickly without warning. Her saddle slipped to the left and she fell hard against the tanbark surface. Royalty reared and galloped away.

Jake didn't remember climbing over the railing. He heard the collective gasp from the crowd, but then he heard nothing but the pounding of his own pulse as he ran the length of the track. He thought he heard Mel cry out.

"Mel!" Jake knelt beside her just as she gasped. Her eyes were wide with fright. He removed the derby from her head.

Others quickly joined him, hovering over Mel, poking at her, probing. He wanted to protect her, shove them all back, say she belonged to him.

"Jake, we've halted the class," the ringmaster said, "and called for an ambulance."

"Thanks, Don."

Mel's chest heaved with her effort to speak. "I don't need an ambulance. It was just…my breath…knocked out…"

"Shut up! This is one time you'll do as you're told."

Mel pushed up on an elbow. "Let me up. I can finish the class."

"Damn it, Mel, you don't have to prove how tough you are. You've had a hard fall. The medics are going to look at you."

"You're not my keeper, Jake Hendricks." Mel struggled to move her feet under her, to get momentum to stand. A look of pain shot across her face.

"That's it. You lie back. Flat," he ordered. "You may have a head injury."

Jake took Mel's shoulders in his hands and gently, but forcefully, pressed her back down. The wool fabric of her coat was coarse to his touch. He was hot. She must be sweltering. He longed to remove the constricting garment, but he knew it best not to move her any more than necessary. Already the ambulance rumbled toward them.

Mel threw him a look of exasperation. A feeling of despair clutching at his heart, Jake squeezed his lips together and returned her gaze, not backing down.

Then the paramedics were there, and Jake was pushed aside. He stood, immobile, impotent, while Mel's vital signs were checked, her neck was wrapped into a cervical collar and her body was stretched onto a backboard. At one point, he realized Pop stood beside him, the old man's face like white paste. For once, Pop kept his mouth shut and didn't remark about falls "makin' you tough."

"Someone going with her?" a paramedic asked.

Jake hesitated. He was nothing to Mel. She wouldn't want him along for the ride. It was Pop's place, not his. Making up his mind, he guided Pop toward the ambulance and helped him climb in.

As the ambulance left and the group of people began to disperse, Jake remained stationary, his gaze on his boots. The shock of the sudden accident began to seep into his consciousness. He took a deep breath, hoping to relieve the nerves that cramped his stomach. Nothing worked. He plowed a hand through his hair.

"C'mon, Jake, let's go." Dave's familiar voice was forceful.

The little groom stood beside him, Mel's saddle in his arms.

"The ringmaster wants to finish the class," Dave said. "Pick up Mel's hat and let's go."

"Where's the horse?"

"She's been caught and taken back to the barn."

Walking in a nightmare, Jake followed Dave out of the arena.

"I want you to take a look at this girth," Dave said when they arrived at their stall area. "Something's wrong with it."

"What is it?"

"I think it's been cut."

* * *

Mel's eyes flickered open. She was cold. Only a thin hospital sheet covered her. She pulled it up to her chin, wishing she was back in the motel room listening to Pop's snores.

Instead, the emergency room doctor had decided to admit her overnight. Now she lay flat on her back, disgusted with herself and her situation. She'd been winning the class. Royalty would have been the stake champion and positioned very nicely for the World's Grand Championship in August. Not now. Not since Mel had lost her balance and toppled off the horse's back.

She could kick herself. She'd never fallen off like that. Why now, just going around a sharp turn? It didn't make sense.

Nothing made much sense anymore. Not her physical reaction to Jake. Not her longing for the daughter she'd given up. Not the overriding guilt she felt for things long done and gone.

Pale light seeped through the curtains at the window. It must be early. She sighed and shut her eyes. The doctor said he wouldn't discharge her until midmorning.

"Good morning, Melody."

Lenny! Mel's eyes flew open. Her ex-husband stood next to her bed. Fear slammed through her body causing her to tremble. Eyes wide, she breathed quickly.

"What are you doing here?"

"I thought I'd offer you my support. I saw that horrible accident last night." Lenny peered at her with eyes that didn't register his concern.

"I don't need your support." She turned her head from his unwelcome perusal.

He came nearer and touched the side of the bed. Mel's flesh crawled. Pushing up on her elbow, and wincing at the effort, Mel tried to remove some of the disadvantage she felt lying flat in the bed. Her efforts simply put her at eye level with the man she'd grown to hate.

"You were doing so well too," he said with a sweet tone of irony in his voice.

Her stomach tightened. Sweat broke out on her body, causing her flesh to chill even more. "Get out of my room."

"Now, Mel, is that the way to act?"

"Get out of my room! I'll push the button for the nurse." Flinching as a pain shot through her hips, Mel fumbled for the button.

"Why do that? This is just a friendly little visit."

"You and I haven't been friends for a very long time. I said get out!"

As she grabbed the button, Lenny caught her hand. "You wouldn't want me to tell Jake Hendricks, would you?"

Mel went very still. "Tell him what?"

"About Cory."

Her senses spun. She'd never told Lenny about Cory. What did this man know?

"Take your hands off me!"

"Then say you'll have dinner with me." Lenny spoke softly, but the menace in his voice was plain.

"Don't threaten me."

"But you won't listen to me otherwise."

Mel's gaze held his for one endless moment, and then she broke eye contact, glancing away. Her breathing was shallow. Lenny meant what he said. Whatever he knew—or thought he knew—he would use it against her. She had to do what he asked. Once. Just once. If for nothing else but to discover what he knew.

Maybe when she wasn't half naked in a hospital gown tied at the back, she would not be at such a disadvantage. With advance warning, she might be able to cope with her ex-husband. It was a chance she had to take.

"When?"

"In two weeks. Before Shelbyville. I'll take you to the Old Stone Inn. You always enjoyed eating there."

"Whatever," she said, dismissing him and looking away. "Just let me know."

"That's my girl."

Mel heard the triumph in his voice. She'd lost again. Why hadn't the divorce ended it all?

"I'm not your *girl*," Mel said, but when she looked back, he was gone.

She let the tension seep away from her like the air from a balloon. Slowly, she slid under the thin sheet, her body shaking from shock. She clutched the edge of it. Lenny was blackmailing her, using whatever knowledge he had to make her do what he wanted.

But what did he want? Sickening fear blossomed again in her belly.

If Lenny knew Jake had fathered her child, she must keep the news from Cory. It served no purpose for the little girl to know who her birth father was. Not now. Not when she was so happy.

What would Jake think when he learned he had a daughter?

Mel had never dreamed she'd face the day when Jake found out about Cory. For a teenager, tomorrow never comes. Consequences are overlooked.

Soon she might have to pay for the mistake she'd made. This time, other people might have to pay too.

* * *

"Damn me, darlin', the doctor said bed rest, and that's just what you're gonna do," Pop told her.

Mel crossed her arms in front of her chest in frustration. "But, Pop, tonight's the championship."

"An' we don't need you there."

"Pop's right, Mel," Vanessa said. "We can take care of everything. Your health is the most important thing you have to worry about. You gave us quite a scare. We thought you had a concussion."

Mel sighed. She didn't like this fuss. She must be Pop's daughter after all. "I've only got a bruise," she offered, but knew her battle was lost.

"Yeah, a bruised tailbone. C'n hardly walk." Pop shuffled around the bed and glared at her. "Could've been a damned lot worse."

Mel had to admit the two of them were right. Her pain had been so great she'd expected something worse too. Nothing as simple as "take your prescription and you'll be fine in about ten days." Putting on her blue jeans a few moments ago had been agonizing, so she hoped the promised ten days flew by quickly.

An orderly brought a wheelchair to the door and announced Mel's ride had arrived. She crawled out of bed, barely able to walk without grimacing. A bruised tailbone was embarrassing. Good grief. She'd fallen off horses before and never received a bruise like this. Gingerly, she slipped into the wheelchair for the ride to the hospital entrance. Vanessa lowered the footrests.

"Jake's got it all under control," Pop said from behind.

"I bet he does."

"We're only showing Dreamcatcher tonight."

Pop wasn't telling her anything she didn't know, but Mel bit back a barbed retort. After all, he was her dad, and he was only keeping up conversation.

"Did I tell you Cory won the walk and trot championship?" Vanessa asked from behind.

"No!" Mel twisted to look at her and felt a sharp twinge of pain.

Vanessa hurried to walk beside the wheelchair. "Don't turn. I know it hurts."

Mel wrinkled up her nose and drew her brows together. She hated admitting weakness.

Vanessa had a delighted look on her face. "Cory was first on all three judges' cards."

"That's great!" Mel said as she clutched the arms of the wheelchair. "Cory will put the farm on the map faster than the rest of us."

Vanessa nodded. "I'm already planning my advertising spread in the *Show Horse Report*. It should be grand."

They reached the lobby. A bank of glass windows allowed the summer sun to thrust its way into the waiting area. In the glare, a single figure waited by the sliding glass door. A shiver skittered down her spine. Jake!

"What's he doing here?" she asked too quickly.

"Takin' you home." Did Pop hide a conspiratorial grin?

"Shouldn't he be at the show?"

"I said he had it all under control." Pop nodded at Jake who came toward them. "'Sides, he volunteered."

"It figures."

Jake offered his hand. "Mel, let me help you."

Feeling a flush creep up her face, Mel simply gave him a blank look. For a tense moment, he stared at her and then stooped over to flip the footrests up. Mel climbed to her feet, wincing as the pain shot down her back. When he took her elbow, she was glad for his support.

"Y'all drive careful," Pop said after Mel had clambered ungracefully into the cab of Jake's truck.

Looking down at her father, at his thinning white hair and his gnarled hand resting on the open window, Mel smiled. "I'll be okay, Pop. Don't worry about me."

"Damn straight, you'll be okay. Just wanted to warn that boy, there." He backed away from the truck.

"See ya'," Mel said with a slight wave.

"Take care of yourself, Mel," Vanessa called as they pulled away. "We'll look after the horses."

And then she was alone with Jake.

Mel pushed the button to shut the window. A thin stream of cool air from the dashboard hit her face. The summer sun beat through the passenger-side window. She was hot. The air conditioning barely made a dent in the uncomfortable cab. Or maybe it wasn't the temperature. Maybe it was the tension that crackled between them as the truck threaded through traffic.

She glanced at Jake, only to discover his eyes glued to the road. Minutes dragged by and neither one of them spoke. Mel's uneasiness increased. She needed to break the silence. She needed to thank him for the ride and tell him she was sorry. Sorry for what? So many things. Her list was long and rambling. Yet, she dared not broach the subject that lay near her heart, the subject of the child they shared.

"I'm sorry about screwing up the class," Mel said instead. "I think I had a good shot at winning."

She saw him chance a glance at her before his gaze returned to the road. "You *were* winning."

"I don't know how I lost my balance." She shook her head. "It isn't like me."

Mel noticed Jake's grip tighten on the steering wheel. "It's easy to fall off if your girth has been cut."

Chapter Eight

"What?"

At a stoplight Jake looked at her. "The girth had been cut just enough so motion and the rider's weight finally severed it. That's why you fell, Mel. Someone wanted you to fall."

"Why?"

Their gazes locked. His eyes moved as he searched her face. The light turned. He looked away and stepped on the gas. "I don't know if someone was out to hurt the farm or you."

Mel rubbed her forehead in confusion. "Me?"

"Yes, remember the jog cart? Now I'm not so sure that was an accident."

Suddenly, the truck cab was too cold. Mel shivered and turned her head toward the passenger-side window. A spike of fear shot through her.

Lenny. Was this "someone" Lenny? He was going to blackmail her. Could he be trying to kill her too?

"That's why I wanted to take you home," Jake said.

Mel glanced back at him. "What did you say?"

"I wanted to get you away from the show. I'm not sure if you're safe there."

"Do you think this person could be the same one who set the barn fire?" Mel asked. Her stomach felt rock hard. "What if I'm not safe at the farm either?"

Jake sighed. "I hadn't thought about that."

Mel didn't need this added complication. Not with Lenny's threats hanging over her. "Maybe we should tell the police."

"They'll want suspects."

Maybe Jake had heard the ugly rumor about Vanessa. But she did have a motive. Money. Greed.

"Our suspects include you and Vanessa," Mel said in a monotone voice, "but I know you two didn't do it."

"Are you so sure?"

Mel glanced at him once more, noticing the slight movement in his jaw. She realized he wanted confirmation from her. "Yes."

Moments passed as she studied the furrowed line of his brow. His sandy hair seemed lighter, as if the sun had bleached it surfer blond. She longed to run her fingers through it and see his dimpled smile directed at her. She longed to feel his arms around her, warm and secure.

Mel turned away, remembering the night of the rain storm and the desire that had overwhelmed her. As the same feelings swept over her, she understood something else. Jake truly was concerned about her well-being.

"Okay, who else do we suspect?" Jake wanted to know. "I don't have a clue."

Mel chewed her lip. She couldn't mention Lenny. Not until she learned what he wanted. Slanting another look at Jake, she said, "There's that realtor. He's a real slime ball."

"What realtor?"

"The one who wants to buy Royalty Farm," Mel answered. "I met him the other night but wasn't impressed."

"In that case, the motive would be ruining Royalty Farm so Vanessa will sell it." Jake tapped a thumb on the wheel. "Doesn't sound as if you'd be involved in that one."

"Maybe I was in the wrong place at the wrong time," Mel suggested.

"It could be a disgruntled employee."

"Do we have a disgruntled employee?"

Jake checked for oncoming traffic and pulled onto the interstate highway. When he faced front again, Mel saw the tenseness in his jaw. "That's something we need to find out."

* * *

Mel was sick and tired of being sick and tired. She had literally been on her back for five days. Bedrest. She hated it. Pushing the controller button, she flipped off the television and stared at the darkened screen. Pop's living room was dim, cool, and confining. She hadn't been this inactive in ages.

Not anymore. She was done with being an invalid, no matter what Pop and Jake said. Mel forced herself up from the cluster of pillows propped at her back and sat up. She pulled on her paddock boots, stood, and with only a twinge of pain in her hips, left the house for the barn.

It was late July in Kentucky, and it was hot with no break in the weather expected for several days. Red clay dust swirled around her boots as she walked slowly towards the scene of the fire. The sun beating upon her bare head was a welcome change from Pop's cool house. Mel squinted to adjust to the bright glare.

Jake stood in the outside riding ring near the now leveled training barn giving Cory a riding lesson. Controlling her emotions when she saw them together, she strolled up to the railing and leaned against the wooden fence.

"Hup there! Show that horse, Cory!" Jake called, his words coming to Mel as if in a dream. She never thought she'd see Jake interact with his daughter.

The little girl spurred the big gelding into a faster show trot and headed down a straightaway.

"Keep those hands up!"

Cory responded immediately. She elevated her hands, squared her shoulders, pulled her body upright, and lifted her little chin. Her sandy hair bounced up and down with each post as she rode into the turn. If she saw Mel standing at the rail, Cory didn't acknowledge her. Her concentration was complete, a look of pride and confidence in her carriage.

Mel's stomach turned over. She recognized herself in her little girl's demeanor. She recognized the same stubborn determination, the same desire for excellence she had shown at that age. Would someone at the farm make the same connection?

At the same time, she also identified Cory's willingness to seek approval, to please the man who was giving her a lesson, and that bothered her. Mel remembered how it had felt to want to please Jake. Once he had wanted to please her. Cory was a byproduct of their longing to please each other. Mel regretted again her mistake. Maybe if she'd been stronger, she would never have given in to the passion that had overcome her good sense.

"Okay, walk and come on in and line up," Jake instructed.

He stood in the center of the ring, tall and proud. He tilted his head and switched a crop on his jodhpurs, his thigh muscles defined beneath the jean-like fabric. Cory rode over to him and nudged the back of her horse's front legs with the toe of her boot. The gelding stretched out and Cory poised herself for inspection. Jake circled around Cory pretending to be a judge. Once, he positioned her left leg and heel. Another time, he moved her hands higher.

Mel clutched the rough rail to control a sudden trembling. *Oh, my gosh!* The two mirrored each other. They had the same shape face and the same color of sandy hair. The only difference was Jake's misplaced dimple, high under his left eye. Cory's dimples were more normally placed next to her mouth, and when she smiled at her father, her dimples seemed to light up her whole face.

Would Jake see the resemblance too? Would he realize the child sitting on the back of the bay horse was a miniature of himself? Mel swallowed hard, regretting for the hundredth time they weren't a family. Couldn't be a family.

Again, an emptiness gripped her soul. She'd made a mistake, and now she fathomed how big a mistake it had been.

"Mel." Vanessa came to stand beside her. "Glad to see you up and around."

"I couldn't stay at home any longer," Mel said.

Vanessa didn't look at her but across the riding ring. "You stayed longer than I thought you would."

"I was being cautious." Had she also been trying to avoid Jake?

Cory turned the horse and headed toward them. "Hi, Vanessa. Mel!" she called with a wave of her hand. "Are you feeling better?"

"Yes, thank you." Mel felt a flush of pleasure at Cory's concern.

"Hey, that's good. Did you see me ride? Isn't Tia spectacular?" Cory reached down and hugged the neck of her horse.

"I think you're both wonderful," Mel said, a wistful note to her voice.

"Hop down, Cory. We need to go to the dentist." Vanessa opened the gate and took hold of the horse's bridle.

"I need to put Tia away."

Jake came up from behind. "I'll put your horse away, kiddo."

"Thanks, Jake." Cory dismounted and gave the gelding a final pat. She followed Vanessa to the car but turned before she opened the door. "Hey, Mel, I hope you don't mind Jake giving me a lesson. You can give me the next one."

Love tinged with regret surged through Mel. "I'd like that, Cory."

Cory waved again and climbed into the car.

"Cute kid," Jake said casually.

"Yes, she's a charmer."

Jake led Royal Tiara to the barn. Mel fell in beside him.

"I'm glad you're feeling better."

"Thanks."

They were quiet as they walked. A deep yearning burned inside her. She felt hot, not from the summer sun, but from being near Jake. His tan face was set, jaw immobile. Glancing down at her boots, she wished she didn't feel a swell of desire when she was with him but was able to remain distant, uncaring.

Maybe that had been part of her problem. She had never gotten over losing Jake. He'd been a third person in her marriage to Lenny, even though she had tried really hard to make the marriage work. Now, it was even harder to pretend an aloofness, especially when she'd seen him with his daughter—the daughter they should be parenting together if the universe was aligned properly.

"I haven't made much progress," Jake remarked.

"At what?"

"Finding a disgruntled employee. I've watched all our caretakers—Sam, Jose, and even Dave. I still don't have a clue."

Mel hesitated a second, and then continued walking on. No, she wouldn't think about Lenny. Not until she had dinner with him.

"None of this adds up." Jake scrubbed a hand over his face. "I must find out what's going on. I don't want to see anyone hurt again."

"You care?" She couldn't help being snarky.

"Of course, I care." Jake halted the horse and faced her. "What kind of comment was that?"

Mel stopped too. "You say you care, but I seem to remember a time when you didn't care enough about us here at Royalty Farm. You cared more about your career."

"Damn it all, Mel. You're talking about us, not this farm." He pointed at her and jabbed the air for emphasis. "You know I've always had your well-being at heart."

He clucked to the horse and walked on...fast. Mel couldn't keep up. When she got to the barn, Jake had already stripped Royal Tiara and put him in the cross-ties. She peered at Jake through the metal bars of the stall.

Her pulse raced. His betrayal had bothered her for years, eaten away at her. In the past, she'd always sidestepped it, never confronting him. Not now. She felt an overpowering need to get her hurt and anger out in the open. Maybe it had something to do with the daughter she'd given away.

"I don't know how you claim to care about me," Mel said quietly through the bars.

* * *

Jake glanced up from where he brushed the bay horse. He took a deep breath before he answered, "Mel, you think I left this farm because of my job offer in California."

"Well, didn't you? That's what you told me at the time."

Jake felt empty, powerless over Mel's misunderstanding. "I know that's what I said, but that's not the total reason."

"What is, then?" Mel demanded. "Isn't it about time you explained?"

Jake threw down the hard brush and confronted her at the stall door, his hand gripping the metal chain of the cross-tie. "I told you I had a new job because you wouldn't accept the real reason. You had marriage on your mind. You wanted to get engaged."

Mel bit her lip. Her eyes narrowed. When she answered, her voice was low but jeering. "I thought we had a good relationship. I believed we were in love. I didn't know you didn't feel the same way until you walked out on me."

Jake heard the anger in her voice. He lifted his hand from the cross-tie and ran it through his hair in a gesture of frustration. "Damn it, Mel. We did love each other, but we were too young. You were just eighteen, and I had just turned twenty-one. Neither one of us needed to be married. You had college to get through. Pop had already paid for your first semester, remember? We would have ruined our lives if we had married that young."

"What? Our lives are a raging success right now?"

"You *are* a success. I've kept up with your career. You're a well-respected trainer." He gave a half-hearted shrug and turned back to the horse. "The only thing I'd consider ruined is the mess the fire made out of Royalty Farm."

"But that was out of our control."

"Precisely." Jake turned around. Why couldn't she understand? He wanted her approval. "We were too young, Mel.

Too young. I did what I thought was best for you. For us. Can't you see I was thinking of you?"

"Sure." She forced a laugh. "Thinking *for* me is more like it."

"You just wanted to get married. You weren't thinking about the consequences. If I had married you then, you wouldn't have gotten your college degree."

Mel's eyes were blank. "I married Lenny before I got my college degree. Then I finished college. I did both, Jake. I did *both*. When you left, you took the options away from me. You didn't let me choose what I wanted."

It was all over and done. *History*. Neither one of them could change a thing.

He came over to where she faced him through the bars of the stall. He grasped the hard metal and searched her eyes. "Mel, I wanted to marry you. When I came back to Kentucky two years later, I was going to ask you. You were a sophomore then, but *you* had taken that option away from *me*. You had already married that guy."

His palms grew wet. He hated to hurt her. Unfortunately, he'd hurt her before, so that was nothing new to their relationship. "Mel, I did what I did ten years ago because I loved you. I didn't expect you to get married before I could ask you. I'm sorry."

She spun away from him. "I might not have gotten married then if you'd said what you're saying now."

Did he imagine the shake of her shoulders? Was that the sound of a sob when she reached the barn door?

* * *

By the time she'd reached Pop's white frame house, Mel had controlled her tears. She had not controlled the abject misery in her heart. If she'd only waited. It was a mighty big if.

I was such a fool!

At twenty, when she had married Lenny, she'd been under so much pressure from him. Lenny had been persistent. He wanted her. She had fed into his persistence and accepted his proposal. In retrospect, she had married Lenny because Jake had rejected her.

If Jake had spoken up, her marriage and subsequent divorce could have been avoided. If she'd known he loved her, she would have told him about the baby. Things would have been different.

A cold ache settled around Mel's heart. Her gut ached, her mind numb. Those forks in the road, those choices. She had not taken the right one. Now she paid the consequences for not speaking up herself.

When Pop came home, Mel still sat in the darkened living room, facing a blank television. The old man flipped on the light, and grumbled, "It is as dark as sin in here, darlin'."

Mel lifted her chin out of the palm of her hand. "I like it like that."

His face did not visibly change, but he came toward her with his shuffling gait. "Weight of the world on them shoulders, huh?"

How did he know? He always knew. Just like the time she and a sixth-grade classmate had stolen a candy bar from the drugstore. Pop had known then. Maybe her face reflected guilt too easily. Whatever it was, she had to own up to something because Pop would not let it rest.

"I had an argument with Jake." She hoped that would satisfy him.

"Ah, a good boy, that one." Pop eyed her before going on, "Too bad you never forgave him."

Mel straightened up. "Forgave him for what?"

"Goin' off to California. Makin' a name for himself."

"That was a long time ago, Pop," she said and settled back in her chair.

"Some things never forgiven stay with us a long time. We often live to regret them."

That was all Pop said. That was all he had to say. He left the living room, turning out the light and thrusting Mel back into the darkness she'd created in her own soul.

Chapter Nine

It was Mel's first day back on the job. Jake found her cleaning Dreamcatcher's hooves in his stall. With the stallion's bent leg balanced against her hip and his hoof cupped in her hands, Mel's backside presented a pretty, provocative picture. She had tucked her auburn hair behind her ears and tied it with a ribbon. She looked as she had eleven years ago when he first fell in love with her.

Swallowing hard, he curbed his physical craving, much as he would control a horse before changing gaits. Once he'd flirted with Mel by whistling. This was not the time to play games, not after he'd hurt her again by his revelation of past love. Mel needed his support, and for once in his life, he was prepared to give it to her.

"Glad to see you're back," he said quietly.

She dropped the hoof, stood up, and glared at him. Jake shifted under her humorless appraisal. She had dark smudges under her big eyes and her face was pale.

"I hope you're feeling better."

"Yes, thank you. My butt is fine."

Jake heard the anger in her reply. As he assessed her demeanor, her expression altered. Then slanting him an irritated look, she turned back to her task.

Mel picked up Dreamcatcher's rear hoof, presenting him with another fine display, her jodhpurs taut against her backside. Was she deliberately insulting him? He made a sound of amusement deep in his throat. Being supportive might be harder than he thought.

"Look, Mel, I'm sorry I upset you."

"Upset me? What you did changed my life."

"I'm talking about a few days ago, when I told you my real reason for going to California. I didn't want you to continue thinking it was because of my career." Jake glanced at his boots. "You'd thrown that up to me one time too many."

Mel dropped the horse's hoof, tossed the hoof pick into the grooming box, and came over to him. "I don't understand why you never told me."

"I tried to explain it to you," he said.

"But if I'd known..." Mel didn't finish her sentence and turned away.

What had he been thinking so many years ago? He should have explained himself better. Unfortunately, what he'd done couldn't be undone. He had to go on from here and try to establish a new future with Mel.

She picked up a cotton blanket and lifted it onto Dreamcatcher's back. Jake helped her pull the light sheet into place. He hooked the front buckles as she tugged the strap beneath the horse's barrel.

"We can't change what happened, Mel, and I'm sorry. Now that I'm back, I don't want to push you, but maybe we can be friends again."

He'd said what was on his mind, and a weight had lifted. Jake stepped out of the stall to evaluate her reaction.

Mel unhooked the cross-ties, unbuckled the horse's halter, and stripped it off. Picking up the box, she also left the stall and hung the halter on the door. Pulling it shut, she turned and raised her head to look at him. The green and brown flecks of her hazel eyes held him enthralled. The lift of her small chin and the squaring of her shoulders enticed him.

He wanted to kiss her. He couldn't help it. She had that kind of effect on him, on his mind and his body.

"I still consider you my friend, Jake," Mel said with quiet dignity. "I suppose we could try being friends."

Her agreement startled him. He wanted more than friendship. Surely, she knew that. Yet this was a good start.

* * *

Mel watched the misplaced dimple pop out under Jake's left eye when he grinned big and wide. His eyes lit with delight. She couldn't believe her simple statement had such an effect on him. Disconcerted, she turned toward the tack room with Jake at her heels. He was trying. He had admitted his mistake. He said he cared for her still. The thought warmed her as a stab of remorse reminded her of her own lie.

No, it wasn't a lie. She hadn't lied to anyone about Cory. She just hadn't admitted the truth.

Her stomach churning with sorrow, she tried to justify her actions to herself. She had good reasons for giving up Cory. What kind of life could she, a single teenage parent, have provided for the child? She'd been determined her error wasn't going to ruin her daughter's life. Because of Mel's sacrifice, Cory had been blessed with a mom and a dad for the first eight years of her life.

Maybe she shouldn't judge herself too harshly. After all, she'd only been eighteen and had done what was right at the time, given the circumstances.

All these thoughts swirled in her mind as she hung up the cross-ties. Jake took the box from her and placed it on the floor. Her daily tasks done, she glanced at Jake. He was quietly watching her. She didn't know what to say to him. She felt tongue tied, like a student giving her first speech.

115

She looked up at him with a tentative smile. "Now what?"

"Good question." He grinned at her. She wished he would cut it out. His smiles disarmed her, causing her to feel lightheaded. "We could clean tack," he said.

That's not what she'd meant. She had been wondering about their relationship. But if he wanted to help clean their borrowed tack, maybe it was just as well.

One step at a time.

"Okay, sir, grab a sponge and a saddle. I'll get the new bottle of Neatsfoot Oil from the truck."

"Yes, ma'am," he replied as she went out the door.

Mel didn't realize how the murky stable shielded them from the early August sunshine. It was still unbearably hot. A slow drop of perspiration dripped between her breasts. She heard the low rumble of thunder in the distance and glanced at the sky. Although ominous clouds were forming in the west, for the first time in a long time, she felt good, hopeful. She wanted to enjoy Jake's company and the tiny bit of truce they had called.

* * *

They worked together for an hour—sitting on stools in the tack room, cleaning the bridles, bits and saddles, and chatting about horses and shows and the heat. Jake wanted this kind of conversation with Mel, one that was normal and easy and mirrored the comfortable companionship they used to have, back when they were in love.

Jake finished with the bridle and set it aside. He glanced at Mel. A bead of perspiration lined her upper lip. Her hands were slick and wet from the Neatsfoot Oil that she had applied to a saddle. She lifted her hand to scratch her nose. She was so cute with a streak of oil across her nose and a smudge of dirt on her brow.

"Here," he said and leaned forward with his towel. "This is fairly clean. Let me repair your makeup."

Mel scowled, but he ignored her and dabbed the blotch on her forehead.

She snatched away the towel. "I can do that myself."

"A little to the right," he directed, as she tried to remove the oil from her face.

Her efforts only made the smudge worse, and she must have known it. Mel shoved the towel toward him in exasperation. "Oh, here."

Scooting his stool nearer, Jake took the towel from her hand. Gently, he rubbed the smear along her nose and the one on her forehead. Then he took her wrist, holding up her right hand, and began to wipe each oily finger with the towel, slowly, one at a time. Her eyes darkened with desire. Jake sucked in his breath. He searched her face, almost desperate for confirmation. Did she feel it too? This pull, this attraction? As if they had never been apart.

"I like truces," he murmured as his grip tightened on her wrist.

Jake pulled Mel forward. When she didn't resist, he touched his lips to hers. Her eyes fluttered shut, and her lips parted under his pressure. Her response sent his stomach diving. He let go of her wrist and held her shoulders. She coiled her arms around his neck, and he clutched her to his chest. Deepening his kiss, Jake tasted the saltiness of her lips.

* * *

Mel found it hard to breathe. Jake consumed her senses. He was so insistent, ardent, and his urgency increased hers. She kissed him back unable to get enough of him. Her mouth opened. She greedily coveted every part of him.

Jake moved slightly and slipped his hand up her T-shirt. His fingers scorched the damp skin of her back. She gasped against his lips. He drew a quick breath and assailed her mouth again.

"Oh, Jake," she moaned.

His breathing pounded in her ear. "God, Mel," he murmured. "I can't believe this."

It was good. Mel knew it. Just as she knew that if they didn't stop, they'd end up on the tack room floor. But she didn't care. She was older now, wiser. She could handle him, and she felt surprisingly feminine and desirable.

For a moment, he held her mouth with his, and then released it. He searched her eyes. With her arms secure around his neck, Mel looked back at him, at the sky blue of his eyes, wanting to see into his soul, wanting to read what was in his mind.

"Mel, I…" His voice cracked with emotion.

At that moment, Dave ran into the tack room. "Jake!"

Mel jumped out of Jake's embrace and stared guiltily at the little groom. Fortunately, he didn't seem to notice their compromising position.

"The sheriff phoned," Dave said out of breath. "A horse was struck by a train near the Oldham crossing. He thinks it was one of ours."

Jake stood up. "What?"

"The sheriff said the horse must have jumped a fence."

"If he's talking about one of the mares in the north pasture, that doesn't make sense," Jake said, and looked at Mel for confirmation "Those horses don't jump fences."

"With all that's been happening around here, I wonder if someone turned them out," Mel thought out loud. She didn't say her ex-husband's name, but a familiar uneasiness clutched her.

"Damn." Jake glanced at Dave. "You go out to the crossing. Take Pop with you. He'll know if it's one of ours. Mel and I will ride up to the north pasture and see what we can find out." A boom of thunder rattled the barn. Dave turned to leave. "With this rain coming on, better take Mel's four-wheel drive. I'll call you when I know something."

Mel grabbed keys and tossed a rain poncho over her head. Jake picked up a toolkit and his rain gear and followed her to the Jeep.

"Want to drive?" Mel asked, ready to toss him the keys.

Jake shook his head. "You know the way better than I do."

They climbed into the four-wheel drive as the first drops of rain began to fall. By the time they reached the north pasture, the wind had risen, and driving rain slashed against the windshield. The wipers clacked back and forth, not offering much help. Mel strained to see as the vehicle bounced over the bluegrass field.

Driving slowly along the perimeter of the fence, she considered the situation. Royalty Farm could not continue suffering losses. Too much was at stake. Although Vanessa had never said anything, Mel felt her friend was close to giving in to that scummy realtor. Bert Noble's eldest daughter didn't have the love of the farm like his adopted daughter Cory. Mel wanted to preserve the farm for the little girl. Because of her sacrifice, this farm was Cory's birthright. Gripping the steering wheel, Mel peered through the windshield.

"There's the break," Jake said suddenly. "Hell. Someone has removed the boards."

Mel pulled to a stop, put the truck in park, and stared at the opening in the weather-beaten, white rail fence.

Even in the darkness caused by the downpour, Mel saw tenseness in the way Jake's mouth was set. Her knuckles were white as she continued to grip the wheel. She imagined how he felt, and she wanted to reach out and comfort him.

Looking away, she wished he would reach out and give *her* comfort, tell her everything would be okay—that they'd find this evil person who was ruining Royalty Farm—that somehow, some day, they would be a couple again, even a family.

"I'll see what I can do to fix it," Jake said. "You stay here."

Mel opened her mouth to protest, but he was already gone. Watching through the rain-smeared windshield, she saw him lift the railing in place. He struggled to hold the railing and swing the hammer at the same time. Mel threw open the door and ran to help.

"I told you to stay inside," he yelled above the noise of the rainfall.

"Oh, shut up," she growled. "I'll hold the board. You hammer."

Jake allowed her to take the railing from him. In a few minutes, the fence was back in some sort of repair, and they retreated to the truck.

"Thanks." Once inside he pushed back the hood of his poncho. Water dripped from his face and hair.

"No problem."

His gaze flooded her with warmth. To cover her reaction, she turned on the ignition and put her hand on the gear stick.

"Really." He leaned toward her. "I appreciate your help. I'm glad we're a team again."

Jake covered her hand with his. Mel trembled at his touch. Maybe it was the cold rain, she tried to tell herself, knowing full well it was the feel of his fingers on hers. She didn't know what to say to him. What did he want from her? What did she want from him? Before she could overcome her uneasiness, Jake's cell phone rang, and he lifted his hand to answer it.

"Yes," he acknowledged, not looking away from her. His eyes mirrored the horror of whatever was being said on the other end of the call.

Mel barely heard his responses to the person on the phone because she was so focused on his eyes. They seemed to bore a hole through the mask of indifference she wore to cover her hurt. They worked on her heart, melting its icy cold and replacing it with a bubbling cauldron of love and affection.

"Okay, we'll go by the shed and see how many we can find." Jake put down the receiver. Shifting in his seat, and looking away, he ran his hand through his wet hair. "That was Dave."

"Yes?"

Jake looked back at her. "He said Pop identified the dead mare as one in foal to Royalty's Reverie."

Mel cursed inwardly and shut her eyes. This was a double tragedy—a prize mare in foal to the stallion lost in the fire. She swallowed hard and opened her eyes to find Jake still looking at her.

"Pop said we had twenty-five mares in this pasture, twenty-one with foals by their sides, not yet ready to be weaned. Four

121

mares and foals have been rounded up on the Neely property. Let's go by the run-in shed and take a count of what's there," Jake suggested.

"Okay, let's go." Mel threw the truck into gear, glad for the action.

The run-in shed was a quarter mile away. Through the rain and the haze, it was hard to see, so they climbed out of the Jeep to count the horses. Only nine mares and six foals had sought shelter in the three-sided building. Frustrated by the low count, Mel climbed into the truck. Jake joined her, and she drove back to the farm.

They entered the tack room in time to catch the end of a heated discussion.

"It's them bums at Neely Hills!" Pop hollered, arms gesturing.

"Now, hold on, Pop," Vanessa cautioned. "Jim Neely has his men out searching his property."

Cory stood behind her big sister, eyes wide with fright and excitement. Everyone in the room turned when they became aware of the newcomers.

"How many did you find?" Pop asked

"Nine mares and six foals." Jake went over to Cory and tousled her hair.

"Cut it out! You're wet!"

"You would be too, kiddo," he told Cory, "if you'd been outside in the rain."

Dear God. Mel's heart ached at the easy banter between them.

"Fourteen damn horses, countin' the dead 'un, and ten foals," Pop ticked off the number.

"This is too much like the fire," Vanessa murmured, her eyes dark and troubled.

Mel felt it too, that same sense of déjà vu. She'd been powerless during the barn fire and even more powerless now. It was like her marriage to Lenny. During those years, she had been totally out of control, and she loathed that feeling. Sucking in a deep breath, she straightened her shoulders. *Not again.* Not if she could do something about it.

"I imagine the rest of the horses escaped through the break in the fence. We better get out there and look for the rest," she said to the assembled group.

Jake agreed. "We need to find those horses before something else happens to them."

"If they're off our property, we can't round them up with the Jeep. We need to be on horseback. I'll saddle that old gelding in the near paddock." Mel picked up a lead line, knowing she couldn't take a chance on riding a valuable show horse.

While Dave helped Mel bring in and saddle up, Jake put the tack on one of Cory's lesson horses.

"Take this cell phone with you." Dave thrust it into Mel's hands. "You might need it."

Mel tucked the phone into the pocket of her T-shirt and tugged down the poncho. Dave held the horse steady as she mounted. Jake was already on the back of Cory's horse. He glanced at Mel and smiled grimly.

She didn't smile back. "After you," she said with a nod.

He tipped his head toward the open barn door. "No, ladies first."

Mel looked away and pressing a leg into the side of her mount, rode out into the steady downpour.

Chapter Ten

Lightning seared the late afternoon sky. Mel trembled, involuntarily pressing her legs against the sides of the old gelding. The horse snorted and lunged forward as a thunderclap shook the earth. She steadied the animal while the hammering rain continued to soak her to the skin. Ineffectual as her poncho was, it did provide some protection from the howling wind that seemed to force them backward with each step they took.

Yet the poncho didn't provide any shelter from her fear. What would she do if she found more horses dead or injured? Who could have possibly broken down the fencing?

Mel led the way along the gravel road and turned onto a little used, country back-road. It bisected the Noble property with that of the Neely's. After about a mile, she halted in front of a gate, leaned down, and pulled it open.

"This pasture is parallel to ours," she called over her shoulder.

"I remember," Jake shouted back, his face determined and just as wet as hers. "Go ahead. I'll get the gate."

Mel rode on, forcing the skittish gelding into a slow jog.

Skirting the fence, with Jake close behind, she urged the horse forward. She was glad Jake was with her. Whoever had damaged the fence could be lurking in the rain and fog. He could be out there somewhere, ready to strike again. Mel didn't want to dwell on it. She didn't want to reflect too deeply on who could be responsible for the vandalism at Royalty Farm. If it was Lenny, as she suspected, she didn't want to believe he had some perverse reason to hurt the farm and people she loved.

Soon they came to a crest of a hill. Pausing, Mel let the horse's head drop while she waited for Jake to catch up.

"Damn! This storm is nasty!" he said when he rode up beside her. He was so near that his knee brushed against hers. "Thanks for coming along, Mel. I'm glad for your help."

She thought he was going to reach out and touch her hand as he had done in the Jeep. Taking a long, shuddering breath of control, Mel lifted her chin and stared stolidly back into his eyes.

"Just doing my job," she said.

"I think it's more than that," he replied, "but I'm not going to argue with you now. We've got to find those horses."

They rode on again, heading for a clump of trees on the horizon. The whistling wind whipped the poncho taut against Mel's body. The wet reins slipped through her hands, and she gripped the leather tighter, her fingers aching from the effort. Her heart ached too, with an overwhelming sense of dread. Maybe after things settled down, after the World's Grand Championship, she and Jake could concentrate on their relationship. Maybe they could sort out the muddle they'd made of what they once had together.

As suddenly as lightning lit the sky, the wide-eyed face of Cory flashed through Mel's mind. Try as she would, she knew she couldn't avoid the facts any longer. If she and Jake were to ever have a relationship based on truth and trust, she had to tell him about Cory. She squeezed her eyes together and bit her lip in resignation. Just as she knew the rain had soaked her to the bone, Mel knew what she had to do to make it right between her and Jake.

And she must make him promise not to tell Vanessa or Cory, not to disturb the only life their daughter knew.

And she was even more afraid.

* * *

Lightning shattered the sky. Jake ducked his head in a futile attempt to shield his eyes from the rain. He admired Mel. No other woman he knew would ride out into a storm. They took a chance of being struck by lightning, but there was no other choice. They had to gather up those horses. Royalty Farm couldn't absorb much more hard luck. He'd seen Vanessa's books.

Mel stood in her stirrups and pointed over her horse's head. "Jake!"

Sheltered under the knot of trees were five mares and five foals. A hurrah emerged from Mel's lips as she spurred the gelding forward. Jake laid his calves into the side of his horse and galloped after her.

Several yards from the trees Mell pulled to a halt and waited for him. "I don't want to spook them," she said. "How should we go about this?"

Jake considered for a moment. "They're ours, I assume."

"Yeah, Pop said the Neelys didn't have horses in this field."

Jake observed the line of her jaw, the slope of her nose and the lay of her lashes. Although wet from the torrent of rain, she presented a perfect profile. Jake longed to touch her cheek, to wipe the water from her lashes. He longed to shield her from the rain—to wrap her up into his arms and protect her—to love her and never let her be hurt again.

"Call Dave and tell him we've found more horses."

Mel nodded and fumbled for the cell phone beneath her poncho. She pulled it out, opened it and punched the number. Jake couldn't hear the conversation above the noise of the rain, so he urged his mount closer.

"Got Sam, his assistant," she told Jake. "He said Dave and Pop have gone down the highway where the folks at Carter's farm found five more on their property."

"That leaves one more mare and foal," Jake said after doing the calculations. "Damn it! Where can they be?"

Mel looked back at him, her eyes wide and serious. When she looked at him that way, she reminded him of little Cory. Jake smiled inwardly at the quick thought and turned to consider the group of mares.

"We have two ropes." Jake rode slowly toward the herd, assessing them with a practiced eye. "The best thing is for you to lead two mares. The rest should follow. I'll continue looking for the other lost mare."

He selected the one he thought to be the dominant female and leaning over and letting his reins drop, grabbed the halter. Then Jake threaded the lead line over the horse's nose, through the loops of the halter, and buckled it. Picking up his reins, he angled his horse and gave the rope to Mel. Next, he cut out another mare, buckled on the remaining lead line, and handed the horse over to Mel.

"I'll follow you to get them going," he said.

She was reluctant to leave him. "Will you be okay?"

It pleased him that she was concerned. "Sure. How about you?"

"I'll be all right. Go on. Get out of here."

Without comment, Mel rode away. Jake followed up the crest of the hill, herding the horses and making sure the mares and foals trailed her.

"I'll take them to the paddock by our barn," she shouted through the downpour, "and come back for you."

"No, don't. I'll be along shortly. One mare can't be hard to find."

Jake watched them go until the haze and the lengthening twilight swallowed them up.

* * *

Stupid, stubborn man! Jake hadn't returned, and it was almost nine o'clock. Why hadn't he used his cell phone to call and tell them what was happening?

Mel sat on the top of the battered, metal desk in the old barn's office and kicked her boots against the sides. The noise made an irritating clank in the too quiet room. Pop sat on a well-used sofa, silently drubbing his fingers on the arm. Dave had left, saying he couldn't sit still, and had gone out to join Sam in a smoke.

Dave came back in. "Rain's stopped."

Pop looked up. "Something's wrong."

Brilliant. Mel had assumed that something was wrong two hours ago. She hated this inactivity.

She jumped up and fumbled for her keys. "Well, let's go find Jake."

"Not so fast, darlin'," Pop came back. "I don't want you goin' alone."

"I'm taking the Jeep this time. Dave can take the farm truck and cover our side of the north field," she suggested.

"Still don't want you goin' alone. Take Sam."

When Pop was in that mood, Mel knew an elephant couldn't move him. "Okay," she agreed, even though she considered the assistant groom good-for-nothing.

But taking Sam satisfied Pop.

Soon Mel and the groom drove toward the Neely property, the headlights of the four-wheel-drive vehicle cutting bright swatches through the drenched pasture.

"Keep your eyes open and let me know if you see anything," Mel ordered.

She concentrated on the left side of the Jeep, scanning the white fence line that looked like a translucent ribbon against the dark, rolling field. Ahead lay the same clump of trees where she and Jake had earlier found the mares and foals. Seeing it deserted sharpened Mel's fear. She gripped the steering wheel until her nails bit into the palms of her hands, and she wrestled with an overpowering sense of urgency.

Ahead the fence ended abruptly, turning in a perpendicular line to the east. Mel pressed the brakes, and the Jeep lurched to a halt. Staring at the edge of the Neely property, worry tightened her stomach. Somehow, they had missed Jake. Damn!

"What do we do now?" Sam asked, hunching low in his seat. His voice was thick and surly.

Mel allowed his question to meet a long silence. Turning the Jeep and heading back the way they'd come, she finally blurted, "We keep on looking."

Several minutes later, driving up a slope, Mel spotted Jake's horse standing riderless near several trees. Her knuckles went white on the wheel.

"Look, Sam!" Mel gunned the Jeep. "How did you miss that horse?"

He shrugged indifferently. "Easy in the dark."

She was furious at Sam's nonchalant attitude, the passive, dumb look on his face, and at the impotent fear that clogged her throat.

As the Jeep jerked to a halt, the horse bolted a few yards away. Fighting a rush of panic, Mel threw the vehicle into park, opened the door, slid out, and followed the gelding.

She lifted her arms, spread eagle. "It's okay. Easy, boy. Easy." Without any luck, Mel shouted at Sam over her shoulder, "I can use your help!"

The groom seemed reluctant to leave the vehicle but got out slowly and circled to the right. After a few minutes of working together, they surrounded the horse, cutting him off. Mel easily caught his reins.

"We got another problem, miss," Sam said in his monotone.

Now what? The groom pointed toward the side of the hill where the jeep had rolled backwards.

"Damn! I thought I put it into park!" Tossing the reins to Sam, Mel stumbled over the rugged terrain to reach the Jeep. To her horror, it had sunk up to its fenders in mud.

"How could this happen?"

Her throat aching with unshed tears of frustration, Mel stared blankly at the vehicle. It was as if some invisible hand toyed with her, wreaking havoc on everything she'd tried to do tonight. First, there was the accident at the railroad crossing that killed the expensive mare, then the thunderstorm and perilous search for the horses. Now Jake was missing, and she was no closer to finding him now than she'd been an hour ago when she set out on this wild goose chase.

And that sorry excuse for a groom was no help at all.

Jerking open the door, Mel grasped a powerful Halogen flashlight from the floorboard. After she pushed it on, she flicked off the ignition and pocketed the keys. By the beam of the flashlight, she confirmed that the gear shift was in neutral. She could have sworn she'd set the shift into park.

Okay. All was not lost. She still had the cell phone. But no signal. There'd been one earlier this evening.

This was the last straw. Tears of helpless rage slipped down her cheeks. Backhanding them, Mel stomped up the hill to where Sam held the horse.

"This phone won't work." She held it up as if he could see it in the black night around them.

"You got it wet today," he offered. "Maybe it shorted out."

That sounded logical, something an electronic thing would do, and Mel didn't know much about electronics. Fighting the punch-drunk fear and anger overwhelming her, she considered what to do. Sam wasn't much help. He seemed, in fact, to be throwing up barriers. Maybe not in reality, but his very passivity bothered her.

"You ride back to the farm," she said in a choking whisper. "Have Dave call the sheriff. Tell Dave to come back here with the truck. I'll keep looking for Jake."

"Don't know about that," Sam answered. "Pop wouldn't like you being out here alone."

"Pop's not here," she screamed. "I'm in charge. You do what I say!"

"Right." He threw her a look of hostility, mounted the horse, and jogged away.

Motionless, she sorted out her two emotions, pushing the fear aside and hanging on to the sharper anger. She knew how to cope with anger, using it to navigate the darkness surrounding her. Like the fury that had been her skipper during the long months of her divorce, Mel knew how to channel her rage and how to turn it into a constructive force.

The sound of the horse had long ago died away. Mel walked toward the shadowy trees that stood like watchmen in the distance. Other night sounds masked the absolute silence of the night—the ratchet of crickets and the low-pitched rumble of bull frogs. Slowly, the after-rain mugginess rose in a mist from the pasture and seeped into her senses.

She was hot. Sweat tickled her breast. She touched her tongue to the saltiness that also laced her upper lip. Balling her left hand into a fist, she swiped off the wetness. With her other hand raised, she aimed the beam from the flashlight into the gloom.

Where could he be? Where in this deserted pasture could Jake be?

Casting light around the field, Mel paused a moment. She shut her eyes and shifted her stance. Then she focused on her raspy breathing. That's when she heard it. Somewhere in the distance. Mel picked up a subtle cadence of a creek. Not having been here in years, she'd forgotten about the shallow stream that meandered through the property.

Opening her eyes, Mel began to walk and then trot toward the cluster of trees. She knew instinctively Jake was in there. Mel perceived his nearness, his danger.

She stopped, wishing her breath didn't echo in her ears. "Jake!"

Tangled in the brush somewhere had to be an opening, a trail of some kind. As the lengths of flashlight stabbed the snarled undergrowth, panic slammed through her. She had sidled forward only a few steps when the light revealed a path plunging into the darkness. Without hesitation, she followed it into the blackness below.

"Jake!" she shouted again, flashing the light ahead of her.

"Mel!"

"I'm coming!"

Now she remembered this ravine from trail rides as a kid. It had been a scary ride back then—down a steep path, over fallen trees, across the shallow creek and up the steep bank on the other side, the horse's neck and withers next to her nose as she leaned forward to give him his head. In the dark, the trail seemed even more treacherous.

Mel saw the frantic mare first. She pawed and tossed her head as she balanced on a firm ledge several feet above the creek. Was Mel just imagining it or was the water rising?

She fanned the light out away from the mare, searching for Jake.

"Mel! Damn, I'm glad you got here! Are you alone?"

"Yes. Sam's gone for help. Where are you?"

"Down here!"

Taking a few more steps, Mel pulled up short. There in the creek with water up to his waist, Jake stood with his arms outstretched, stabilizing the head and neck of a small foal. The gangly colt was contorted with its fore leg stuck in a fork of a buckeye tree that was precariously perched over the creek. Without Jake's support, the horse would drown in the rising water.

"Oh, my God!" Mel scooted on her haunches down the loose embankment. "How long have you been in that water?"

"Not long really," he said. "But you'd be surprised how cold it is."

In the flashlight beam, Mel saw his heartening smile. He was trying to ease her fear.

"Couldn't you free his leg?"

"That trunk is too shaky. With my weight, I couldn't chance it." He shook his head. "This is, unfortunately, all I could muster in the time I had. I was praying the cavalry would save the day before I had to abandon the colt."

"Cavalry, huh? I'm afraid all you've got is one small, female horse trainer that you almost refused to hire." Mel couldn't resist the barb. It lightened the mood, causing her to ignore the thud of dread that sounded in her ears.

She positioned the flashlight on the bank to shine on the tree. Then she inched herself onto the tree trunk.

"Mel, don't try it. It's too dangerous."

"You've done it now, man," Mel joked. "Them's fightin' words."

"Be careful," Jake warned. "That colt is spooked, and his hooves are sharp."

Well, duh! Without responding, she concentrated on the panicked foal. He was a delicate creature with a fine head and well-shaped legs—legs that could easily be broken. Jake was right, the little horse had hooves like razors, and if she wasn't careful, they could cut her to shreds.

"Easy. Easy," Mel crooned while she slowly straddled the tree trunk.

Too bad she had taken off her poncho. She could throw it over the hind legs of the colt. There wasn't anything else. *Except my T-shirt.*

Mel pulled her shirt over her head. Holding it by the sleeves, she stretched it out. Without looking at Jake and trying not to think about what kind of picture she presented in her bra and jeans, she flung the shirt over the spindly legs.

It worked long enough for her to crawl out on the trunk over the colt. He squirmed beneath her like a fiend.

"Easy, darlin'," she used Pop's endearment. "Easy, boy."

Carefully, she extended her right hand to grab his slim foreleg, and at the same time, tried to keep the free hoof from flailing her face. Moving slightly, she stretched out with her left hand, pressing her face against the slim neck. Steam lifted from the warm horseflesh.

"Be careful!"

Inwardly cringing, but outwardly refusing to show fear, Mel gripped the left leg and loosened it from the wood. When she freed the leg, the colt thrashed trying to stand. It was impossible, and in a sudden whoosh, they both plunged into the icy water of the creek.

Jake broke her fall. He fell back under the water.

Mel and the colt struggled together. She found her footing, and somehow righted the foal. With all the effort she could muster, she shoved the wriggling horse toward the embankment. He scrambled out of the creek onto the shore and was greeted by his mother.

The cold and the force of the water sucked her breath away. "Jake!"

Jake's head popped up right in front of her face. "I'm okay!"

As he gained his balance, his hands closed around her arms and steadied her. From the creek's edge, the meager light of the flashlight cast weird shadows across Jake's face. She couldn't see him as much as feel him—the ripple of his muscles beneath his soaked shirt rubbing against her bare shoulders, the solid rock of his chest pressing against her cheek. With the water surging around them, he held her there for a heartbeat. She let him, soaking in all his strength.

"You were magnificent," he said, stroking her dripping hair.

A droplet of water slid off his hand and rolled down her nose. She blinked up at him and shook her head no. She didn't feel magnificent. She felt scared and weak like a child.

"I couldn't find you." Her voice sounded plaintive, even to her own ears.

Jake anchored her tightly against him. "But you did. That's all that matters," he said as he touched his lips to her hair. "Now, let's get out of this water before we drown or freeze to death."

Chapter Eleven

Jake stood at the paddock gate watching the rescued colt and its mother, but in his mind, he saw the top of Mel's bowed head and the twin mounds of her breasts against his chest. In his imagination, he felt her sports bra straps crossing in the back where he placed his hands. Locked in his arms, frigid water swirling around them, she'd turned to him for support. He liked that. Jake smiled at nothing in particular, his thoughts of Mel blinding him to the fierce August sun. He had never been much of a daydreamer. Not until Mel came back into his life.

His love of her was not a daydream. The desire he felt was real and uncomfortable. Jake shifted his stance and placed a booted foot on the lower rail of the fence. He rested his arms against the upper rail and leaned forward. Mel had been worried about him. She'd searched alone through the darkness to find him. Her concern was like a warm caress.

Mel had needed him too—needed him to carry the little colt up the slippery bank and lower him into the truck Dave had brought. He'd freed her Jeep from the mud, an easy thing to do just by putting it into four-wheel drive and rocking it back and forth. Mel had not thought of that. After all, she was a *typical* female.

He smirked at the idea of Mel being typical. He'd better never say that to her face. She'd never let him live it down.

When he'd needed her, she had come to his rescue. She'd taken a big risk to release the colt. She was as brave and courageous as she was goodhearted and beautiful.

"Must be thinking about Mel," a high-pitched little voice said.

Jake glanced down to find Cory staring up at him, a dimpled grin spreading across her face.

Moving his foot off the rail and facing her, only an elbow resting on the fence, Jake asked, "What makes you say that, kiddo?"

"Oh, you've got that silly look on your face," she teased back.

He pulled his elbow down and crossed his arms in a defensive move. "What look?"

"That look you have on your face whenever you look at Mel."

Jake felt his face grow hot. Satisfaction blazed in Cory's eyes as if she knew she'd hit home. Flipping her blond braid, she twirled around and took off running toward the barn.

He chased her and caught up with her. "Am I that obvious?"

She slowed and sauntered along, trying to hide a smile. "Like a lovesick cat."

"That's bad."

"Yeah, when my cat got like that, my mom got her fixed." Cory was serious.

"Stop that!" Jake laughed. He snatched her up, swung her around and up, and set her on his shoulders.

Laughing too, Cory patted his head. "Put me down, you meany."

"I'm not mean. I'm a five-gaited horse and this is the World's Grand Championship. You're the world's best female rider, and this is your very first time to ride in Freedom Hall."

Cory fell into the playacting. "Okay, trot. Pick up those hooves!"

Jake trotted in a circle around the dusty parking lot of the barn.

"Now, canter!" Cory ordered, whipping the air with a pretend riding crop.

Changing his gait into a skipping lope, Jake continued to have fun, even though this was getting to be more like work than play.

"Stop," she said. "Now reverse."

Jake stopped and changed directions. "Slow gait," he said through his huffs and puffs, and started ambling around in a circle.

"Rack on!" Cory whooped.

Jake tried valiantly to comply, but it was too much. He racked into the dusky barn and tumbled the little girl over his head onto a bale of straw.

"Silly!" She succumbed to a spasm of giggles.

He collapsed onto the sawdust of the barn floor with his back against the straw. "Silly? I'm not silly."

Cory snickered and tackled him around his neck. Through his fit of laughter, Jake imagined what it would be like to have a daughter like Cory, one who was as horse-crazy as Mel.

* * *

Mel paused on the threshold of The Old Stone Inn in Simpsonville and scanned the tables. Her fists clenched to control a shudder that filtered through her body. She wasn't ready for this encounter. She had barely recovered from the panic and trauma of the previous day. Being unable to find Jake had affected her more than she had realized. Yet she had to find out what Lenny knew.

"May I help you?" the hostess asked.

With a faint smile of acknowledgment, Mel turned to the woman. "Yes, I'm to meet someone."

"Ah, the gentleman is already here." The hostess gave Mel a sweet smile. "Follow me, please."

Mel fumbled with a ball of rising anger. Did the woman assume she and Lenny were having a romantic rendezvous? Maybe anger was a good thing to hold on to.

Lenny sat in an isolated corner with his back against the wall. It was so like him to have a commanding view of the area, to already have the upper hand. Mel drew a deep breath, lifted her chin, and crossed the floor.

"Here you are, dear." The hostess placed a menu on the table and turned away. "Enjoy your dinner."

"Melody, so good to see you," Lenny said as if she were a long-lost lover, not an ex-wife who hated his guts. He stood and pulled out her chair.

Unable to ignore him, she let him seat her. Her skin crawled when his hand grazed her back.

Lenny returned to his seat and favored Mel with a look of dark amusement. "I'm glad you accepted my invitation."

"Don't play games with me, Lenny. What do you want?"

"Want? I just want to have dinner with you." He handed her silverware wrapped in a white cloth napkin. "Here, relax. You used to love this place."

Mel snatched the silverware from him and opened the napkin, laying it in her lap. He was doing it to her again. Like an intangible shadow, Lenny had a way of skittering away from an issue. She'd never been able to pin him down in their marriage. How could she hope to do so now?

"You're up to something. I want to know what it is." She'd fallen back into the same old defensive patterns.

His smile was slow and ingratiating. "Why do you ask?"

She caught her breath. Was he putting down another trap? She was too afraid to ask Lenny the real question. What did he know about Cory?

"I ask because I'm just a little curious about anyone who threatens me. You've been following me around, showing up in the strangest places," she said instead.

"A cocktail party is strange?"

"Coming all the way from Missouri is strange," Mel snapped.

"Melody, darling, The Lexington Junior League Horse Show is a very prestigious event," he replied, his voice oily. "It coincides with the Saddlebred auction at Tattersalls."

Mel made a sound of bitter amusement. "I thought you gambled away all your money. You can't afford the auction."

She opened the menu, hoping to buy herself some time to regain control. Lenny had always enjoyed giving her a hard time. Being contrary was one of his games.

The waitress arrived to take their drink order. "We'll take the house red wine," Lenny said, winking at Mel.

A shard of alarm plunged through her veins. She didn't have to buy into his control any longer. "I'll have a Coke," she told the waitress.

Touché. She'd made her point. She saw it in the smugness of Lenny's gaze. He was entertained. Like a cat with a mouse. And like that hapless mouse, Mel felt cornered. She returned Lenny's unyielding gaze and tried to keep her expression bland.

"I suppose you'll want the baked chicken," he reflected, turning his eyes to the menu, "or will you contradict me on that too?"

"I don't know what I want. I'm not very hungry."

The wine and Coke arrived, and while Lenny sipped his drink, Mel stirred the ice in her drink with her straw. If she actually ate or drank anything, she knew she would hurl.

"I worry about you, Melody."

"No you don't."

Lenny sipped from his glass, his eyes boring into her over the rim. "You're getting in over your head at Royalty Farm."

"What do you mean by that?" Mel stiffened. "You're not responsible for those *accidents*, are you, Lenny?"

"Melody, Melody. Do you mean that horrible barn fire? What a thing to accuse me of." He flicked off her charge as if it were a pesky fly. "I know you don't mean it."

"You don't know anything about me, Lenny." Her voice was hard.

"Oh, that's where you're wrong, darling." He smiled. "I know about you and that trainer, that Jake Hendricks. I made inquiries about him."

Mel's hackles rose like an aggressive dog. She sat forward. "Why? What business is he of yours?"

"You might say he's been my business for many years."

The waitress came again. Mel sat back. What did he mean?

"I don't dare order for my lovely wife," Lenny said in an ingratiating whine.

"Ex-wife," Mel growled.

The waitress turned to her. "Ma'am?"

Mel glanced at the woman. "I'm not hungry."

"Oh, come on," Lenny interjected. "I'm buying."

"Very generous of you." Mel thought of the many times during their marriage when she'd urged him not to spend so much money.

"Darling, you can be rude to me all you want, but you shouldn't be rude to the nice lady, should you?"

Mel wanted to scream. She wanted to pick up the menu and slap him across his face with it. At the same time, she wanted to kick herself up and down for falling in with this man in the first place. What had ever possessed her? Lenny had come into her life at a terribly vulnerable moment. He'd acted as though he knew how to take care of her, and she had wanted to be cared for. She'd wanted to be protected and cherished and loved.

Fat chance. She had gotten precious little of that from Lenny after the first glorious months of courtship. In fact, after the rush of sex early on in their marriage, there had been little of that as well. Lenny had been traditional, cautious, dependable, but he had also been boring and distant. What had attracted her to the man? It was almost as if she had endowed him with greater depth of character than he'd ever possessed.

When he refused to start a family, the fingers of doubt about her husband had grown. Then he had pressured her to take a job at a more celebrated stable which would mean leaving the kids she loved to teach. When she'd refused, their relationship had soured. Lenny didn't like not getting his way. About a year later, the insurance scam rumors had circulated among the horse show crowd in Missouri. By then, Mel was only enduring the marriage in a vain attempt to prevent another failure. The gambling debts were the last straw.

"You order for me, Lenny. You always knew what was best for me," Mel said, sarcasm dripping like the condensation on her glass.

145

"I'm glad you recognize that." He smirked, then turned to the waitress and placed both their orders.

When the woman left, Lenny smiled again, a smile that never reached his eyes. "Where were we?"

"I don't know, because I don't know the purpose of this whole charade."

"Ah, yes." He looked away and then back again. "You know I always have your best interests at heart, don't you, Melody?"

"No, I don't know that. You were always critical. That's one reason I divorced you."

"If I ever criticized you, it was only to make you a better person," Lenny said. "Sometimes you were too passive. I was just trying to give you spunk, make you stand up and fight for what you wanted. I know you deserved a better job than the one you had at that pathetic kid stable."

"I was doing what I wanted," Mel shot back. "Teaching children."

"But your career was stagnant."

"In your viewpoint. But it was my career. You just wanted me at a fancy stable to make yourself look better among your wealthy horsey set," Mel pointed out. "In fact, that's probably the very reason you didn't want us to have children. It would postpone my *illustrious* career."

"I never wanted children."

Chilled by his hard look and words, Mel drew a deep breath. Her hands felt as cold as his cold heart. She hid them under the table, clutching them together. "You've made that clear."

"Besides, you already had a child." His voice was icy, bitter, unforgiving.

Mel's mind buckled at his words. Had he really said what she thought he'd said? She had never told him about Cory. How did he know?

"What do you mean?"

"You know who I mean. Cory Noble." His words were hushed and carefully measured.

The restaurant noise sounded far away as if she were at the far end of a tunnel. Fear spiraled through her, twisting and turning in her stomach. Totally focused on her ex-husband, Mel tried not to cower under his hostile stare. She felt her face grow hot.

He released his piercing glare for one moment, his gaze dropping to his glass of wine. Picking it up, he drank. His eyes came back up to capture hers once again, and he set down his glass.

She tried to hide her fear. "I don't know what you're talking about."

"Come, dear. You were never good at lying," he said. "I've known about your little bastard since we married."

The earth seemed to open up and swallow Mel into a black void. Her vision blurred, obscured by the overwhelming darkness. Her breath became forced. Why would he call Cory that horrible word? *Bastard.* Her child was *not* a bastard. Her child had a name and a home and a sister who loved her. Mel struggled to respond. She struggled to understand. She felt as if she climbed the edge of a slippery chasm.

"How did you find out?"

"Does it matter?" Lenny shrugged and continued to appraise her. "As I've said before, you don't lie well. You have a very honest face."

When she could reclaim her breath, Mel lifted her chin and replied to his intense scrutiny with what she hoped was a cold look. "You continue to surprise me."

He looked pleased with himself. "I thought I might."

Underneath the table, Mel absently plucked at her napkin. It wasn't important how Lenny knew about Cory. Maybe he'd heard it from that lawyer he'd been tight with once, maybe from a business contact, or a friend of the Nobles. It didn't matter. What mattered was what he planned to do with the information and why he was bringing it up now.

When she didn't say anything, Lenny took another sip of his wine, letting her fret longer.

He set down his glass and continued to look quite content. "Aren't you going to ask how I found out about her father?"

"I'm sure you're going to tell me."

"Yes, you know me well." Lenny sat forward. "Like I said, you're very transparent. I knew you carried the torch for Hendricks from the beginning of our relationship. Remember all those heart-to-heart talks we used to have? How I held your hand and told you everything would be okay? Broken hearts mend, I told you." His eyes hardened. "I fault myself for believing you'd get over him. But you never did. When I found out about the child, well, it was easy to put two and two together."

Terror carved into Mel's gut. Her mouth was dry as she saw again in her mind's eye the naive teenage girl gaining comfort from the older, wiser man. He'd been so understanding. Sympathetic.

"Is that what you meant about telling Jake Hendricks?" Her hands beneath the table trembled, her voice wavered.

"I think Mr. Hendricks would like to know about his daughter, don't you?"

"No, I don't, or I would have told him long ago." Mel drew her mouth into a firm line. She glared at the predator before her. "But it's more than that. Cory is a happy child. She shouldn't be hurt. It would serve no purpose to tell Jake."

"It would serve *my* purpose and, frankly, I don't care about your love child."

"I've known you to be cruel to me." Mel's eyes narrowed. "And you probably did have that horse killed for the insurance money, but I don't understand why you want to hurt an innocent child."

Lenny's expression was void of emotion. "I don't want to hurt the child."

Mel squared her shoulders. "Then what do you want?"

He put his palms flat on the table and leaned toward her. "I want your help with a little business proposition."

Lenny was so sure of himself. Mel had hated that self-assurance during their marriage. For most of their time together, Mel had lacked confidence. It wasn't that way now. She had used her newfound courage to leave him. She certainly could stand up to him now.

"No one gets everything he wants, Lenny."

"Yes, I've found that out." He curled his hand into a fist. "I didn't want the divorce. You got what *you* wanted. Since you destroyed our marriage, I think I should have a little compensation."

Mel barely restrained her anger. "If anything affected our marriage, Lenny, it was your distance, your lack of ability to open up, to really care about another human being," she stated. "And your lies."

Lenny's eyes hardened. "So, it's my fault. Our divorce was *my* fault. I don't think so. What about *your* lies?"

His indictment slammed Mel in the gut. She had not lied. She'd just never told him about Cory. She felt that same old frustration, that lack of control. Her marriage had been a roller coaster ride, and once she had stepped off, she'd regained some sense of respect for herself.

"I think two people are at fault in a divorce," Mel reflected. "I was wrong to marry you in the first place. I was too young, but I tried to make it work. I just didn't have much help from you."

Lenny made a sound of derision. "You made a fool of me when you married me." He sneered as he spoke. "What's done is done though. Right now, I'm going to tell you a little about my business proposal."

She didn't respond. Couldn't respond.

"Remember the money I owe you for the sale of our house? I need it. You don't. Turn your portion of the house over to me, my dear, and I won't tell Hendricks anything."

When she didn't speak, Lenny went on, "He'll be angry with you, you know. He won't forgive what you've done to him."

"Jake isn't like that." Mel said, hoping to convince herself.

"He's a man, isn't he? You lied to him, just as you lied to me."

"I never lied to Jake. "

"Ah, there's a fine line. Let's say, you didn't tell him the truth."

Mel stared. It was as if he had read her silent thoughts.

"Hendricks won't buy your lame explanations. He won't trust you. You took his daughter away from him." Lenny continued to torment her, his voice like a distant roar of water. It was as if she was in a runaway canoe spiraling toward a terrifying waterfall.

"How do you know he even cares about having a child?" Mel tightened her grip on the fabric of her napkin. "His career is all important to him."

"Grasping at straws, darling? I've seen him with Cory. For whatever inane reason, the man is nuts for the kid." He flashed a cold smile, and Mel could not control a shiver.

"You've been spying on us."

"At a horse show, it is so easy to watch what's going on. I didn't spy on you." Lenny shrugged his shoulders. "I observed from afar."

"There's a fine line there too," Mel did not bother to conceal her anger.

"Maybe so, but you might say I don't care." Lenny waved a dismissive hand. "I need the money. Now sign this release, or I'll tell Hendricks." He pulled a piece of paper from his coat pocket and shoved it at her.

His threat was not lost on Mel. "I don't like blackmail."

With a contemptuous smile on his lips, he captured her with a self-satisfied gaze. "It really matters little what you like, my dear ex-wife. Your secret will be safe with me, as long as you do what I say."

Lenny had disregarded her agony. He'd ignored her anger. She might not have the upper hand here, but she could refuse to play his game. Mel rose and tossed her napkin on the table. "You do what you have to do, Lenny, and I'll handle it." She turned her back on him and strode out of the restaurant.

Chapter Twelve

In the half-light of the August night, Mel entered the quiet barn. Her senses had all but shut down. She was numb. Staring straight ahead, she wandered down the center aisle. On either side of her, horses stirred in their stalls. Their soft rustling and a distant train whistle were the only noises. Even her steps were muffled by the dirt under her feet.

Not bothering to flip on a light, Mel was guided by her need for comfort. She entered the darkened stall of Royalty's Dreamer. The mare lifted her head and moved toward her. Mel held out her palm as a token of greeting. The mare's breath warmed her hand.

"Good girl."

That cozy, horsey smell surrounded Mel, soothing her.

"No, I didn't bring a carrot," she said to the insistent horse.

Mel slipped her arms around the animal's neck, resting her cheek against the warm flesh. Shutting her eyes, she nuzzled Royalty's neck. It felt so good, so homelike, so complete.

Why did life have to be complicated? Maybe that was why she loved the simplicity of the horse business. Feed, groom, exercise, muck the stalls, and feed again. Get up the next day and do it all over again. Day in and day out.

Mel shifted her stance but continued to hug the willing mare. Lenny's revelation still held her in a deathlike grip. He knew about Cory, *had* known about her for most of their marriage. She'd lived a lie with him. As she had struggled to put Jake and Cory behind her, to be a good wife, Lenny had known her deepest secret. He'd known but never forgiven her. Or forgotten. He'd held that information, waiting for his chance to use it. To blackmail her.

Mel rubbed her cheek against Royalty's neck. What she didn't understand was why Lenny hadn't used his knowledge to block their divorce. It didn't make sense. He had let her go.

Yet, Mel believed him. He would tell Jake about Cory if she didn't sign that stupid paper. Cold fingers of dread slithered down her spine. She swallowed hard and grasped the horse tighter. Lenny would tell Jake, but hadn't she decided to do that herself? Hadn't she concluded that their relationship must be based upon trust? She must tell Jake and do it before Lenny got a chance.

"Who's there?"

A flash of light swept across Mel's face. Alarmed, she opened her eyes to see a dark shadow behind a large flashlight.

"It's me," she called out as she dropped her arms from the horse's neck.

"Me, is it?" Jake lowered the light from her face, so she could see his features in the dusk. "Well, me, what are you doing here?"

Mel thought she heard amusement in his voice and automatically stiffened. Why did she have that reaction to Jake? Why was she defensive with him? The arms of rejection had a long reach, messing up her life for many years. She shook herself mentally. It was time to forgive. She needed to make the effort.

"I'm just visiting Royalty," Mel countered. "What are you doing? Spying?"

"I 'resemble' that remark."

He was laughing at her. She saw the humor in his eyes as he came nearer. She saw his dimple, high under his left eye.

"You're *so* cute." Mel rolled her eyes.

"Not as cute as you, sweetheart," he replied, coming nearer.

"Oh, cool it." She left the stall, pulling the door shut. "What *are* you doing here?" Although she acted angry, Mel didn't mind his banter.

When she turned around, Jake was standing near her. She looked up into his eyes. The light was fading fast with only the shaft from the flashlight providing illumination. But in that muted environment, Mel sensed a sudden tension, a sexual attraction. She licked her dry lips, feeling herself go warm and then hot. He continued to stare, his empty hand opening and closing into a fist.

It was as if their visual connection sobered him. Jake glanced away. When he looked back, his expression was almost tender.

"Actually, I've moved into the office and set up a cot," he said. "Thought it wouldn't hurt to keep a better eye on this place."

"Sounds like a good idea." Mel's eyes faltered under his disconcerting scrutiny. She began to walk down the aisle. "You're spending the night?"

"And every night until things are settled around here." He fell into step by her side. "I thought you went out to dinner."

Mel avoided his leading statement. "I did. I'm back."

"I see."

She felt the question in his response, as if he wanted to know more. Uneasy, her nerves drawing taut, Mel fumbled to change the subject.

"Let me see your humble abode," she said.

It was a mistake to look at him. His eyes were soft, affectionate. The barn grew darker by the second. At the end of the aisle, a horse kicked at the wooden wall of its stall. Mel felt her heart almost hit the wall of her chest. She swallowed hard, not daring to look away for fear he'd think she was rejecting him.

"Come right on in," Jake said with boyish eagerness. "You won't recognize the place."

Passing within a hand'sbreath of Jake as he ushered her into the brightly lit office, Mel caught the faintly spicy scent of him. She paused on the threshold to regain her composure and adjust to the brightness within the room. The air conditioning was on, and the room was uncomfortably cold. She shivered from the temperature. Or was it Jake's nearness?

Jake crossed the room to turn up the thermostat. Given time to recover, Mel glanced around. The old desk and sofa had been pushed into a corner to make way for an uncomfortable looking canvas cot. He had placed a bundle of blankets at the foot and tossed a pillow on top.

"It may be primitive, but it's home for as long as necessary," Jake said, the deep timbre of his voice holding a note of amusement. "Come on in. No sense air conditioning the whole stable."

Mel moved into the room, and Jake shut the door. When he turned to look at her, she felt like a rabbit in a snare. Being alone with him in a small space wasn't a good idea. It felt too intimate.

As she stood, returning his expectant look, she realized she longed for him, for his touch, for the feel of him.

"So, why did you stop by?" The gentle roughness of his voice beckoned Mel.

How could she admit she'd needed the contact and the warmth of another living creature? His eyes were too intense, stripping her bare. She recognized the passion in them even across the room.

She turned away and off-handedly picked up his pillow. "I have a habit of hugging horses."

Jake walked nearer as she squeezed his pillow to her breast. "And why is that?"

Mel felt the bewildering closeness of him. Swallowing hard, she turned "I've always thought that with a good horse to hug," words tumbled inanely from her lips, "I'd have no need for a man."

Jake tossed the flashlight onto that sofa. "I wouldn't be so sure about that," he said, the implication of his words hanging like destiny between them.

Desire knifed through her. She drew a sharp breath. Jake watched her as she struggled with this new, but familiar, sensation. She gripped the pillow tighter, hoping it would protect her. From what?

Herself.

For as surely as she knew this growing ache would never be assuaged without its natural outcome, she knew Jake would not make the first move.

Continuing to clutch the pillow, she raised her right hand and lightly stroked his cheek. His skin was warm and rough with a day's growth of beard. He sucked in his breath. Reaching up, he grasped her hand and held it tightly against his cheek.

"Mel." He spoke her name almost sighing with relief.

She should tell him about Cory before things got out of control. She should bare her soul, just as she longed to expose her body to the man who held her hand in his. She should speak. *Now.*

Jake removed the pillow from her grasp and tossed it on the cot. Still holding her hand, he drew her forward. Mesmerized by the scent of him, his very presence, his touch and feel, Mel was unable to speak. He caught her other hand and drew them both up to his chest, tucking them into his larger grasp.

"I won't pretend I don't want you."

"I know," she whispered.

His gaze held her hostage, drawing her captive into his passionate mood. She lowered her eyes, blending her body into his. He kissed the top of her head, and she shivered. When she looked up, he caressed her cheek with his lips, and her skin quivered. An uncontrollable urgency surged through Mel, blocking out all other thoughts.

When her eyes drifted shut, he kissed her lashes. She felt their warmth. He pulled her hands up around his neck, forcing her to rise on tiptoe to meet his now relentless kisses. He smothered her whole face with tender offerings of love, finally seizing her mouth with his. Mel responded. Her whole mind was awash with sensation, just as her body was alive with a throbbing and a desperate need.

His kisses grew deeper, more insistent. It was as if he had a goal—to draw her out of herself, to make her one with him.

He buried his face in her hair and hugged her tightly to him. Mel thought her ribs would break. Yet she hugged him back, wishing he would never leave, hoping they would never be apart.

"I have protection," he said against her hair. "We were stupid to do it that one time before without it. It's lucky for us you didn't get pregnant."

But I did. Mel loosened her grip on his neck to look at him. Jake's face was contorted with indecision. Fine lines tracked out from his eyes. Shadows softened the skin beneath them. Mel reached out and with one finger, touched the place that would be his dimple when he smiled.

"We were too young back then," he said. When he smiled down at her, Mel felt the indention in his cheek. "Maybe things have worked out for the best. At least, we found each other again."

Mel withdrew her hand and tried to pull away from him. Jake wouldn't let her. She fought to keep the fear from reaching her eyes.

"What's the matter, Mel?" he asked in a quiet voice. "Don't you feel it too? This attraction that draws us together?"

"Yes." She was breathless. "But there are things I need to tell you about my past."

"I don't want to know what happened in your marriage. If I find out that bastard mistreated you, I'll kill him."

Mel froze, feeling rooted in the spot. He was talking about Lenny, of course, but he had used that disgusting word that her ex-husband had used today. It sickened her. The lie she'd live sickened her.

"It's not about Lenny," she told him, trying once more to pull away.

"Don't, Mel. Let me hold you. It's been so long."

She allowed him to draw her once more into his arms. He cradled her head under his chin. She couldn't talk. Could barely think. For ten years, she'd searched for a fulfillment she'd never found. But here it was in Jake's arms—the contentment and peace, she'd always longed for.

"I'm hoping there may be a future for us," he admitted in a low voice.

Mel shut her eyes, knowing the solace of his arms would soon be gone. "What I have to tell you might affect our future."

Jake just held her tighter. "Then don't tell me now. Right now, all I want to do is love you."

Mel was silent feeling the rhythm of his beating heart and the increased cadence of his breathing.

"Please."

* * *

The soft strands of Mel's auburn hair brushed Jake's nose, tantalizing him with its lavender scent. He tightened his arms around her slim shoulders. She felt so good to hold.

How had Mel ended up in his arms tonight? He'd resolved not to touch her, to control himself. But her presence in the stall had bested his resolve. Mel had looked so lost, so alone. He'd wanted to comfort her and ease whatever pain that caused her eyes to grow wide with grief.

His good intentions had backfired.

He wanted to lose himself in her, really lose himself forever. Only when he had truly made her his own, would their lovemaking reach perfection. That would come. They had time.

Holding her in his arms was like heaven, something he'd longed to do for ten years. He wasn't beyond pleading. Not this time. "Please," he whispered again.

Lifting her head, Mel responded to his request with a smile and a breathless "Yes."

Chapter Thirteen

The next night, Jake's features were grimly set. "I suggest Professor Plum, in the conservatory, with a knife," he said and glanced around Vanessa's dining room table at those playing the board game.

Mel checked her detective's notebook, discovered she had Professor Plum, and lifted the Clue card so only Jake could see it. The provocative look he thanked her with sent shivers sliding through her body. The card shook in her hand as she returned it to her pile of suspects, rooms and weapons.

"Thank you." Jake checked off the suspect. "Your turn."

Mel took the die from him and tossed it. She moved her Miss Scarlet playing piece two spaces toward the lounge.

It was Pop's turn. Mel absently watched as he picked up the die with his gnarled fingers. She was very much aware of Jake sitting beside her. The renewed sense of intimacy she felt whenever she was around him was disconcerting. Unsettled, she tried to keep her gaze from his, but it was difficult. Every time she looked his way, he would glance back, giving her that *we've got our own secret* look.

"I suggest Mrs. White, in the ballroom, with a revolver," Pop said and turned to Cory.

The little girl shook her blond braid and everyone looked expectantly at Vanessa.

"Here's one." Vanessa slid the card across the table. Pop made a big show out of picking it up and concealing it as he surveyed its content. Then he passed it back to Vanessa.

Spending last night with Jake was not the only secret she kept from everyone, Mel thought with a guilty observation of the table. Cory, the love child she'd given up so long ago. Vanessa, her friend, who didn't know the truth about the baby

161

her mother and father had adopted. Pop, who would never really know his only grandchild. And Jake.

What can I say to Jake?

She'd better find a way to tell him soon if she didn't want her vengeful ex-husband to do it for her.

Yet, her agonizing secret wasn't the only misgiving Mel pondered as she watched Cory make her move. What *about* last night? What had it meant? Had it been a simple matter of easing their sexual tensions? Or did it signify more?

Mel glanced again at Jake. His hair was slightly ruffled as if the wind had caught it. His blue eyes held a devil-may-care look. Was he pleased with himself? When he grinned at Cory, his dimples enhanced the boyish quality of his features. She looked away, suppressing the urge to reach out and touch the misplaced dimple high under his left eye.

Whatever might become of their relationship, Jake had wanted her last night. He'd made her feel womanly and desirable. But more than that, he'd protected her physically when they made love, as he had not protected her ten years earlier. Sure, times had changed, but Jake had changed too. He was more mature, more caring.

Jake might be more mature, but he still possessed that quirky sense of humor. He still loved to tease her and hear her fuss. Funny, it didn't bother her liked it once had. They'd fallen into a comfortable habit that was becoming part of their relationship.

Cory scooped up Mel's playing piece, drawing her attention back to the game. "I suggest Miss Scarlet." She thought for a moment toying with the piece. "In the hall, with a candlestick."

Cory put Miss Scarlet and the candlestick in the hall and turned to Vanessa. Her sister shook her head.

"Jake, got a clue?" Cory asked since he was the next player.

"Not me, kiddo."

After both Mel and Pop also failed to show a Clue card, Cory burst into an impertinent grin. "Well, let me see," she said, drawing out her words dramatically. "I suppose I'm just going to have to accuse Miss Scarlet in the hall with a candlestick."

"No, not a candlestick!" Jake exclaimed in mock shock. "Mel, how could you?"

"You don't know I did it," Mel retorted. "Cory hasn't proven a thing."

Cory snatched up the envelope marked "Confidential" and stole a furtive look inside. Thrilled with herself, she plopped all three winning cards on the table.

"You did it," Jake accused Mel.

"With a candlestick." Mel agreed trying to ignore the flutter of sensation filtering down toward her toes when he teased her.

Jake raised his brows in a meaningful look. "You're a very dangerous woman."

"Well, damn me, not as dangerous as Miss Noble here," Pop said to Cory. "You won again, darlin'."

"Maybe she has a career as a detective," Jake suggested.

"Not me. I'm gonna be a horse trainer." Cory was animated by the amount of attention she received. "Let's play again."

"No, it's my bedtime," Pop grumbled and lurched to his feet. "Being shut out twice by a little tike like you just don't sit right with me."

Cory pulled a face. "You're just jealous, isn't he, Mel?"

"Pop is very competitive," Mel agreed with a smile.

Vanessa had been picking up the playing pieces and turned a motherly look at Cory. "Bedtime. Sounds as if Pop has just the idea for you."

"Ah, sis," Cory complained. "It's not dark yet."

"No whining, child," Pop said. "Get on up to bed with you."

Cory grimaced. "Okay, Pop. Will you take Major home with you? Vanessa won't let him in my room at night, and he likes to sleep with someone."

Pop motioned to the white and black setter. "Sure, I'll take the mutt. C'mon, Major."

"Mel and Jake, will you stay for coffee?" Vanessa asked as she put the top on the game box. "I have a new espresso machine I want to try out."

"Want help?" Mel asked Vanessa.

"No. Let's take it in the library though."

"That's fine. I'll be along in a while, Pop," Mel told her father who shuffled to the door with Cory and Major in tow.

"Take your time." He looked meaningfully between the two of them. "Take *all* the time you want."

"I wonder what that look was supposed to mean," Mel muttered as she and Jake entered the library.

"Probably that Pop would like to see us get together." Jake rested his left hand on the back of her neck.

Mel controlled her breathing and faced him. "My father always liked you better than the man I married."

His hand moved to her shoulder, binding them together with an assured intimacy. He lifted his right forefinger and touched the tip of her nose. "I'm better looking, I'm sure."

"You were always an arrogant SOB."

He shrugged his shoulders. "Hey, the truth hurts."

Truth. Yes, the truth would hurt. A fierce guilt stabbed at her heart. With her eyes turned up at his, she measured Jake's droll expression. He moved his hand to cup her cheek in his palm, as if he were trying to read her thoughts. She leaned into his hand, drawing comfort from its warmth.

"Do you get the distinct impression this whole thing was a set-up?"

Mel straightened, fighting down an unexpected fear. "What do you mean?"

"You and me showing up at Royalty Farm." Jake's eyes lightened. "I have a feeling Pop planned it all along."

The feathery touch of Jake's fingertips tied Mel to him. She searched his eyes. "What are you saying?"

"Pop O'Shea, matchmaker," Jake said with a laugh. "Did he tell you he hired me as a trainer?"

"No."

"And he failed to tell me you were divorced and coming home." He nodded his head. "I rest my case."

Mortified that Pop might have manipulated them like that, Mel turned from him as Vanessa came in the room with a tray. Jake hurried forward and lifted the tray from her hands.

"Here, let me help you." He placed the tray on the coffee table.

"I tried some new Irish cream flavored beans for this cappuccino," Vanessa explained, and sat down on the sofa. "There's no alcohol in it, but I can get some Bailey's if you want."

"No, this is fine." As she settled beside Vanessa, Mel took up a cup and sipped the frothy coffee.

Jake joined them. "This is good."

"Umm," Vanessa acknowledged while she cradled her coffee cup near her lips.

For a few minutes, they savored their drinks. The hot liquid was soothing. A slow, rosy warmth settled over Mel causing her to feel drowsy. She watched Jake from over the rim of her cup.

"Cory is the funniest child," Jake remarked after a bit. He sat down his cup. "She's such an expert at Clue."

"I wish she could solve our mystery," Vanessa said with sudden bitterness.

"Yeah, the sheriff and the state police could use some help," Jake scoffed. "They're as slow as Christmas."

Vanessa placed her cup on the coffee table. "The sheriff did tell me the results of the state fire marshal's arson report."

Mel watched her employer's tense features. How did she remain calm under the circumstances?

"I'm afraid the arsonist may be in my employ," Vanessa reported.

Jake sat forward. "How's that?"

"They believe the fire was started in the bedding straw of that empty stall. Liniment was used as an accelerant. All it took was a match."

Jake cursed. "What's more common in a horse barn than straw and liniment?" He stood up and strode to the picture window looking out toward the burned rubble.

Mel scrutinized Jake's slumped shoulders. This thing with the fire was getting to him. She wanted to go to him, to drape her arms around him and comfort him. At the same time, she was relieved the arsonist couldn't have been Lenny. He didn't have access to anything at Royalty Farm. Anything but her. He'd gotten to her for sure. Her cozy drowsiness ebbed to be replaced by a nagging fear.

"Jake and I have been afraid the perpetrator was someone at the barn," Mel commented.

His mouth was rigid when he turned around. "Whoever this guy is, he's good," Jake told Vanessa. "I've been keeping my eyes open for a few weeks but haven't noticed anything strange."

Vanessa nodded. "I wanted you both to be aware of this. No one else needs to know."

"Good idea," Jake conceded.

Thirty minutes later, Jake and Mel said their goodbyes and left the main house. Outside, darkness had fallen, and the night was black with summer heat. Mel was quiet, her mind a jumble of confused thoughts. Jake caught her hand as they started down the gravel road toward the barn.

"You don't mind me seeing you home?"

"You're going my way, aren't you?" Mel's voice was light and teasing. She didn't want to give him the satisfaction of knowing how the feel of his warm grasp disarmed her.

He gave her hand a squeeze. "Yes, and I hope we continue to go the same way."

"And what does that mean?"

"It means…" He stopped and turned to her.

She stared up at him, the night air heavy around them. He ruffled his hair with his free hand and looked away from her.

"I don't know how to say it without just saying it." His expression was tender. "I want to get to know you again. I want us to be like we were."

"As if nothing ever happened between us?"

167

"I know it can't be like before." Jake's voice was gentle. "We had something special when we were kids. I'd just like to try and recapture that same feeling, but I'd like to make it work this time."

"Yes, we *had* something special," Mel avoided a direct answer, aware Jake didn't know her words held another meaning.

Mel turned from him and dropped his hand. She started once more down the road.

Catching up, he draped his arm over her shoulder as they walked. "I know things came between us."

"Yeah, my marriage."

"You wanted to tell me something last night. Was it about your marriage, Mel?"

Breathing hard, Mel continued to walk. Anxiety, raw and cutting, severed her concentration. She had to tell him but make him promise not to interfere with Cory's life. The feel of his fingers, now absently caressing her skin, spurred her desire to confess. Overhead the stars winked and grinned at her, almost daring her not to yield to her fears. Everything would be okay the universe seemed to say.

"No, not my marriage. Something more. Something more important to both of us."

She stopped once more and looked up at him. Unbidden, tears of anguish pooled in her eyes. In the darkness, she didn't think Jake saw them. He was looking over her head anyway.

"When I went to college, I failed to tell you about something that had happened to me. I should have told you, but I was scared. I was stubborn too. I thought you didn't love me, so I wasn't about to beg you to marry me," Mel rambled on, trying to find the right words.

"I'm sorry, Mel." Jake glanced back at her. "I haven't been paying attention." He inclined his head toward the barn. "I turned the lights out before I left for dinner."

Mel followed his gaze. "Maybe Pop turned them on when he checked the horses," she suggested, not understanding the sharp edge to Jake's voice.

"But Pop would have turned them off before he went home to bed." Jake dropped his hand from her shoulder.

The absence of his touch alarmed her. Jake's logic was plain, and an ugly panic twisted deep inside her stomach.

"I have a bad feeling about this one." Jake raced toward the barn.

Mel ran after him. They entered the bright, but quiet aisle of the barn. "Things look okay," Mel said out of breath.

To be sure, she walked quickly between the row of stalls, searching each one and counting the horses. Mel turned back to face Jake who stood at the end of the aisle, the garish overhead light emphasizing the concern on his face.

"All accounted for," she said.

Jake shook his head. "I don't know. Something's still wrong here. I feel it." He crossed the aisle and pulled open the door to the tack room. "Oh, God."

Mel sprinted the length of the corridor and followed him into the tack room.

"Oh, no," Mel moaned, heartbroken by what she saw.

Lengths of leather reins were slashed in half and dumped like so much garbage on the floor. Each saddle was ripped from pommel to cantle, splitting each back wide open. Saddle pads were shredded.

Jake smashed his fist into the wall. "What kind of sick jackal did this?"

"We've got to have this tack for the show tomorrow." Mel shook her head in denial. "What are we going to do?"

Jake turned to the door. "Call the sheriff for starters. Damn it, Mel, why is this happening?"

He paused beside her, cupping her chin in his hand and raking her face with his gaze. Mel's lips trembled. She wanted to comfort him. To ease his grief, to make things better. She wanted to erase his tormented thoughts.

"We'll get through this," he said to her, offering her the solace she sought to give.

"Yes," she whispered.

"Together," he added with a pointed look in his eyes.

"Yes."

Jake lowered his mouth to hers, plundering her lips just as deliberately as someone had ransacked the room. It wasn't a gentle kiss, but one full of heartsick passion and despair. Mel answered him, shutting her eyes, losing herself in the taste of his lips and the force of his hunger.

"Oh, Mel," Jake took her in his arms. "Why is life so tough? Unfair?"

She was breathless. "I don't know."

It felt good to be wrapped in his arms. The solid strength of his chest, its rise and fall in a steady rhythm, gave Mel a sense of security, false as it may be. He kissed the top of her head, nuzzling a moment in her hair.

"We'd better make that phone call. Maybe the sheriff can catch this creep." Jake said pulling out his cell phone when they left the tack room.

The door to the office stood slightly ajar. Jake pushed it open and stood aside for Mel to enter the air-conditioned room where they planned to make the call.

A low, threatening growl greeted them.

"Major?" She flipped on the light by the door. "No!"

Major lay loyally beside Pop, guarding his master who was crumpled on the floor, the cot upended beneath him.

Chapter Fourteen

Even at midnight, the ER waiting room was hot and crowded. A baby wailed, and a man leaned against the admissions desk shaking his fist at the harassed nurse behind it.

With taut nerves, set jaw, and a scowl on his face, Jake roamed the stuffy room hardly able to control his rage.

Raking a hand through his hair, he glanced at Mel, who sat in one of the dozen impersonal chairs lining the wall. Her beautiful features were punctured by worry and fatigue, her arms crossed defensively in front of her and her eyes cast downward. Jake wanted to comfort her, but he didn't know how.

What could he say? *Pop will be okay. He'll make it.* Right. Pop was an old man with a heart condition. Based upon the time he'd left Vanessa's house, he'd been unconscious for at least an hour. Jake had difficulty swallowing. *We'll get through this, Mel. Don't worry.* Jake had said those empty and useless words to her in the tack room before discovering Pop.

Conscious of a deep need to find solace, he sat down beside Mel. She didn't move. He slipped his arm around her shoulders, drawing what warmth he could from her. She looked up at him and smiled slightly, then looked away again. A cold knot of anguish settled in Jake's gut. Silently, he pulled her toward him, hugging her, a gesture that seemed natural and right. He never wanted to release her. He never wanted to let her go through life alone again.

"Mel! Jake!" Vanessa rushed across the waiting room toward them "What happened to Pop?"

Jake stood up. "We don't know." He shook his head. "Mel and I found him unconscious in the office. Someone had vandalized the tack room."

173

"Yes, I saw that before I came over here." Vanessa nodded. "It took me more than an hour to find a sitter for Cory. How's Pop?"

Jake drew her aside. He tipped his head toward the swinging doors at the end of the corridor. "We don't know that either. The doctors are working on him."

"Oh, poor Mel," Vanessa said taking a deep breath as if in an effort to calm herself.

"Tell me about it." His reply was derisive. He still couldn't believe they'd found Pop lying on the hard office floor.

The old man's face had been turned, so that he'd been able to breathe. That had been the only blessing. Pop's face had looked like bloody pulp. He'd never seen such a mess. Fortunately, Mel had acted like a pro until the paramedics arrived. Although anxious, she'd cautioned against moving him in case he had a neck injury. That advice from the same stubborn woman who'd insisted on sitting up after falling from the horse in Lexington.

Now they waited for word. Jake hated his inactivity and the uncertainty.

"I know this isn't the time to talk about it, but what about the show in Shelbyville? It starts tomorrow. Without tack…"

"We're going," Mel spoke up. A hard, determined expression in her eyes had replaced her earlier blank stare. "It is what Pop would do. You know that."

Vanessa walked over and sat down. "But Mel, we don't even know how badly Pop is hurt."

"He'd want us to go."

Vanessa clutched her purse on her lap. "This horse show business seems unimportant in the face of all that's happened."

174

"That's just what someone wants you to think." Mel's eyebrow furrowed. Her words were careful. "The same someone who set the barn on fire may have tried to kill Pop."

Vanessa shifted uneasily. "I see your point."

An ER doctor entered the waiting area. Dressed in green, he looked like someone's kid brother. "Miss O'Shea?"

Uneasiness twisted in Jake's gut. When Mel stood, he crossed the floor to stand beside her, placing a light hand on the back of her neck. With that gentle touch, he tried to link himself to her, hoping he conveyed his concern and caring.

"Your father is awake," the doctor said.

"How is he?"

"He suffered not only a concussion, but a fracture of his zygomatic arch, his nose, and possibly his superior orbit. We're going to do an MRI to be sure on that. Afterwards, the plastic surgeon will evaluate next steps. Right now, Dr. James is sewing up his scalp laceration."

"Laceration? Is that where all the blood came from?" Mel asked.

"Yes, and from his broken nose."

Mel paled. She searched the young physician's face as if unable to comprehend.

Jake allowed his hand to caress her shoulders. "Just what do all those fancy words mean, doctor?" he asked.

"Uh, yes. Let's see." The doctor rubbed his chin. "The zygomatic arch is the cheekbone. The orbit is the rim around the eye. These bones and nose serve as a cushion to protect the brain from frontal injury. It's kind of like the impact system in an expensive car."

Time felt like it had slowed. Jake's stomach quivered as the facts sank in. "So, all those fractures probably saved his life?"

The doctor nodded. "Yes."

"Will he need surgery?" Mel wanted to know.

"Uh, we don't know the answer to that right now. That's why we're doing an MRI. It's more detailed than regular x-rays or CAT scans."

Vanessa came forward. "What could have caused those injuries?"

The doctor looked at her. "I don't know, ma'am. Had to be a large flat object though, something able to make that kind of severe impact."

"Something like a shovel," Jake suggested.

"Yes, the flat end of a shovel could do that kind of damage." The doctor nodded his head once more.

Mel took a deep breath. "When can I see him?"

"Uh, you can see him just a moment before we take him up for the MRI."

"I'll wait here," Vanessa said.

As the doctor led the way into the examination room, he turned to Mel and Jake. "There may be some retrograde amnesia. He seems pretty foggy about what happened to him."

Mel approached the bed with slow steps. Against the sterile surroundings of the ER, Pop was a shrunken shadow of the great trainer he'd once been. Several tubes protruded from his body leading to various bags and monitors.

With pain in his chest, Jake stared at the old trainer's face. One of his eyes was swollen shut, the other one closed. Pop's face looked like a deflating basketball, his cheek mushy and swollen, and his nose caked with dried blood. Clutching his hands into fists, Jake vowed to find the monster who had done this.

Mel stroked Pop's forehead, her eyes bright with unshed tears. "Hey, Pop."

The trainer cracked open his good eye. "Hi, darlin'."

"Jake is here too, and Vanessa is waiting outside. We're all worried about you."

"Yeah, this damn dizziness," he complained. "If it would just go away,"

"The doctor said you were to have more tests. They'll fix you up."

"What happened to me anyway?"

"We hoped you could tell us," Jake said. "I'm sure the police are going to ask you."

"Don't remember a thing. Are the horses okay? The horses weren't hurt, were they?"

"No, Pop. The horses are fine. Nobody touched them," Mel whispered and glanced uncertainly at Jake.

The old man really didn't know what hit him, quite literally. Jake found it gut-wrenching.

"Don't worry 'bout me. As long as them horses are okay, I'll be okay. Did you say someone hit me? Why aren't you at Shelbyville? We got to show them two young 'uns."

"We're going tomorrow," Jake said, hoping to allay some of Pop's fears.

A nurse motioned for them to leave. An unsure looked crossed Mel's face. "Can't I stay?"

The nurse nodded. "As long as he doesn't talk."

"Do you hear that, Pop?" Mel bent near him. "You're not supposed to talk."

"Damn hard thing to expect from me, ain't it, darlin'?"

Jake had to grin. "I'll step out." He placed his hand against the small of Mel's back. "Will you be all right?"

When she turned to him, sadness etched her features. Jake lifted a fingertip and stroked the softness of her cheek. Her eyes softened a moment. He smiled encouragement and walked out of the room.

Vanessa waited for him at the door. Jake shook his head. "He looks bad."

His boss touched his sleeve. "Oh, poor Pop."

"Vanessa, will you stay with Mel? I want to go back to the barn and take a look around." Jake fought down an urgency that was like a sudden storm within his mind.

"The sheriff has already checked the place over."

"Right," Jake acknowledged, "but he wasn't looking for anything particular. I'm looking for a shovel."

"Suppose there would be fingerprints?"

"If the guy who attacked Pop is one of your employees, I doubt if the sheriff will find strange fingerprints," Jake speculated. "I thought it might help if I located it. There may be other clues. Besides, I'm doing no good here. I really need to get out of this place awhile."

"I understand. Well, you take care."

"Will do." Jake made it to the door before Vanessa called him back.

"Oh, Jake! I forgot to give you this." She hurried toward him. "This letter was delivered to my house by mistake, I guess. I forgot to give it to you at dinner."

"Thanks." Jake took the white business envelope and turned it over. It had been mailed from Lexington, but there was no return address.

Absently, he tucked it into his pants pocket, tossed a farewell wave at Vanessa, and fled the commotion of the emergency room.

* * *

Pop had been taken into surgery. Now Mel and Vanessa sat in another waiting room. Yet, Mel still couldn't relax.

With a great weariness, Mel rested her head on the back of a chair, slouched down in the seat, and closed her eyes. Her insides were doing double-time to some obscene, demanding drill sergeant of fear. Her head throbbed to the relentless cadence of her troubled thoughts. Somehow, Lenny's hand had written this scenario. He was involved with the barn fire and Pop's attack. She was sure of it.

But how? He had been nowhere near the barn. The only way into the property was past Vanessa's house. The gravel drive made a passing car very obvious. If a vehicle had somehow slipped by in the darkness, it certainly would have been heard by someone. The only other way into the farm was through the fields, past the Neely's property. Lenny wouldn't have known how to come that way. Walking wasn't part of her ex-husband's repertoire, and he didn't know how to ride a horse.

Just the same, Mel knew he was implicated. A nagging voice inside her head told her so. Lenny had a habit of getting what he wanted. Just like the insurance scam of which she had no proof. Yet there would be no future for her if Lenny had his way.

Jake's hand upon the back of her neck had been like a velvet caress. Amidst the chaos of her emotions, he'd been like a steady rock—her support, her friend, and now, she thought with a smile, her lover. To thwart the evil around the farm, Mel had to speak up. She had remained silent long enough.

She opened her eyes and sat up. "Vanessa."

"I thought you were asleep."

"No, just thinking."

"I know. I can't stop beating myself up over this. I feel I'm somehow to blame."

"I don't think you are. It's more likely me," Mel said.

"If I had told the sheriff sooner about Kyle Bishop's offer for the farm, if I hadn't let Bishop think I was willing to sell, this might not have happened."

"Don't do that to yourself." Mel leaned forward and grasped her hands. "You said the state police investigated the realtor and found nothing."

"Well, somebody has got to be behind this evil. It's not random." A look of anger crossed Vanessa's face. "I hate not knowing. It's just like when I lose something. I can't stop looking for it until I find it again."

Keeping her gaze averted, Mel took a fierce breath. "I don't think Bishop was involved. I think it was my ex-husband."

"Your ex-husband?"

She felt Vanessa watching her. "I don't know for sure. It's just a feeling."

"What makes you think that?"

Mel considered her longtime friend. It was time to tell her. She couldn't have Vanessa blaming herself because for far too long Mel had kept too many secrets. "I had dinner with him two nights ago. He wants me to sign a release, so he can have all the money from the sale of our house. I refused, and he threatened me."

A wave of shock passed over Vanessa's face. "What made him think you'd do what he says? You're divorced, after all."

"I know," Mel hedged. "He seems desperate for money, and I just have the feeling he might do something to hurt the people I love to get his way."

"Could he be involved with the fire or Pop's attack?"

"I wouldn't put anything past him."

"Right now, you can't blame yourself."

"I just wanted someone else to know," Mel said. "In case."

Vanessa stood up. "Want some coffee?"

"No thanks, I couldn't drink it. You go get some though."

"Okay. I'll be back in a minute."

Mel watched the other woman leave the waiting room. She had done it. Spoken her fears. It was a relief to share at least one of her secrets with her friend. Sure, she hadn't told her everything she knew. How could she do that? How could she tell Vanessa her beloved little sister was really Mel's daughter?

She didn't want to disrupt Cory's life, even though an ache as wide as the Grand Canyon split her heart when she thought about her daughter—even though she wanted Jake and Cory to be part of her family. It was too late for that now. Cory belonged to the Nobles, not her.

The same sense of responsibility to do what was best for her daughter she'd held years ago, remained strong today. Cory was happy and healthy. The little girl didn't need Mel to come into her life and disrupt it.

Maybe when she was grown. But not now. No, not now.

* * *

Dawn approached when Jake pulled up to the remaining barn at Royalty Farm. The early morning gray sky matched his mood, for his mind had been churning continuously during his drive from Louisville. Had he missed something? What obvious clue had he overlooked?

Was he such a poor judge of character that he couldn't pick out the criminal among the farm's employees? He had discounted Dave because he had been with Pop for years, but he had had just as much opportunity to vandalize the farm as Sam or any of the other caretakers.

The stable was the same—dark and quiet, with the familiar scents of sawdust, manure, and horseflesh that he had smelled most of his life. Although he didn't turn on the overhead lights, the horses heard him and began to come awake in their stalls— circling, snorting, and pawing. Morning meant feeding time to demanding, hungry horses. Dave and Sam would soon be here to do the honors, so Jake just walked quickly down the aisle, his footsteps muffled in the dirt of the barn floor.

If his steps were barely audible, Pop's attacker would have also been soundless. Jake pulled up short and took a deep breath. The old guy hadn't had a chance. Even with Major to warn him, Pop probably had little premonition of an attack.

Flipping on the light switch, Jake surveyed the tack room. With the saddles and bridles a muddle of destruction, the room remained as he had seen it last. The sheriff hadn't disturbed a thing, but he hadn't been looking for a shovel. Stepping over the slashed saddles and bridles, Jake moved to the end of the room where the grain bin was full of a honeyed mixture of rolled oats and corn. It smelled sweet and delicious. Jake eyed the grain bin.

The shovel was missing from the bin.

If the sheriff's men hadn't moved the vandalized tack, they wouldn't have removed the shovel. Only Jake had talked to the doctor and only he knew what to look for.

Suppose the attacker had heard Pop come into the barn and go into the office. The bad guy must have been afraid Pop might step into the tack room to turn off the lights. Terrified of discovery, the attacker could have picked up the shovel, followed Pop to the office, smashed him in the face, and fled carrying the weapon. Where?

Leaving the tack room, Jake paused in the darkened aisle. He narrowed his eyes. A manure spreader was parked at the far end near the door.

The flat bed of the wagon was filled with the previous day's work—manure, wet straw, and dirty sawdust. This could be a perfect place to hide a large tool. Picking up a fork used to scoop manure, Jake reached over the side of the wagon and jabbed into the waste material. He circled the machine, poking and prodding with the fork.

Suddenly, he struck something hard. With a rush of adrenaline, Jake lifted the tool out of the manure with the tines of the fork. If he touched any part of the shovel, he could disturb the fingerprints or other evidence. Not wanting to do that he left the shovel on top of the manure. In the coming dawn, he could see dark stains on the back of blade.

His theory that the attacker was an employee of Royalty Farm seemed valid. How else would that person have known where to find a shovel and where to hide it?

Going into the office, Jake turned on the lights. Blood discolored the concrete floor. The sofa and cot had been pushed aside to accommodate the paramedics. Fingerprint powder dusted the furniture where the sheriff's deputies had been busy.

Fighting his queasy stomach, he pulled his cell phone from his pocket to call the sheriff. As he did so, the long white envelope Vanessa had given him fluttered to the floor.

He picked it up and discovered his name was printed in block letters on the front with the address of Royalty Farm beneath it. Turning it over, Jake examined the back. Whatever was in it didn't take up the whole space inside. Jake shifted the object to the bottom. Next, he tore the opposite end and shook out a glossy photograph. When nothing else fell out after he shook the envelope again, he picked up the photo.

Only the name of the film maker was on the back and a very faint date stamped into the paper. It was ten years old. As he turned over the photo and held it up to the light, Jake saw a lone figure who looked vaguely familiar.

It couldn't be.

But it was.

A picture of a very young and very pregnant Melody O'Shea.

Chapter Fifteen

Five minutes away from the call of the final class at the Shelbyville Horse Show, Mel rubbed a trace of mud from Jake's black boot. Spine rigid, head erect, he sat unmoving aboard the back of Dreamcatcher. His blue eyes hooded by the brim of his black felt Homburg, Jake stared straight toward the show ring activity. His only hint of emotion was the tic of his jaw muscle. It moved slowly in a rhythmic manner.

"Are you okay?" Mel asked, sensing his tenseness. It wasn't a typical tenseness, the kind she would expect on the night of the five-gaited championship. There was trouble behind it. Trouble she didn't understand.

"Sure."

"I'm glad you decided to show only three horses this week," she said aloud, hoping to draw him out. "It's a good thing we were able to borrow tack." She looked up at him expectantly. When he didn't respond, she went on, "I didn't count on Royalty winning so easily tonight. Now it's Dreamcatcher's turn."

Nothing.

Mel stepped back from Jake's motionless side and traced a hand over Dreamcatcher's well-defined flank. The stallion's skin twitched at her touch. She ran her hand along the animal's muscled hip, up to the dock of his tail. Something had changed between them.

Jake hadn't talked to her since the night of Pop's attack, five days earlier. Oh sure, he'd spoken to her briefly about the daily, mundane aspects of life around a show barn. But he hadn't talked with her in the same intimate way, comforting her with his hand straying to her back.

Untying the string that held Dreamcatcher's tail looped up to keep it from collecting dirt, Mel combed through the coarse black strands. The week had been crazy, flying by in a blur of activity. From waiting for Pop to awaken from his operation, to sitting by his bedside, to juggling her duties at the farm and preparing the horses for the show in Shelbyville, Mel had hardly had time to think. Now was the first time she perceived the difference in Jake. No longer having his undivided attention and support, she felt a tremor of uneasiness sweep through her.

"Ready?" Jake asked with barely a glance at her.

"Yes." Mel spread the black tail out so that it flowed to the ground like a fan.

"Okay. Let's go."

As Jake pressed his legs into the stallion's side urging him forward, Mel flicked her comb through the tail once more. Dreamcatcher started his trot, heading up the incline into the lighted arena, and Mel scrambled to find a spot on the rail.

Sounds and smells of the horse show carried well on the cool breeze. Laughter from the catered dining tent to her right mixed with the rhythmic organ music that changed beats with every change in gait.

The crowd had picked a favorite horse and whooped and hollered with every pass. To Mel, so near the action of the circling horses, the thud of the hooves on the tanbark and the clucks and hups of the riders were like familiar echoes from her childhood.

She leaned against the white railing. Her thoughts tumbled in disarray as she watched Jake make pass after perfect pass. Yesterday, Cory had won her equitation age group in walk and trot. Next show season, the little girl would graduate to the canter classes. Walk, trot, and canter were a horse's three natural gaits. Maybe someday Vanessa would buy her a five-gaited pony, and Cory would also be able to show the slow-gait and the faster rack.

Cory was instinctive in the saddle. Like her parents. Like her grandfather. Mel smiled slightly at the thought. The little girl had loved horses from the very first. Pop had bragged about her, not knowing she was his grandchild. Mrs. Noble had always been good about sending Mel Christmas snapshots of her daughter— Cory at eighteen months being held on the back of a pony; Cory at two and a half, being led down the aisle of a barn; her first blue ribbon at age three on the back of an ancient, but safe, white pony.

A pang of guilt tore through Mel. She hadn't found time to tell Jake about his child. Things had been too hectic. It had slipped her mind. In other words, she had used every convenient excuse to avoid the inevitable. Uneasy, Mel glanced at the crowd, wondering if Lenny was there. Was he watching her even now as he'd done in Lexington?

Mel's blood ran cold in her veins. What if Lenny had already told Jake? Maybe that was why Jake was so distant.

Her throat felt raspy and dry as she picked Jake out of the circling horses and riders. He was decidedly the most handsome trainer in the class. Erect, not stoop-shouldered like some of the older men, Jake had an aristocratic air about him. He carried his natural grace well, his athletic ability allowing him to make the most of a big horse like Dreamcatcher.

I love him so much. The wayward thought drew Mel upright. She pressed the railing, sucking in her breath as her heart skipped the required number of beats for someone in love. Lowering her lids, she allowed the sights and sounds and smells of the horse show to meander around her unnoticed while she dove inward to search her soul.

187

She loved Jake Hendricks. Always would. She was sorry his career and her secret had gotten in the way of what they'd once had between them. She was sorry they still did. Whatever happened in the future, she could never erase that first love from her heart.

"Come in and line up now and face the ringmaster," the announcer directed.

Bumped back to reality, Mel watched the riders and horses whiz by, many of them showing off for the last time before the judge. When most were safely parked out in front of the ringmaster, Mel angled along the railing to stand across from Dreamcatcher.

"You looked great!" she called to Jake.

He acknowledged her praise with a curt nod of his head and settled himself deeper into the saddle, flicking the tail of his riding coat over the back of the saddle to smooth it out.

Mel bit back another comment, dismayed by his lack of response. A grim expression marred his attractive face. Mel longed for the laughing Jake, the guy with the quick wit and practical joke. She longed to see the misplaced dimple high under his left eye. Chewing her bottom lip, she sucked in her breath.

The judge came down the row, taking one last look at each horse. As he approached, Mel raised her towel and shook it into the air to catch Dreamcatcher's attention. The moment the judge walked by, the stallion pointed his ears forward to watch Mel, the picture of a classic American Saddlebred.

It wasn't a surprise when Dreamcatcher's name was called for the blue ribbon. Mel whooped and scrambled over the railing, meeting horse and rider at the center of the arena. After the winning photo was snapped, she pinned the long blue ribbon on the Dreamcatcher's brow band and collected the silver plate.

Another trophy for Royalty Farm.

"Pop should have been here to see this," Mel told Jake as they made their way back to the barn after the victory pass.

Jake looked down from the back of the stallion. "He'll be there for Louisville."

Something about his face, its passivity and indifference caused Mel to snap. "I'm glad you've allowed yourself to speak more than three words to me."

"What do you mean by that remark?" His voice was hard.

"You've been giving me the silent treatment all week. I don't know why and I don't like it."

They arrived at the stabling area before Jake had time to reply. Vanessa was there and Cory, and when Jake dismounted, the little girl leapt into his arms giving him a big hug.

"You won! You won! You won!"

"That I did, sweetheart."

At the head of the horse, Mel saw Jake's dimple pop out under his eye and a grin spread wide across his face. For a moment, jealousy twisted in her gut, but she tucked the silver plate under her arm and busied herself by removing the blue ribbon from Dreamcatcher's brow band. Dave came and led the stallion away.

"Cory, get down," Vanessa admonished.

Cory pulled a face. "Oh, sis."

Vanessa shook her head. "It's not very ladylike."

Blond braid swaying, Cory slid out of Jake's arms. "Oh, okay," she grumbled and pushed down the skirt of her party dress.

"You look mighty fetching, Miss Noble," Jake complimented.

He took the ribbon from Mel's hand and offered it to Cory. "To the mistress of Royalty Farm, our championship ribbon."

Intense anguish knifed Mel's heart. In a different world, everyone would know Jake was honoring his daughter. She put the winning trophy on a table and turned back to see Cory presenting a little curtsy to Jake's formal bow.

"Congratulations on your win, Miss Noble." The voice of Sheriff Vickers interrupted the charming scene.

Jake offered the officer his hand. "Sheriff."

"I wanted to talk with you folks." The man nodded to acknowledge all of them. "Thought you'd have some time now."

"Cory, go help Dave put Dreamcatcher away," Vanessa ordered.

Cory held the ribbon tightly in her hands. "In my best dress?"

"In your best dress."

"You're just trying to get rid of me," she said with a pout.

"Do what your sister says." Jake sounded firm.

Cory's eyebrows drew together. "I know when you're going to talk about something important. I may be little, but I'm not dumb."

"Go on and get out of here." Vanessa laughed and shook her head as Cory scooted away. "Sheriff." She offered him a seat.

He settled down in one of the director's chairs clustered near the entrance to the barn where their horses were stabled. Vanessa sat down with him.

"Mel?" Jake looked at her, offering her the last seat.

"No, I'll stand." Her nerves were like brittle ice. She couldn't have remained seated if she had tried.

"How's your father, Miss O'Shea?" Sheriff Vickers asked.

Mel leaned back against the wooden side of the barn and propped a booted foot against it. "He'll be home tomorrow. Thank you for asking."

"Sorry thing to happen to old Pop. To all of you folks." The sheriff shook his head. "This business at the farm is bad news. Bad news."

"Have you found out anything more?" Vanessa wanted to know.

"That's why I've come to talk to you folks. As you know, my office has been working with the state police on this case." He nodded at Jake. "That shovel you found, Mr. Hendricks, may have been the weapon used on Pop. Unfortunately, we are unable to know for sure. With the chemical and bacterial interaction of the manure, we were unable to identify the stains as blood stains. Then of course, the latent prints on the handle belonged to several of your grooms. No conclusive evidence there."

"What a shame," Vanessa mumbled.

"Seems like it's time for us to consider the motives for these crimes." Vickers rubbed his chin. "Now, the motive for arson usually falls into three categories. First, we take a look at arson for profit. Did someone commit the crime to collect the insurance?"

Vanessa shifted uneasily. "I know you considered me."

"Mighty logical." He nodded. "But you know we ruled you out right away. Although you have some money difficulties, your insurance won't even cover the cost of your reconstruction, so burning down the barn with all the horses in it would have been a stupid thing for you to do."

"I'm glad you realized that, Sheriff," Vanessa said dryly.

Mel swallowed hard. She hadn't understood Vanessa was that bad off financially. It made winning at Louisville doubly important for the future of the farm.

"And we checked out that realtor you told us about. He could profit from your bad luck, but he has an alibi. He may not be the most popular guy in these parts, but he's clean, Miss Noble. Come to find out he's bought the property on your other side. He can build his subdivision without buying Royalty Farm."

The sheriff leaned forward. "Now, the second thing we've got to think about is them nut cases. No logic here. These are the folks that burn down the place because they like to see a fire."

"But other things were done here. Not just the fire," Mel brought out.

"I'm getting to that," the sheriff said. "The third motive we have to consider is revenge."

Mel's breath caught. *Lenny?* She'd come to the farm to make sure Pop and Cory were happy and healthy. Instead, problems seemed to have come with her, problems that threatened the way of life for her daughter.

"You folks seem to think someone on your staff done the deed." The sheriff fiddled with his fingers. "Now, let's count what happened. First the fire, then the slashed saddle girth."

"Someone tampered with the jog cart," Mel reminded.

"We couldn't prove that though." Jake glanced at her.

Mel held his gaze for a split second before he looked away. "But we couldn't *not* prove it."

"Then someone turned them mares out," the sheriff continued. "And vandalized your-all's tack. It's our guess Pop surprised that person, and the perpetrator attacked him."

"It's too bad Pop hasn't been able to remember anything about it," Vanessa reflected.

"Now, all these things that have happened leads us to believe that someone has easy access to your-all's place. Someone's familiar with your movements, knows just what to do to cause a little trouble."

"But he's caused more than a little trouble." Mel put her foot down from the wall and began to pace. "He could have killed my father."

"What have you done, Sheriff, to interview my employees?" Vanessa asked.

"Well, we talked to all of them. Your man Dave, there, is clean. All the others. But there's something strange about Sam Samson."

"Like what?" Mel stood behind Vanessa's chair and gripped its back.

"Found to have been spending a bit more money than usual at a casino over in Indiana. Checked out his bank records. Come to find out he's put a lot of money in his checking account recently. Drew some of it out to buy a new car."

"He had enough money to buy a new car?" Jake asked.

"Yep. Brand-spanking new car."

Mel's throat went dry. "Oh, my gosh."

"The fellows from the state police are heading out to your place right now to pick him up. We want to talk to that boy one more time."

Vanessa rolled her eyes in relief. "Well, thank goodness."

"Question is, ma'am, where did he get that money? Was somebody paying him to do what he did, supposing he did it—which we haven't proven, by the way."

"So, you're saying that you may have found the person who set the barn on fire and attacked Pop, but there may have been someone behind him?" Jake tried to clarify the situation.

"That's the look of it. And we ain't tied this to Sam. He's just mighty damn suspicious." Sheriff Vickers nodded his head and climbed to his feet. "Just wanted you folks to know. And I'd keep an eye on old Pop when he gets home. Wouldn't want someone surprising him again, thinking he can identify his attacker."

A chill coursed through Mel's veins. She hadn't thought of that possibility. Was Pop still in danger? She glanced at Jake, who had risen to shake the sheriff's hand one more time. She longed for the comforting connection of her hand in his. She needed him now. She needed his support and his caring. The very essence of him was what she wanted. A look of love. A smile of happiness. She yearned to see the affection in his eyes as he watched her mere movements.

Mel had taken his presence at the farm for granted this past month, thinking he didn't care for her, believing he had never cared for her. His leaving ten years earlier had been a festering wound, staining her life and influencing her actions. Now she knew he had cared about her and left Royalty Farm because he loved her then. He hadn't known about the baby. Jake had left because she hadn't told him.

"Well, at least, we know something," Vanessa said and stood up.

"Do you think I should have told the sheriff about Lenny?" Mel felt guilty, as if she had kept another secret.

Vanessa's gaze roamed over her. "Let's see what they find out from Sam. We can always tell him tomorrow."

Jake joined them. "What about Lenny?"

Mel couldn't answer him, could hardly look at him.

Vanessa answered instead. "Mel's ex wants her to sign over their property in Missouri to him."

"Has he done something to you?" Jake demanded.

Mel met his gaze. "Not really. I had dinner with him, and he wanted me to give up my share of the house we owned. He said he needed the money."

"Why didn't you tell me about this dinner?"

"We were busy. It slipped my mind."

"Seems like a lot of things slip your mind." Jake swung away from them and headed into the barn. "We've got to get the horses loaded."

Vanessa lifted her eyebrows. "Well, that was rude."

Mel could tell she was curious about Jake's manner. "I guess I'd better help out."

"And I guess I better take Cory home to bed," Vanessa said.

Together they headed into the barn. "Don't worry, Mel." Vanessa patted her arm. "Things have a way of working out."

How? Things had never worked out for Mel. Although she'd fought to get her college degree and build her reputation as a trainer, her personal life had always been a shambles. She'd given up her baby and her only love. She'd married a selfish liar. Now Pop had been attacked, and his dream of the world's best show stable at Royalty Farm was in jeopardy. And it might be her fault.

The "poor me" voice in her head played and replayed the scenarios of her life over and over again. Mel fought the immobility of self-pity. How could she make things turn out happily ever after? How could she make her dreams come true?

"Come on, sweetheart, we've got to go home," Vanessa said to the perky Cory, who had come out of a stall with a bridle in hand.

"Now? I'm helping Dave."

"I'm sure your absence will help him too," Vanessa said with a smile.

"Meany." Cory lifted her nose in air. "I think I'll get myself another mother."

Breath caught in Mel's throat. Absolutely motionless with dread, she watched the little girl until she realized Cory was just kidding.

"You scamp! Give that bridle to Dave and get going."

"Okay, Vanessa." Cory grinned. "Thanks, Dave. See ya', Jake and Mel." With a wave of her hand, the little girl pulled Vanessa away from the stalls.

Mel was busy the next hour helping Jake, and Dave pack all the equipment and then load the three horses onto the Royalty Farm truck.

"I think I'll ride with Dave," Jake said as the little groom climbed into the truck cab.

"No, ride with me." Mel reached a hand out and touched his sleeve. "I'd like to talk to you."

He didn't say a word but slammed the door of the truck and followed Mel to her Jeep. The fairgrounds had cleared out quickly. Only workers from barns like theirs were left, packing up and loading horses. The lights in the arena blazed in the distance. Yet, in the field where Mel had parked, it was quiet and dark.

"Why have you been giving me the silent treatment?" Mel confronted him when she reached her side of the Jeep.

Jake regarded her across the roof of the vehicle. She couldn't see his eyes or read his mood.

"Something has happened, and I don't know what it is." Her breathing sounded like pounding horses' hooves. She swallowed once. Thinking he wouldn't answer, Mel reached for the door handle.

"I can't figure you out."

Mel paused. "What do you mean?"

"I don't think you ever tell me the truth."

She held her breath.

"It makes me wonder if you've ever been honest with me. Our whole lives."

"I don't know what you mean."

"Get in the car and I'll show you." His order sounded ominous.

Mel slid into the driver's seat, and Jake climbed in the passenger side. He left his door open, so the overhead light cast a cruel glow around them. Grim-faced, Jake fumbled in the pocket of his white dress shirt and pulled out a folded piece of paper. Mel could see the question and hurt in his eyes, but she didn't understand.

"Someone sent this picture to me in the mail."

She was breathless. "Who?"

"There was nothing in the envelope but this photograph."

Mel didn't have to guess who had sent whatever was in Jake's hands. *Lenny.*

"Take a look at this and tell me who this is." Jake unfolded the rumpled picture and thrust it at her.

She took it into her trembling hands. A crease obscured the face of the person in the picture. She slanted the photograph to better catch the light. When she did, heat flushed through her body. How had Lenny gotten this picture? She'd forgotten it existed, because she'd lost it years ago. Or maybe Lenny had stolen it years ago.

Mel didn't know how to answer Jake. She couldn't speak, even if she knew what to say, because her mouth felt full of cotton balls. One of her worst nightmares had come true.

Jake grabbed her wrists and shook them once. His features hardened with anger. "Tell me that's not a picture of you! Tell me you were never pregnant!"

Chapter Sixteen

Mel's face paled. With her wide hazel eyes, she stared at him as if he were a monster. Jake felt the pulse points of her wrists, the steady *ta-dum, ta-dum* seeming to mingle with the throbbing pulse in his fingertips.

"Take your hands off me."

He dropped her wrists. "Gladly."

Her gaze didn't drop. She held his with a defiant look and even lifted her chin aggressively. Jake wanted to shake more than her wrists. He wanted to shake her whole body so the truth would tumble out of her reluctant mouth.

Curling his fingers to make fists, he fought back the urge to hurt her, just as he had been hurting all week. The thought she'd been pregnant and not told him was a festering wound.

"Are you going to answer me?" He controlled his voice with effort.

"I think you know the answer."

"No, I don't know the answer," he snapped. "Why do you suppose I've been so distant this week? I *don't* know the answer."

Her eyes grew wary, but Mel continued to resist him with her silence.

"I believe *you* know the answer, and I want the truth from you." Jake looked away, a crushing sense of defeat in his heart.

"That's me."

He hardly heard her. She'd put the photograph on the seat between them. The narrow space separating them was like a vast gulf. Intense agony in his soul, Jake picked up the crumpled picture and held it under the overhead light as if seeing it one more time would make the truth go away.

"Where was it taken?"

"At college."

"How old were you?" He was afraid to hear the answer.

"I had just turned nineteen," she said in a weary voice.

"You weren't married until you were twenty. You and Lenny didn't have any children, did you?" Jake placed the photo once more between them, hesitant to touch it any longer.

"We didn't."

Her reluctance to give him any information irritated him. If he had to drag it out of her question by question, he would. "Then what happened to this child?"

"I gave the baby up for adoption."

"Adoption?"

"Well, my options were few because I wasn't married. I refused to have an abortion. What else was I to do with a child?" Mel turned the questions on him, her voice rigid with a growing anger.

"You could have raised the child yourself," Jake said, his eyes narrow.

"How could I do that? I had to go to college, remember? You told me I had to get my degree. You said I was too young to be married, remember? So that meant I was certainly too young to raise a child alone. Besides, I didn't want to deprive the child of a complete, two-parent family."

"You thought solely of yourself and gave up the child?" Jake's breath came in irate gasps. He would never give up his own child. "You put your own selfish welfare ahead of the child?"

"Selfish? Like *you* were selfish, I guess, to go off to California and pursue your great career," she spat out.

A wind of realization blew through Jake's clouded brain. *I'm the father.*

Somehow, he'd known it from the moment he'd seen the photograph. Mel's anger made sense. Years ago, she'd thought he didn't love her, and so she'd kept quiet about the child. *His child.*

"It's my child, isn't it?"

She glanced away. Jake grabbed her chin and drew her head around to force her to look at him. The delicate bones of her jaw were like putty in his grip. Her skin was soft. Her eyes were wide with an unspoken fear, but he sensed something more. A raw hurt…a determined defiance…a shattered love.

"Isn't it?" he asked again.

"Yes."

"Was it a boy or a girl?"

Mel tried to drag her eyes away. He wouldn't let her. In fact, he pinched her so hard, she winced. He was almost glad. Glad to hurt her as he had hurt—as he *was* hurting.

"It is a girl."

"Damn." His curse was almost a prayer. Jake removed his hand from her face, the contact between them severed once more.

"Don't worry, she's all right."

He jabbed a finger at her face. "How do you know?"

She turned from him and looked out the window. "I just know."

"You know who adopted her. Where is she?"

Mel's silence stretched forever. His heart began to harden toward her. She didn't care about his feelings. He'd lost a chance to know his daughter, and it didn't seem to bother her.

"You know, but you won't tell me."

"No, I won't tell you."

"Why?"

"Because you don't need to know."

Jake was furious. He'd never felt such fire running through his blood as he felt now. He wanted to put his fist through something hard. He wanted to shout to the top of his lungs so the whole world would know his frustration and his fury.

Instead, he curbed his voice to a moderate tenor. "What makes you believe I don't need to know?"

"Because she is healthy and happy, and she doesn't need birth parents showing up to confuse her. She has a family, and we're not going to mess that up."

"Why would seeing her for myself mess things up?"

"You might be tempted to tell her who you are," Mel said unable to meet his eyes.

"I suppose you don't trust me to do the best for the child? You *hurt* my feelings, Mel."

"So? You don't think I haven't been hurt?" she shot back.

"You run off and have my baby and don't even tell me."

"You were in California."

"I was in California because you didn't tell me the truth."

"You wouldn't marry me. *We were too young.*" It was Mel's turn to repeat his words. "If we were too young to get married, we were too young to parent a child."

"But you didn't give me a choice. You didn't let me decide."

"It seems we've had this argument before," Mel said quietly.

Jake took a deep breath and glanced away. She was right. They had argued about his decision to go to California. He hadn't told her the truth then, that he loved her. He'd been afraid she'd talk him into doing something stupid like getting married while they were both too young and before she'd gotten her college degree.

But he'd had her best interests at heart. This wasn't the same. Mel had taken away something precious from him. His own daughter. This was something that could never be replaced. Mel's actions were out of spite, because he wouldn't marry her. Because he never admitted he loved her, she'd taken out her anger and hurt on him in the worst way imaginable.

He took another tactic. "How was it that you didn't have to tell them the name of the father?"

"I told them I didn't know."

The answer was too simple. "So, you acted as if you'd slept around and didn't know who the father was? You labeled yourself a slut. Mighty clever of you, Mel."

"It wasn't like that, because the father was never an issue. His name wasn't required." She was quiet, subdued.

Jake's anger grew. "Seems as if they would want to know the paternity of the child."

"Not if the state had no stake in raising her. I put her up for private adoption. Her records are sealed."

His daughter's records were sealed, just like his heart.

"Let's go home," he said, and slammed the passenger-side door, throwing them into deep darkness.

* * *

Because things weren't settled between them, Jake was in limbo. Last night they'd driven home in silence, helped Dave put away the horses, and gone their separate ways.

On this rain-soaked Sunday afternoon, he was in an ugly mood as he walked to Pop's house to visit the old trainer.

Jake didn't like the falling-out with Mel, but there was nothing he could do. She had wronged him. Wronged their child. He refused to let her remain in control. Now that he knew the truth, he wanted a say-so in this part of his life that she'd kept secret from him.

"I came to see Pop," Jake said when Mel opened the door.

She glanced warily at him and stood aside to let him pass. Her hair was loose, not bound in a braid or a formal bun for showing. The auburn strands, curlier because of the humidity, framed her pale face. Her hazel eyes seemed wider, the circles under her eyes darker. The lift of her chin told him nothing had changed between them. For a moment, he longed to cup her face in his hands and smother it with repentant kisses. But it was a fleeting urge. In annoyed silence, he entered the darkened living room. He had nothing to repent.

"No, Pop, don't stand." Jake went forward to the sofa and shook the old man's hand. "How are you doing?"

"Damn terrible. Feel like warmed horse shit."

Jake couldn't suppress a grin at his simile. "That's terrible."

"Damn right. Sit down, boy. Take the weight off your mind." Pop waved a gnarled hand toward a worn easy chair.

Jake settled into the seat and leaned forward, clasping his hands. Pop looked like a bruised melon. His face was red and purple and swollen, especially under his eyes.

"Can't eat a damn thing either except this soft baby food stuff," Pop complained. "Soup and mashed potatoes and pudding."

"Well, I'm sure you'll soon regain your strength," Jake said.

Pop frowned. "Damn dizzy too."

"Some of that is from the effects of the anesthesia, not just the concussion," Mel explained to Pop. "The doctor told you you'd be dizzy and exhausted for a while." She stood behind the sofa, as if the heavy piece of furniture protected her from Jake.

"I thought I'd report on the call from the sheriff this morning," Jake said.

"Yeah, what's goin' on? I feel like a horse put out to pasture. Can't remember bein' attacked, so folks treat me as if my whole mind is blank."

"I told you what the sheriff told us last night at the show," Mel protested.

Jake smiled. "Well, that's why I wanted to fill you in. When the sheriff's men got here last night, Sam was gone. Now the state police are looking for him."

"Damn coward," Pop grumbled. "Sounds guilty to me."

"That's what Vickers thought."

"I can't believe that scalawag Samson was strong enough to knock me out."

"He surprised you," Mel said, her hand clutching the back of the sofa.

Jake watched her fingers grip the fabric, her eyes shrouded, her features closed. "I don't understand his motive," he said.

"I'd say greed," Pop reflected. "It's one of the oldest motives in the world,"

"But who paid him?" Jake asked.

"Strange things happen in life," Pop mumbled.

Jake pinned Mel with his gaze. "Yeah, I know."

She flushed and returned his examination look for look.

Pop seemed to sense the tension in the room. "Must be my nap time. Doc said to get plenty of rest." He grappled for a handhold on the arm of the sofa. Jake sprang forward to help him stand.

"Don't like bein' puny," the old man grumbled.

Jake supported his arm and helped him toward his bedroom door. "I agree with you, Pop."

"Nothin' worse than bein' beholdin', that's for sure. I haven't been the best patient. Mel has been a real trooper though." Pop paused at the threshold of his room. "You ease up on her, boy. Give her her head. Things'll work out."

Pop shuffled into his bedroom and shut the door behind him. Jake turned to find Mel had gone to the window. Her back to him, she looked out at the rain.

"His spirits are good." Jake walked toward her. "You can gauge it by the amount of complaining he's doing."

"His bark has always been worse than his bite," Mel murmured.

"At least, he's predictable. There's no guess work where Pop's concerned."

Mel swung around. "What is that supposed to mean?"

Jake shrugged. "Just what I said."

She turned from him and fled to the sofa, picking up the pillow that had fallen to the floor and placing it against the cushion.

"You sound defensive," he jabbed at her from across the room. "Must have been carrying around a lot of guilt for a lot of years."

Mel twirled, her eyes flashing. "I have nothing to feel guilty about."

"In your opinion."

"I did what I thought was best at the time. I had no choice."

"Are you trying to convince yourself?" Jake didn't recognize the spitefulness in his voice. It was hard for him to acknowledge the real depth of his anger. Troubled, he turned from her, breaking off the fight and staring at the barn in the distant haze.

Mel didn't break it off. She came at him, her voice hushed but high-pitched. "I don't need to convince myself. I did what I had to do for the child. She was my first concern."

Jake didn't believe her. He didn't believe his child was better off with a distant stranger. Without him. Without her real mother. Without her real family.

Feeling the tension in his neck and shoulders, he faced Mel. "Besides wondering why you never told me, I'm wondering who else is involved. Who sent me that picture? Do you know?"

Mel pressed her lips together and stared down at her hands. "It was my ex-husband."

"That doesn't make sense." Jake cocked his head to the side. "Why would that man get involved?"

"Blackmail."

The word was ugly, but precise. Jake's breath hitched. "Are you going to tell me why?"

Mel crossed her arms, but she didn't back down. "I told you Lenny wanted me to give him the money from our house."

He took a step toward her. "But if he sent the picture, he's ruined his little blackmail scheme. Why would he do that?"

"I refused to give it to him," Mel said. "He had no control over me. He was angry, so he sent it to you."

"He has nothing to hold over you?"

"No, I suppose not."

"Unless he tells me the name and location of the child." Jake dropped the truth between them.

She looked away. He saw the uncertainty race through her eyes. He knew she hadn't thought of it that way.

For a moment, Jake felt sympathy for the woman across from him. He wanted to go to her and crush her into his arms. He wanted to kiss the top of her curly auburn hair and dribble kisses down her neck to the base of her throat.

Sucking in his breath, he understood he couldn't take pity on Mel. Too much was at stake. "If you tell me the name of the child, your ex-husband will have nothing to hold over you. You'll be free."

"I can't." Her voice was small, like a child's.

His anger flared again. "Why can't you?"

She squared her shoulders. The hazel depths of her eyes were ablaze with new determination. "I hate it when birth parents change their minds and show up to take an innocent child away from what she knows. From her family, her school, her friends, her life. I won't let you do it. It's not fair."

"But I can't *change* my mind. I didn't have a choice, remember?"

"I didn't either." Her words were like venom. "It wasn't my choice to get pregnant. It wasn't my choice for you to run off to

California. I *chose* not to abort the baby. I *chose* to give her up for adoption. I chose life over death."

He let her words sink in, suddenly glad for Mel's decision to let their daughter live.

She continued speaking quietly, "But they weren't real choices. If I had my way, you would have married me. We would have been a family. But I won't harm an innocent child because of our mistakes."

He couldn't let it go. His betrayal was absolute. "You had another choice. You could have told me you were pregnant."

"I didn't want it that way. I wanted you to love me for myself. I didn't want to force you into something you might have hated the rest of your life."

Tears pooled in her eyes. At the same time, she set her jaw and wouldn't tell him what he wanted to know. They were at an impasse.

"There's nothing I can say to convince you?"

"Pop said something to me once about forgiveness." Mel sounded as if she were in a far-off tunnel.

"Forgiveness? You want me to forgive you? That's asking a lot when so much is at stake."

"Yes, I suppose so."

Long moments of silence shouted through the room. Outside the rain splashed haphazardly on the steps of the porch. The gutters, crammed with debris, spilled like a waterfall near the multi-pane window. Jake noticed a spider had made a home in the corner of the window sill.

"Maybe it has more to do with trust," Jake offered after the silence had intensified.

"You didn't trust me when I was eighteen."

Jake looked at her ashen face. "And you don't trust me now."

"How can I?"

"I'm the one who was betrayed," he reminded her.

"I'm the one thinking about what's best for a precious little girl."

"Neither one of us will compromise?"

"I can't," she whispered. "It should be her *choice*, when she is older. When she is more mature."

He looked at her, fixated, sick with anguish. "You've never wanted her to know you?"

Mel glanced at the floor. Suffering shifted across her face. "All the time. I've ached for her to know me. I've cried at night because we will never be a real family, the three of us, like it should have been." She raised her head.

"How did your ex-husband find out? Did you tell him?"

"No. I never told him. Somehow, he figured it out and kept his knowledge secret from me."

"That's a strange thing to do," Jake commented.

"You have to know Lenny. He has his agenda. He tries to accomplish his goals no matter what stands in his way."

Were Mel's words prophetic? At the moment, he was willing to do anything. "I suppose I could ask Lenny for the name. You seem sure he plans to use it against you. Maybe he'll tell me."

"Maybe he will," she said in an emotion-choked voice.

Silence settled around them once more as they appraised each other. Mel didn't look away. Jake clenched his jaw. He felt like a battered football player after a losing game.

Her eyes were over-bright. Walking to the door, she opened it and stood aside for him to leave. Outside the rain had increased, coming down hard and steady.

"I guess we have nothing more to discuss."

"I guess not."

Jake stepped out the door and into the storm.

Chapter Seventeen

The water from Sunday's rain had drained enough from the sandy outdoor arena by Monday afternoon to allow Mel to give Cory's riding lesson outside. The summer sunshine felt good after the dismal weather the day before. Mel welcomed the heat on her face, just as she welcomed the opportunity to interact with her daughter. There had been too few times like this over the years.

"Push with your left leg as you're going around the corner," she directed.

Cory followed the instruction, laying her leg into Royal Tiara's side. At the trot, the gelding responded by sticking near the corner rail instead of swerving outward as he had been doing.

"Now tickle your reins a little. Get the horse's head up." Mel stood in the center of the arena as Cory circled around her along the rail. "Use tiny bumps. Like this." She raised her hands to demonstrate. "Bump straight up, not back. Yes, that's right. Good job. When you raise the horse's head up, he'll pick up his hooves higher."

Cory came around the corner and headed into the straightaway. "Now use that whip on him, once. Push him into the bridle."

The little girl took instruction well. She responded with the correct signals, and the huge horse reacted with a springier, more animated trot. Cory and Royal Tiara presented an elegant picture at the two-beat diagonal gait. Mel bit her lip. She was so proud of her daughter. It was tough being her mom. Her heart broke many times because she could never acknowledge Cory as her own.

"Walk," Mel drawled, instructing Cory to stop trotting to let horse and rider catch their breaths.

Jake and Vanessa watched from the outer rail. Mel kept her back toward them while she followed Cory with her eyes. Was she wrong not to tell Jake about Cory? A familiar tightness filled her chest. What was best for Cory? After all, she no longer had a typical family. Both her adopted parents were dead. Her new "mother" was single. Just as Mel would have been if she'd kept her daughter.

Had she done the right thing? Suppose she'd kept Cory but still married Lenny? At that time and in that same state of mind, she might have made the same unfortunate mistake. Living with Lenny would have been bad for Cory. But maybe Lenny wouldn't have wanted Mel with the extra baggage. After all, he'd always been possessive of her time and attention. He didn't want a family.

Funny thing, these *what if* games. What if Jake had told her he loved her? Her whole life would have changed.

Energy seemed to drain from her, and her body felt cold. She shouldn't do this to herself. She'd beaten herself up over the *what if's* for far too long. She must deal with the reality of today.

"Go ahead and pick up your trot," Mel said. "Get your diagonal."

"Trot, Tia." Cory's tiny voice carried in the hot air.

What was best for Cory now? Fists clenched to control a sudden trembling, Mel turned to watch her daughter circle the arena. The girl was happy. She loved her older sister, and Vanessa loved her. Cory loved Royalty Farm and the horses. She was bright and pert, but respectful of her elders. Because Cory felt loved. Because she *gave* love.

Mel's heart wrenched painfully as it had so many times these past years. She had her answer in the smile and the lift of the chin of a very confident and content little girl.

214

She'd been right to give Cory up. What kind of life could Mel have given her? At age eighteen she'd had no money. Pop had never been well off. It wouldn't have been fair to put the burden on him. She'd been fighting her own demons then, and how long had it taken her to overcome them? Ten years? Ten years and a divorce from a man who had wanted to control her thoughts and her actions.

Mel squeezed her eyes shut. It was all the more important to solve the mystery of who was trying to ruin Royalty Farm. Winning the World's Grand Championship became critical as well. If Royalty Farm went under, the shine might disappear from Cory's eyes. Mel could not control the what if's. The past was gone, but she had some say over the future.

She opened her eyes. "Come on in and line up."

Cory trotted over to Mel and stretched out the horse. Jake joined them smiling up at the little girl.

"I'll pretend to be the judge." He walked around horse and rider, inspecting them.

Suppressing a small grin, Cory raised her chin.

"Keep your hands even." Jake came up to Cory and took hold of her wrists. "Arch your wrists over like this." He positioned her hands. "Nice, very nice."

Cory retained her composure, but Mel saw the gleam in her eyes. She was pleased by Jake's attention.

"Good job, Cory. Now go put your horse away." Mel dismissed her.

"Walk, Tia." The girl nudged her horse out of the stretch, and they walked toward the gate Vanessa held open.

"Changed your mind since yesterday?" Jake asked. "Are you going to tell me the truth?"

"No."

He made a sound of bitter amusement and followed horse and rider out of the gate.

Stalemate. So, that's the way it was going to be.

She'd made the right decision when she was young. But what about now? She wasn't so sure. Maybe she should tell Jake. Maybe she should trust him. Taking a deep breath, she fought uncertainty.

Suddenly, Dave burst out of the barn and ran toward them. "Jake!"

By the time Mel had joined Jake and Vanessa at the gate, Dave had reached them. "The sheriff called," he said panting. "Sam is dead."

Vanessa's hand went to her mouth. "My God!"

"What happened?"

"Vickers doesn't know. All he knows is the state police found Sam's body floating in the Salt River in Bullitt County. Appears he was murdered."

"How can they know?" Vanessa asked.

"It's pretty clear what happened, because Sam had a bullet hole right between his eyes."

Mel's pulse quickened. Who would have killed the pitiful little groom? More importantly, *why* was he killed?

* * *

After supper Jake found time to catch up on his chores in the tack room, but his mind drifted elsewhere. Now that he knew about his daughter, he couldn't remove her phantom-like image from his mind. Where did she live? Was she truly happy and well?

Jake rubbed Glycerin soap onto the old leather of the borrowed saddle Cory used for the shows. Cory was adopted and well-adjusted, eager to please and content with her life. Even though her adopted mother and father were gone, Cory seemed perfectly content with Vanessa as her substitute parent. Was his daughter happy like the Nobel's adopted child?

He buffed the saddle in a circular motion, applying pressure. What if Cory's biological parents showed up? How would that affect her life? Jake hadn't looked at it that way.

Suppose someone took Cory away from Royalty Farm? Vanessa would be crushed. Pop and Dave and Mel, all the people who loved the child, would be crushed too. Jake had to admit he wouldn't like the idea. Maybe Mel was right. Maybe he should view the problem from the eyes of his daughter. As much as he wanted to see her, what would his sudden appearance do to her and the people who loved her?

Unlike the borrowed saddle, it wasn't as if his child's adoptive parents had ever planned to give her back to her biological parents. What did he have to offer a child being a single man with a job that was transient at best?

Jake paused a moment to massage the sudden pain in his temple. He wanted the finest in life for his own flesh and blood. Ultimately, he wanted the child loved and safe and secure. Who was he to disturb his child's life? What arrogance made him think he could do more for the child than her adoptive parents?

Mel said his daughter was happy. How could he find out?

And then it hit him.

"Cory!"

Like the sudden, swift kick of a horse, he knew the identity of his daughter. In that instant, he saw the resemblance, between himself and Cory, between Mel and the little girl.

How could he have been so blind? So stupid?

He laughed at himself. Until last weekend, he hadn't even known his daughter existed. Now with an intense insight that tightened his stomach and compressed his heart, he knew all about her and could give her a name. Cory was *his* child.

With a grunt, Jake dropped the rag and picked up the oily sponge used for Neatsfoot Oil. The slippery liquid coated his fingers as he rubbed the sponge on the saddle. The dry leather quickly soaked up the oil. The last time he'd cleaned saddles, Mel had helped him. He recalled the smudges of dirt on her translucent skin, and how he'd wiped a blotch from her nose. Desire flared as it had then. For an instant, he wanted to yank Mel into his arms and kiss the stubbornness from her heart.

It all made sense now. Although he was still angry at Mel's lack of trust and her deception, he understood now the care she'd taken by placing Cory with the Nobles. Where she could watch over her. Where she could judge her well-being.

How it must hurt her to come home for visits and see her daughter. For the first time in a week, Jake fully appreciated Mel's sacrifice, the great depth of her character, and the abundance of her love for their child.

He looked up when he heard the door of the tack room click open. Mel stood in the doorway.

"Oh, I didn't know you were here. I'll come back later." She turned to leave.

"No, don't go away."

She paused on the threshold and stared at him with an exhaustion in her face that was easy to see. Their disagreement had taken a bitter toll on her. The natural circles under her eyes were darkened. Her mouth was set in a solemn line, and the marks of a frown blemished her forehead.

"I don't want to bother you," she said.

"You just want to avoid me."

Her chin came up.

He was sorry he'd picked a fight. "Actually, I could use the help." He tossed the rag at her.

Mel snatched it out of the air. "What do you want me to do?"

"Take care of the headstall there." He nodded towards the bridle hanging by a hook from the ceiling.

Stroking the leather with the soapy rag, Mel began cleaning the long reins. She was silent. Jake cast wary glances her way— watching how her slender fingers moved, how her eyelashes curled against her cheek. Her hair was pulled back with a ribbon. The profile of her cheek distracted him, just as the soft pout of her lips charmed him.

Would she ever tell him Cory was his daughter? He had a stubborn streak too. He wanted her to be the one to open up.

"Have you heard any more about Sam's murder?" he asked after a moment.

She raised her head. "No. Have you?"

Jake shrugged. "Vanessa called Sheriff Vickers after supper. He doesn't know anything more. The investigation is progressing though."

"Investigation? It sounds so ominous."

"Yes, they think Sam was killed to shut him up."

Mel stopped working. "I suppose that makes sense if someone else was behind the vandalism here."

"That's the thinking." Jake searched her concerned face, fighting down the need to throw caution to the wind and tell Mel he loved her.

* * *

Why does he look at me that way?

Mel turned her back on him in self-defense. The strange light in his eyes plagued her. She didn't want there to be anger between them. She wanted closure to their problem. As long as Cory existed and as long as Jake didn't know who she was, their disagreement would split them like competing political parties.

"After the World's Grand Championship, I think I'll find another job," she observed off-handedly.

"Skipping out, huh?"

"It's not that. I just feel it would be better for us not to work together."

Jake didn't answer her. She looked at him to find that his face and eyes had taken on a guarded and distant expression. Mel fought an aching need to run to him, throw her arms around his neck, and kiss the distance from his heart and mind. To hide her discomfort, she turned around once more.

"Suppose we win?"

"Then you'll have new customers and money enough to hire someone to replace me."

"It's not like you to give up."

"I'm not giving up. I'm just dealing with reality."

"What is reality?"

"The truth."

"Yours or mine?"

Suddenly, his voice was near to her ear. Mel turned quickly into his embrace. The heat of a flush crept into her face as his oily fingertips squeezed her bare arms.

"Let go of me."

"No."

A startling huskiness in his voice made Mel dizzy. She opened her mouth to speak just as his lips came down and silenced her. His kiss was full of passion and need. A tremor rippled through her whole body as she responded.

His kiss stopped just as abruptly as it had started. Mel was left reeling. Only his slippery grip on her arms kept her steady.

"That's my reality," Jake said. "I loved you enough to let you go. It's as simple as that. You owe me the truth."

Mel fought the lump of remorse in her throat. His breath was hot on her face, his eyes unwavering. She owed it to him. He'd done nothing wrong. Pop was right. She needed to forgive. To trust.

"It's Cory."

The gift of her trust revealed itself in his eyes. Their blue heightened into a brilliant sparkle. In one whoosh, Jake swept Mel into a startling, bone-crushing embrace.

"Oh, Mel, I'm so glad you told me," he whispered into her hair.

Something about the relief in his voice made her pull away. "You knew."

"I just figured it out before you walked in."

Mel didn't know how to handle the triumph in his face. She moved away from him. "Now you understand why I didn't want to tell you. I don't want her hurt, Jake. She's done nothing wrong. We were the ones who were wrong. Not to trust, not to open up." Mel shrugged and turned away from him, throwing down the rag.

"I would die before I let anything happen to Cory," Jake said. "Surely you know that?"

Pain throbbed in Mel's heart. "I didn't want to chance it."

"You told me anyway. Why?"

Mel turned to look into his eyes, the love within them a living thing. Was the love for her? Or for her child?

"Yes, I told you because you're her father." For some reason, she felt defeated. All the years she'd kept her secret to herself stretched behind her like a treacherous trail. "I need to go home and see about Pop."

He let her go without comment. Outside the day had drifted into night. Hot as usual in August, the night creatures had just started their ritual calls.

As Mel headed toward home, her footfalls sounded rough in the comparative silence of the darkness surrounding her. A similar darkness enveloped her heart. Why wasn't she happy that the truth had finally been told?

Chapter Eighteen

"Roll the dice, Mel," Cory said.

"My turn?" Mel picked up the die and cupped it in her hand. She blew on it for good luck, her gaze filled with humor.

Jake watched the two of them, Mel on the sofa and Cory sitting cross-legged on the floor. They huddled over a game of Clue spread out on the coffee table, Cory's blond head, a stark contrast to the auburn curls of her mother.

Her mother. Jake was still not used to the idea of having a child, let alone knowing her, and like her mother, being unable to acknowledge her. He knew how Mel had suffered through the years, but she'd never let on. Never done anything to harm the child.

The injustice of the whole situation gnawed at him. Shoving a hand through his own sandy blond hair, he scowled. Whoever said life was fair?

As Mel tossed the die and jumped her squares, Pop's soft snoring erupted into a snort. Cory covered her mouth and eyed Jake with amusement. He winked at her, then Mel took her turn, slipping through the secret passage into the kitchen.

"Let me see." Cory became all business while she shuffled through her cards and consulted her notes. "I'll suggest Professor Plum, in the kitchen, with the revolver."

A revolver. Ironic that they should be playing this game after what happened to Sam.

"Jake?"

"Huh?"

Cory sighed. "You're not paying attention." She frowned and put her hand on her hip.

"I'm sorry." He flipped through his own cards. "Plum, revolver, kitchen? I have this one." He tipped the card with the revolver on it so that only Cory could see.

"Your turn," Cory said after making a mark in her notes.

"Sure." Jake picked up the die and tossed it onto the board. He moved two spaces.

Cory scooped up the playing piece and handed it to Mel. As she did, Jake fought the urge to sweep the little girl up into his arms and hug the stuffing out of her. He wanted to hold her as if the physical connection would miraculously undo all the wrongs and hurt Mel and he had suffered. God help him, he wanted the three of them to be a family as it should have been if Mel had trusted him and he'd declared his love.

He glanced away. To be fair, he hadn't given Mel a reason to trust him. Not with that self-serving story about his own career. He better understood what she'd done, but somehow with knowledge, their relationship had taken a turn for the worse. And he didn't understand why.

"You all just aren't into this game," Cory complained, causing Jake to settle his attention back on her.

"I'm sorry, kiddo."

Cory glanced at Mel and then at Jake. She shook her head and began putting the playing pieces away.

"What are you doing?" Mel asked.

"You all are not interested in playing. I'm not really either."

Jake sat back. "I'm afraid you're right."

"That's okay." Cory nodded her head. "I'll go keep Pop company until Vanessa finishes dinner."

When the game was safely put away, Cory went over to Pop, poked him awake and crawled into his lap. Jake's heartbeat quickened. This was all so sad. Cory might never know her own mother and father. She might never know that the man who was giving her a big bear hug was her own grandfather.

Mel stood up. "I think I'll go outside a minute."

She must have felt the futility too. He climbed to his feet and went with her, unable to remain cooped up a moment longer.

Lightening bugs winked a welcome as Jake leaned against the porch railing. It was hot and muggy even in the dark of night. Mel sat down on the steps.

"It was nice of Vanessa to make her famous spaghetti for Pop. It's a nice send-off before going to Louisville," she said into the darkness.

Jake made a low noise in his throat. "I'll lose ten pounds before it's ready."

"Remember Vanessa's basically an only child. She wants everything to be perfect."

"You sound like a radio psychologist," Jake grunted.

Mel shrugged and fell silent. He wondered if she had been thinking of herself. An only child too. Did Mel want everything to be perfect? Was that one reason she refused to tell him the truth about her pregnancy on that August night so long ago? Was that why she'd avoided him this past week? Jake's mouth tightened.

He longed to touch the woman who sat so quietly at his feet. Something held him back. A perverse quality within himself kept his hand idle on the old, white, porch railing.

Mel broke the silence. "Tell me again what the sheriff said."

Would hearing the details again would make it less real, less grave? "Vickers said they tested the bullet. Your ex registered a gun like the one that probably killed Sam."

"He bought it from a German dealer." Mel's quiet words made Jake's skin tingled with alarm. "A Walther something or other. He was obsessive about the gun, because it was like James Bond's."

He found it hard to breathe as he watched the shadows of fear play across her face. He clutched the railing. "I hate inactivity. They have to find out who's behind all this trouble."

Mel cast a quick, anxious glance at him. "No telling who will be hurt next."

Her words hung in the night air like a prophecy. Jake felt the urge to pull her into his arms, just as he had wanted to hug his daughter earlier. He wanted to embrace Mel and tell her again he loved her. His chest tightened when he thought of all the wasted years.

"It was a lifetime ago," he said, not knowing where he was going with his thoughts. She looked up at him as if perplexed by the turn of the conversation. "I wish we could start again, wipe the slate clean."

She glanced away. "That's like wishing for a winning lottery ticket."

Flinging his hand off the railing in disgust, Jake dropped down on the steps beside Mel. A thread of moonlight laid a ribbon of light across her eyes which were hooded by her long eyelashes. He sensed wariness within her. Carefully, he lifted her chin with a fingertip. As she raised her eyes, his stomach fluttered.

"You're beautiful." It didn't seem enough to say.

Mel's gaze became a challenge and her lips slightly parted. He accepted the invitation and touched his mouth to hers— softly. Not demanding, just asking, until her lips parted. Jake's heartbeat, strong and steady, meshed with hers. He felt the lift of his chest as emotion surged within him like the final notes of a symphony.

The screen door suddenly banged behind them. Dragging his mouth from Mel's, Jake turned to see Cory standing on the porch, hands on her hips, head cocked to the side and a bright grin on her face.

"Vanessa said to tell you all it's time to eat."

She giggled and ran back into the house.

* * *

"Don't bite me!" Mel swatted Dreamcatcher across the nose with her towel. The big bay stallion snorted and pawed the cedar shavings with a polished black hoof.

Poor guy. Mel didn't really blame the horse for acting out. He was as nervous as the rest of them. She didn't know if the horse understood this was the biggest Saturday night of his life, or if he'd just picked up on the tension that severed the air like lightening.

Mel's own stomach cramped with nerves. The World's Grand Championship. Freedom Hall. Louisville, Kentucky.

It was a big night for her too. For all of them—Royalty Farm, Pop, Vanessa, Jake, and most of all for Cory. The little girl's future rode with her two parents on this night.

"I'm becoming too melodramatic," she told the horse. But there was a certain firm truth about her thoughts.

As Pop had planned, Dreamcatcher and Royalty's Dreamer had qualified in earlier events that week. Tonight, they would face eight other horses, the best American Saddlebreds in the country. Tonight, Mel and Jake would also face each other in hopes of bringing the prestige of the Five-Gaited World's Grand Championship back to Royalty Farm.

Mel raked a hard brush over the stallion's coat. Competing with Jake was the difficult part. His mere presence—his strong, muscled body and slow, dimpled smile—always sent shivers through her wayward heart. The memory of last Saturday night's kiss, filled with its dreamy intensity, cast a glow of pleasure inside her.

Dreamcatcher stood patiently between the cross-ties, seemingly resigned—just as Mel had resigned herself to the fact she and Jake remained at an impasse. He loved her. But what sort of future did they have? Her failure to tell him the truth about her pregnancy had created a barrier that might never be scaled.

Mel's hand and brush paused at the horse's withers. With her free hand, she grabbed a chunk of black mane and leaned her forehead against Dreamcatcher's shoulder. His skin twitched beneath her weight. Mel knew as well as she knew the contours of the stallion's broad back that she had created the barrier simply because she found it hard to forgive herself.

Sultry August heat radiated like the pulsing barrage of Mel's bitterness. She was tired of being out of control. Tired of not having what she wanted in life. Tired of never having a dream come true.

Her underarms were already wet, and perspiration trickled between her breasts. Hot air blew from the rattling box fan strapped to the bars of the stall. Dressed for the show, except for her wool coat, hat and gloves, her face pulsated with heat. Mel lifted her head and gave herself a mental shake.

Jake and Dave were down at the end of the aisle helping the farrier who replaced Royalty's Dreamer shoe. Mel's job was to ready this big brute of a stallion. Pop, Vanessa, and Cory were already inside Freedom Hall watching the other classes.

She sighed and gave Dreamcatcher an affectionate pat. Trouble seemed to follow them. Royalty had loosened a shoe less than an hour before the championship. What could happen next?

Mel stepped out of the stall and into the dark shed row. At the far end, three men and the mare were illuminated by a yellow glow, almost like actors in front of a spotlight. Concentrating on the horse, they didn't see her come into the aisle. Mel sighed again. Could she ever forgive herself?

Then thoughts of Cory brought a smile to Mel's lips. She wandered to the tack room where three long blue ribbons were proudly displayed. The little girl had won her age group championship aboard Royal Tiara on Tuesday. Mel fingered the smooth ribbon, remembering how Cory had taken her victory pass along the rail like a pro. Grinning from ear-to-ear, her chin high, her hands up, and her posture erect, Cory had thrilled the crowd as well as her family.

Family. She wished she was part of Cory's family. Choking back a tear, Mel wouldn't cry. Not now. This wasn't the place. She stifled the pangs of longing and regret that had been eating her alive these past weeks.

The stallion snorted. Mel glanced back at the open door of his stall and saw him try to toss his head in his cross-ties.

"Easy, boy," she said, wandering back toward the horse.

Through the metal bars above the wooden stall, she noticed the whites of the horse's eyes roll with fear, and then he tossed his head as if one of the cross-ties had become unhooked. Mel's adrenaline spiked. She ran toward the stall.

"What's going on?"

In the stall, Lenny half turned, giving her a scathing look. His left hand was flat on Dreamcatcher's neck. In his right, he held a hypodermic needle.

"What are you doing?" Charging him, Mel knocked the needle free.

"Bitch!" Eyes filled with loathing, Lenny grabbed her arms.

"No!" she screamed in helpless rage.

Suddenly, Lenny's fingers were wrapped around her throat, his fetid breath hot on her face. Pain engulfed her. Mel brought her hands up to his wrists, clutching them, trying to drag his fingers from her throat. The ligaments of his arms bulged beneath her hands.

In that split second, Dreamcatcher reared. Lenny pivoted to get out of the way and thrust her toward the horse as he fled. Mel fell back under the hooves of the frightened creature and hit the sawdust with a thud.

"Mel?" Jake's voice, filled with fear and confusion, sounded far away.

Mel threw her arm across her eyes, shielding her face from the dangerous hooves. The stallion's front legs came down right beside her. A left hoof glanced off her arm.

"You bastard!" Lenny shrieked.

She heard the sounds of flesh hitting flesh. Someone howled. Fear clawing at her heart, Mel pushed herself up on her elbow, rolled out of the way of Dreamcatcher's hooves, and then struggled to her feet. Stumbling into the shadowed aisle, she saw two shadowy forms clash in a death-like embrace.

"Dave! Get the police!" Mel shouted to the groom. "Lenny tried to kill me."

With a muffled oath, Dave darted away as Lenny threw a mighty right hook that caught Jake squarely in the face and dropped him to the ground. Flinging a disgusted glance at her, Lenny escaped down the shed row.

"Jake!" She ran to him, kneeling by his side, and threw her arms around his neck.

He folded her into his arms, his breath coming in heavy gulps. He smelled of sweat, spicy aftershave, and defeat.

"God, I let him get away," Jake muttered fiercely. "What was he doing here?"

"He was in with Dreamcatcher, and he had a needle. I surprised him, and he tried to kill me."

Jake set her away from him at arm's length and studied her eyes. "Did he hurt you?"

"No. You and Dreamcatcher saved the day." She grinned, trying to ease the tension.

Jake assessed her critically. "There's dirt on your collar."

"From where he tried to choke me."

"And dirt and hoof polish on your sleeve." Jake began to unbutton the long white sleeve. Slowly he rolled it upward revealing a deep purplish bruise on the flesh of her upper arm. His fingers were gentle. "That's going to hurt."

"It already does," Mel told him, her emotions beginning to tumble in wild disarray. "What about your face?"

Jake pulled her toward him once more as if he didn't want to let her go. "It's nothing," he said into her ear, his voice sounding shaky.

Mel wanted to believe him. She wanted a happy ending. She wanted closure. Her nerves, strung so tightly, began to relax, and she started to shiver.

"Cold?" he murmured into her hair.

"No, just reacting to all that's happened. Shouldn't we do something?"

"Dreamcatcher." Jake rose and hauled her to her feet.

With a quiver in her stomach, Mel followed him to the stallion's stall.

Chapter Nineteen

Forty-five minutes later, Mel sat quietly on the back of Royalty's Dreamer in the dim make-up area behind Freedom Hall. The palms of her hands inside her black leather gloves were wet. Her face was grim.

"Do you see him?" she asked Dave, who held Dreamcatcher's bridle. The stallion was riderless.

Mel twisted in her saddle and searched Stopher Walk, the covered walkway that lead from the stables to the entrance of Freedom Hall. Jake had gone with the police and hadn't returned. It was almost time for the Five-Gaited World's Grand Champion.

All around her, other trainers sat motionless on the backs of sleek show horses. Many of the men had been rivals of Pop, and three had already won the championship over the years. Their lined faces spoke of experience. Their hands, resting on their reins, were calm and confident. Mel felt young and green beside them.

Mel's chest tightened. "What are we going to do if he doesn't show up?"

"You go give 'em what for!" Dave said offering a grin, as if he were trying to boost her confidence.

Mel smiled in response for she was suddenly incapable of speech. Suppose Jake didn't make it back in time? Suppose the future of Royalty Farm was hers alone to salvage? Mel squared her shoulders and sat straighter in the saddle. This was something she could handle. She'd handled a lot worse lately.

"Where's my number 25 horse?" the paddock master's voice blared from the loudspeaker.

Perched on a high platform, the man had a bird's-eye view of the makeup area, and it was his responsibility to make sure all

233

the horses entered Freedom Hall at the proper time. "Get on your horse, Jake. We haven't got all day."

Mel felt, rather than saw, Jake come up to stand beside her. She swallowed slowly and looked down at him.

"You made it."

Jake put his hand on her lower leg, connecting with her in a moment of pure intimacy. "The police are searching for Lenny. I can't believe he tried to tranquilize Dreamcatcher."

Her eyes explored his face. "I can."

"Thank heavens the horse is okay."

"Thank heavens *you're* okay," she echoed him. What if, in his desperation to escape, Lenny had harmed Jake?

"Now, lady and gentlemen, we're going do this right," the paddock master instructed. "We're going to enter the arena one at a time when I call your number."

With his traditional riding habit and fresh red rose pinned to his lapel, Jake looked as handsome as always. His blue eyes held a deep yearning, a simple look of sadness and, yes—love. Flecks of memory pricked Mel's soul. She remembered him as a young man, eager to learn from Pop. She saw him instructing Cory and swinging the child into his arms. She saw him staggered by Lenny's fist. Mel reached down and softly touched his cheek with a fingertip.

"Will they find him?"

"I hope so." His misplaced dimple appeared as he smiled in encouragement.

She removed her fingertip reluctantly. "You'd better mount."

Jake nodded and took the reins from Dave and swung into the saddle. He pivoted the stallion and urged him forward until they were face to face. Mel searched his eyes, the roguish dimples now in repose, the line of his mouth drawn tight, his brow furrowed.

"Tonight is an important night for us both."

He didn't need to say he was thinking of Cory. One of them had to win for their daughter. A renewed sense of urgency raced through Mel's blood.

Slowly, Jake stretched his hand forward and cupped her cheek in his palm. Even through his gloves, she could feel the warmth of his hand.

"Good luck, Mel."

"Good luck, Jake."

The paddock master's voice blared again. "When the music starts, we go. You're in first, 292."

A crusty old trainer on a horse called Movie Maker broke away from the others and stood poised at the head of the ramp.

Jake smiled once more and removed his hand. Her chin trembled with an intense ache of loss.

Inside Freedom Hall, the organ began to play the opening bars of "My Old Kentucky Home" and thousands of spectators rose to their feet. On cue, the first horse and rider started down the long ramp into the arena, followed by a cortege of running grooms.

Mel shifted in the saddle and straightened her back. With effort, she set her mind on the business at hand. To make a good ride, she needed all her concentration. Shortening her reins and pressing with her legs, she asked the mare to walk. They made several circles as other horses and riders entered the arena. Then it was Jake's turn. He spurred his horse into action and disappeared down the ramp, the bay stallion's black tail billowing dramatically. She heard the crowd roar as the favorite entered the arena.

"Number 640, you're next."

Mel took a deep breath. "Come on, Royalty, it's show time." She clucked to the mare. "Trot, girl."

Royalty's Dreamer didn't need to be urged. Lifting her proud head and stepping out at a lively trot, the horse flew down the ramp and burst into the bright lights and green shavings of Freedom Hall. All around her the crowd cheered, but the mare didn't flinch. Royalty knew her job and set out to do it with the heart of a champion.

The competition was already taking shape as Mel made her first pass down the long straightaway. The contending horses circled and circled the arena, vying for the favor of the three judges who stood like little monarchs in the center of the ring. The striking of the horses' hooves on the green tanbark sounded like muted cannons.

Coming around the first turn, a horse and rider from Missouri rudely sheared in front of her. Stifling a curse, Mel pulled up just in time and swung Royalty around the upstart. Once settled against the rail again, Mel saw other riders challenging Dreamcatcher, cutting in front of him so the three judges could compare their horses with the favorite.

As she pounded down the second straightaway, Mel decided to save her horse because the competition looked like a long one. Since the show at Lexington, she'd schooled the mare for endurance. If she made the final workout, Mel hoped her effort would pay off, and only then would she challenge Jake.

"Waallkk." The announcer's voice was a Southern drawl. "Everyone bring 'em on down to the walk."

Royalty's walk, more of a prance actually, was what the judges looked for in a five-gaited horse. The black mare picked up her dainty forelegs and snapped them out in front of her body. Her lovely, long neck, which came straight out of her beautiful laid-back shoulders arched coquettishly. Her head was high, her ears were alert and pointed forward, and her eyes expressive. She had that show horse attitude that said, *Hey, look at me! I'm something special!*

"Okay, everybody, let's set 'em up and slow gait."

Mel knew Royalty probably had the best slow gait of the whole class. The mare performed the four-beat gait as it was meant to be—slow. Mel sat motionless on her back, gliding around the arena.

"Rack on! Let's see 'em rack!" The announcer's instruction was accompanied by a cheer from the crowd.

The rack, a faster version of a slow gait, was the most exciting part of the five-gaited class and the most difficult.

Mel turned Royalty loose and let her go on. The mare skimmed across the green shavings as if her hooves barely touched the ground.

The class was called back down to the walk, but several riders kept racking past the judges. Saving Royalty for later, Mel simply returned to the walk and found a good place along the rail for the canter.

After the canter, the competitors reversed, striking a trot as they circled the arena again and again. With every step, Mel urged Royalty forward, pushing her up into her bridle and keeping her head set and neck arched. Horses and riders repeated all the gaits one more time, and then the announcer called everyone in to line up.

Once more Mel sent Royalty into a brisk trot past the judges. Then hopping off the mare's back in the line-up, she stretched the horse out into the classic stance.

Jake halted beside her and slid off Dreamcatcher, his eyes sparkling. "Good ride."

"Thanks." Breathless with the excitement of the competition and his compliment, Mel smiled.

Mel held the reins high and kept the horse's attention while Dave removed her saddle and wiped off sweat with a scraper and a towel. He quickly pulled a comb through Royalty's long raven tail and spread it out to touch the green shavings of the arena floor. Jake busily mirrored Dave while his own groom handled Dreamcatcher. When the judges approached, Jake tossed the comb and towel to the groom and took his place at the head of the stallion.

Soon after that, the three judges were near them, walking around Dreamcatcher and inspecting his conformation. The crowd cheered.

When the judges toured Royalty, the audience whooped and hollered louder. Jake caught Mel's gaze and winked. Disconcerted, she tried to retain her composure, knowing the grand show mare, ridden by the only woman in the ring was the sentimental favorite of all the ladies in the crowd.

It was kind of ironic, after all, to be competing with Jake but having the same ultimate goal. The irony went even further when she thought of herself in this position. In the past, she'd shunned the big championships being content with training horses for young riders. Jake was the one with the fancy career, the desire for greatness in the Saddlebred world. Now she and Royalty were sentimental favorites in the Five-Gaited World's Grand Championship.

After everyone was back in the saddle, the announcer called for a four-horse work-out, and, to Mel's amazement, she was part of it. Sultan's Starcross and Movie Maker had also made the cut, and to no one's surprise, Dreamcatcher.

Her nerves on edge, Mel pushed Royalty into a fast trot. She set her lips in a grim line of determination. Now was the time to shine—to show the judges and the world that this little mare had the heart as well as the ability to be a grand champion. Now was her chance to save Royalty Farm for Cory.

Angling behind Jake and his horse, Mel followed them around the ring. The bay stallion's body glistened in the bright lights. His black mane tossed with every springy step and his black tail cascaded behind him. The crowd loved the rivalry between the two of them.

"Ladies and gentlemen, you're watching a brother and sister duel out there," the announcer revealed. "Royalty's Reverie, two time Five-Gaited World's Grand Champion, was the sire of both Dreamcatcher and Royalty's Dreamer. Earlier this summer, both horses were rescued from the barn fire that took their sire's life."

The four horses were asked to trot, slow gait, and rack and then reverse and do the three gaits again. Once Mel saw Sultan's Starcross falter and break from the rack. His rider got him going again quickly. The contenders challenged Dreamcatcher and Jake answered challenge with challenge. During the reverse, Mel backed off, and let the males go after each other. She put Royalty on the rail and worked her hard, hoping that her mare's quality and stamina would show through.

"All right, everybody. Let's come on back in and line up facing the ringmaster."

Mel used the opportunity to make one more pass in front of the judges. She sent Royalty sailing along the rail to the delight of everyone in the crowd. Although winded, the little mare kept going as spiritedly as if she had just stepped into the ring.

The final line-up went quickly. The judges stood behind the contestants, checking the numbers pinned to their backs and writing them down on scoresheets. Then the whole class retired to the end of the ring by the entrance ramp. As she regained her breath, Mel was comforted that she could do no worse than fourth.

Jake rode up beside her. "You did a great job, Mel."

She turned to meet his eyes, their blue reflecting the brilliant lights of the arena. "Thanks, but this class belongs to you."

"I wouldn't be so sure. You never know what the judges will decide." In an old-fashioned gesture, Jake touched the brim of his homburg, a look of respect in his eyes.

At that moment, Mel knew she loved him more than life itself. It didn't matter who won, just as long as one of them did.

Overwhelmed by emotion, she raised her head, ignoring the sounds of the crowd around her and the tension in the air. The massive scoreboard hanging from the ceiling proclaimed in shinning yellow lights *5-Gaited Grand Championship.*

If Dreamcatcher or Royalty didn't win tonight, Royalty Farm was in jeopardy. Tears blurred in Mel's eyes as she thought about failing the people she loved.

"Ladies and gentlemen, we have the results of the class." The announcer paused to deliberately drag out the suspense.

Mel dropped her head to find Jake watching her, a look of love in his eyes. She nervously rubbed the warmth of Royalty's neck.

"The new Five-Gaited World's Grand Champion is…number 640, Royalty's Dreamer, owned by Royalty Farm of Simpsonville, Kentucky, and ridden by Melody O'Shea!"

* * *

Watching the whirlwind of activity surrounding Royalty Farm's stable, Jake slouched in the shadows against a vacant stall some distance away. The lights and noise from the carnival rides from the midway on the west side of the fairgrounds filtered over the mammoth exhibition buildings to the horse barn complex even as an intoxicating mixture of manure and corn dog odors wafted in the air.

Almost midnight, the atmosphere was hot and sticky. Even with the sleeves of his white dress shirt rolled, Jake felt warm. The agitation within his stomach made the palms of his hands sweat.

Mel had won. She deserved it.

Jake shoved a nervous hand into his tousled hair. In fact, both horses had won, Dreamcatcher being called out as reserve champion. One and two. A clean sweep. Hopefully, now Royalty Farm was saved and his daughter and Vanessa had a future there.

Thoughtfully, Jake scuffed the red dirt with his boot. From his vantage point, he sensed the excitement around Mel and Pop. Camera bulbs flashed, and several reporters scribbled on pads of paper. Well-wishers shook hands with Mel, slapped high-fives with Pop, and requested selfies.

Because of the commotion, Jake avoided the post-show celebration. He needed time to think. And after all, this was Mel's time in the spotlight. He didn't want his presence to overshadow her.

He planned to ask Mel to marry him. Would she accept? As he pushed himself away from the stall and walked to join the party at the stable, Jake realized he didn't know what he'd do if she didn't say "yes."

Mel came to welcome him. "Where have you been?"

"Just cooling off."

Her eyes were wide and glowing. She had accomplished a lot, and she had to know it. Her career was made. Mel had entered the ranks of famous Saddlebred trainers, something he'd once dreamed of accomplishing but something that didn't mean much to him any longer.

He reached out a finger and touched the tip of her nose.

She smiled up at him. "Everyone's been asking for you. Come talk to Pop."

Jake allowed himself to be drawn to where Pop sat like a reigning king in front of the championship trophies and ribbons.

"Damn me, boy, we did it!" Pop raised his hand in salute.

Jake grabbed the old man's twisted fingers and shook his hand. "We sure did," he said with a grin. "We blew them away."

Pop squeezed his hand before he let it go, and Jake knew he was saying thanks.

Vanessa broke away from a group of friends. "I've already been offered enough money for Royalty's Dreamer to pay for a new barn," she announced to them, "and three people are shipping their horses to us tomorrow instead of sending them home. They want Jake and Mel to train them."

"A team," Pop said with a knowing look. "What did I tell you? And you thought it was just the prattle of an old man."

Jake glanced at Mel who flushed becomingly.

"I even had an offer for Royal Tiara, but I told them he wasn't for sale. Cory would kill me if I sold her horse."

Jan Scarbrough

"Where is Cory?" Jake looked around. He wanted to share the celebration with her.

"I don't know. She was here a minute ago," Vanessa said.

"Probably went to get something to eat," Pop suggested.

Vanessa looked exasperated. "But I told her not to leave."

"I'll check the stalls," Dave offered.

Alarm shot through Jake's stomach. He stared at Mel, who stood quietly beside him. The look of triumph had vanished from her eyes, and her cheeks paled. She reached out and touched his forearm, her fingers cold on his bare skin. In some immutable way, her touch communicated her fear. He knew what she was thinking.

The way things had been going lately Jake wasn't surprised when Dave returned, puffing from exertion. "I can't find her anywhere."

"Lenny!"

Jake wasn't shocked when the name of her ex-husband slipped like a curse from Mel's lips.

243

Chapter Twenty

Mel was tumbling from the back of a galloping horse. Tumbling and tumbling, she spiraled into an open abyss, never seeming to hit the bottom.

With a start, she opened her eyes to find the glare from the picture window throwing a rainbow of light across her face. Blinking, she adjusted her eyes. The empty space where the old training barn had once been showed through the window, a grim reminder of the summer tragedies.

Her divorce from Lenny had started the events that ultimately caused Cory's abduction.

"Four days without a word." Mel turned to see Vanessa circle the walnut desk and sit down. "I can't believe it."

"What?" Mel couldn't keep the bitterness from her voice. "That Lenny took Cory or that the FBI hasn't found her yet?"

Vanessa glanced at her and wiped away tears with a tissue. "Both."

Hands clenched, throat aching from unshed tears, Mel watched the movement of fear and anger shift across Vanessa's face. Was her own terror as blatantly exposed? Did she look as haggard and disheveled as her friend?

"They'll find her," Jake spoke softly from where he sat facing the desk.

"I'm glad you're confident," Mel snapped.

"How else should I be?" he retorted. "It's hard enough as it is."

Their gazes caught and held. Unspoken emotions of guilt and blame and fear passed between them. Mel longed to snuggle safely into his arms. Like a child seeking a parent's comfort, she wanted to be held and cuddled and told it all would be better.

245

But the adult part of her knew that wasn't going to happen. No manner of cajoling and positive words would cover the truth. Cory was gone and in the clutches of a man who had already killed another human being.

"Arguing won't help," Vanessa cautioned.

Mel's shoulders sagged, and she turned back to the window. "I'm sorry."

Hours of interviews with the authorities had drained them all. After this length of time, it was not surprising they found themselves at each other's throats. Throughout the interrogation, Jake had revealed the secret of Cory's parentage, but asked it to be kept private for the child's sake. Mel was proud of him for that, but it didn't matter in the larger scope of things. What mattered was Lenny's crazed attack on Dreamcatcher and the alarming fact her ex had a gun just like the one that had killed Sam.

Mel rubbed a fingertip across her temple. Lenny was crazed. It was senseless of her to feel any sort of guilt when she had done nothing wrong. Lenny had done it all. Lenny with his sick view of the world and reality.

"At least, we know who's kidnapped Cory," Jake commented as if he wanted something more to say.

"At least, we think we know." Vanessa's voice was weary.

"Who else could it be? Lenny is missing and his behavior the night of the show was criminal." Jake paused a moment and then went on. "It's better to know something, however intangible. I'd hate to be like some families whose kids disappear without a trace."

"But Cory *did* disappear without a trace," Vanessa said, unable to suppress a sob.

Hopelessness filled Mel's soul like a dead weight.

"Why would Lenny do it?" Vanessa asked.

"Revenge," Jake speculated.

Mel turned once more to find his gaze on hers. "Lenny didn't care about our divorce," she said coming forward, a new certainty awakening in her. "About losing me, at least. He only cared that the divorce hurt his pocketbook." Nails biting into her palms, she frowned sadly at Jake. "All I was to him was an entrance to the horse show community. A window dressing."

Mel knew what they were thinking—blaming her arrival for bringing this horror down on the farm. On Cory. She blamed herself. Mel clutched the back of a chair to keep from toppling headlong into the chasm of her fear.

"Why would he take Cory?" Vanessa asked once more in a weak voice.

Mel cast Jake a defensive glance. "My best guess is that it has something to do with his gambling debts. As Pop once said, desperation causes people to do funny things."

The two of them looked at her as if she'd said it all. Mel's glance shifted between them. The look on Jake's face seemed to be a confirmation of the love and respect he felt for her. He wasn't blaming her. She lowered her eyes in confusion. Things were so complex. She wished the slate could be wiped clean. She wished for a new start and for a happy ending.

The ringing landline phone startled them all. Vanessa pounced on it. Her hopeful look said she expected news from the police. Mel watched with mixed emotions as Vanessa's face spiked with apprehension. She touched a button, and a low voice came across the speaker phone.

"You owe me."

"Lenny," Mel mouthed, recognizing his voice on the speaker.

Jake stood up. They both converged on the desk where Vanessa stood.

"Bitch, if you'd just sold the property to Bishop none of this would have happened."

"What does the realtor have to do with it?"

"Shut up! You had your chance. Now I'll take mine. Tell Mel to bring one hundred thousand dollars and come alone. No cops. If you bring the cops, the kid is dead."

"Where?" Jake shouted, lunging toward the speaker.

Lenny must have heard him because he laughed. "She'll know. And she'd like hell better come alone."

The click that severed the connection boomed like artillery across the room. They stared at each other.

"My God, what next?" Still holding the receiver, Vanessa sat down hard in the chair behind the desk.

Hope fluttered in Mel's stomach. "We know where Cory is now."

"Where?" Jake touched her arm, the blue of his eyes filled with questions.

"He's got to be at the only secluded place he knows. His father's fishing cabin near Branson. Why didn't I think of that before?"

"I'll call the police." Vanessa began to dial.

"No!" Jake placed both hands on the desk and glowered across it at Vanessa. "Do you want to sign Cory's death warrant?"

"Jake's right," Mel said. "Lenny has killed once."

248

Vanessa laid the receiver back into its cradle. "But what do we do?"

"Like Lenny said, you give me the money and I'll take it to him."

"He will kill you too," Vanessa whispered.

"I'll have to chance it." Mel couldn't explain to Vanessa that it would be a mother bear protecting her cub. She'd do anything to get Cory away from that monster.

Vanessa searched Mel's face. "It's too dangerous."

"It's something I have to do," Mel assured her, "and it's better than waiting here."

"And she won't be alone."

A look of determination lit Jake's eyes. "I'm going with her," he said.

* * *

Somewhere in the darkness of the night lay Lenny's cabin. Hypersensitive to sound, Mel struggled to hear the slightest indication of Jake's return. He had gone on foot to reconnoiter the cabin.

Gulping down a breath, forcing herself to stay quiet, she waited alone in her Jeep fighting emotions between hope and abject fear, a captive of Lenny's madness.

Had Lenny hurt Cory? Was her daughter afraid? Nothing mattered now, not until her little girl was rescued.

Her future with Jake was something Mel didn't want to think about. She didn't want to think about his boyish smile, wayward dimple, and clear blue eyes. A sudden flush of heat rippled through her as she tried not to recall the way his arms felt— secure and loving, not controlling and loathsome like Lenny's arms had been.

A tiny prick of light gave Mel her first indication that Jake was back. "Someone's there." He opened the passenger-side door and looked at her, his eyes bright with excitement, and flicked off the flashlight. "It's about a half mile away. I didn't get close enough to look inside, but the lights are on, and there's a car in the driveway."

Her hands curled in her lap as she tried to quiet her fear. "It has to be Lenny."

Jake covered her hands with his. Their warmth somehow conveyed concern as well as a deep, abiding trust. Unsettled, Mel sought confirmation in his eyes, but the darkness surrounded them like an enveloping blanket.

"I hate to let you go alone," he whispered.

"I have to. You know that."

"But I'll still worry."

Mel didn't know which way to turn. Part of her wanted to free Cory, but the other part was afraid. She'd have to trust herself—trust the person she'd become, the one who saved horses from a burning barn and rescued a foal from a swollen creek. If Jake trusted her after all they had been through, she certainly could embrace his faith.

"Lenny wants the money. I'll give it to him and take Cory. It will be simple." Mel's voice was uncertain.

Jake squeezed her hands. "I don't trust him. I'll hide in the woods in case you run into trouble."

"Okay." Her chin trembled.

"I wish you'd take this gun." He held up the weapon.

"No. I don't know how to use it. I'd shoot myself or Cory. Let me do it my way."

"Okay." He sighed. "You know how I hate this."

"I know." What more could she say? With a rush of trepidation, she admitted, "Remember, I never stopped loving you."

"And I never stopped loving you," he repeated as he shut the door.

Even in the darkness, she read the truth in his eyes.

And suddenly she felt a sense of peace.

Mel turned on the ignition. That's all she had—her confidence in herself and their love. She had to use both to rescue Cory from Lenny and come back to Jake.

* * *

In front of the open cabin door, Mel stopped the car and turned off the headlights. The dark shadow of a man stood in the doorway, blocking the yellow rectangle of light that gleamed into the otherwise black Missouri night.

"You took your sweet time," Lenny growled.

"It's a long drive from Louisville."

"Did you bring the money?"

Mel left her keys in the ignition and climbed out. Her hands shook. She wanted to flee and run screaming into the darkness. Instead, she marched up to the door. "Do you have Cory?"

"What do you think?" His tone was surly.

"I think you better have her."

She entered the tiny log cabin that smelled of cedar, frying fish, and musty socks. There wasn't much to the cabin. Just a cramped area that functioned as kitchen, living room, and bedroom. Cory sat cross-legged in the middle of a double-sized bed, her eyes wide at Mel's entrance, but her face was unnaturally ashen. Mel smiled at her daughter, trying to send a message of courage and silence.

Lenny shut the door. Mel turned back to him. "Here's your money." She tugged a brown packet from her jacket and tossed it on the coffee table.

He approached the table slowly. His face was grim. Lines Mel had never seen before framed the corners of his eyes. Lips drawn, he picked up the envelope and settled onto a well-worn sofa. Lenny glanced up at her, his gaze filled with loathing. Beads of sweat broke out on her forehead.

"I'm going to count it first."

Mel shrugged. "Sure, have it your way. You'll find it all there." Remembering the location of the bathroom, she headed toward it.

"Where are you going?"

"Do you mind? I have to pee."

Her crude choice of words disturbed him. She'd never talked like that to him, but at the moment she felt vulgar and bitchy. He'd done too much to her and her family.

Five minutes later when she pulled open the bathroom door, Lenny blocked her exit. "It's all there," he said with a sneer.

"I told you it was." She shouldered past him. "I'd like some coffee before the drive home."

Lenny grunted something akin to assent, so she went to the makeshift kitchen and pulled an aluminum pan from a cabinet shelf. After running water into it from the faucet, she set the pan on one of the two burners. It was a low-tech way to make coffee.

Even turned on high, the water still took its time to boil. Finally, a mist of steam slowly rose from the pan. The back of her neck tingled. She knew he was staring at her back. Something was wrong. Just from the edgy way he was behaving, Mel knew Lenny wasn't going to let Cory leave. Or her either.

She struggled to remain calm. Finding a jar of instant coffee and two mugs, she dropped a teaspoonful of dark granules in each cup. "Want some?"

His eyes were cold. She carried one of the mugs to Lenny and thrust it into his hands.

"Thanks." He snorted loudly. "Too bad you weren't this domestic when we were married."

Turning from him, Mel went back to the stove. "You didn't want a domestic. You wanted to be married to a trainer who could win the Five-Gaited World's Grand Championship."

Glancing around with a sickly-sweet smile, she let him know he hadn't gotten what he wanted. "I've done that now."

"You bitch," Lenny growled.

Mel smiled once more. "You told me I was too nice. That I should be more aggressive about my career," she taunted him. "You must be a good teacher, huh, Lenny?"

"It seems so." He spit out the words at her.

"We wondered why you did it, Lenny." Her sudden need for revenge made her bolder. "Why did you burn the barn and kill poor pathetic Sam."

"Sam had it coming," Lenny suddenly admitted. "He botched everything."

"You mean you didn't tell him to burn the barn and beat Pop to a pulp?"

"I told him to make things a little harder, to encourage that Noble woman to sell. Those horses weren't supposed to die. You know I love horses."

"And Pop wasn't supposed to get hurt?" Mel used a dishtowel and lifted the pan from the burner. "The water is hot. Let me pour it into your mug." She came toward him.

Lenny held up his mug. "I was sorry about Pop."

"I bet you were." Mel flashed him another stony smile then tossed the scalding water into his face.

He howled in rage and pain. He flailed with his hands.

Mel dropped the pan and screamed, "Cory, run!"

The little girl sprang from the bed and bolted toward the door. It was locked. Mel hadn't thought that far ahead.

Terror seized her. Frantic, Mel ran to the window and struggled to jerk it open. It was stuck. She tried to think. The lock was a dead bolt, she remembered. Lenny had to have the key. She turned to confront him. To her shock, he came toward her like he was playing blind man's bluff. His hands reminded her of the talons of a bird of prey. She dodged him.

"Give me the key, Lenny."

"If you've disfigured me, I'll kill you." He let the threat hang in the air and advanced toward her again, reacting to her voice. He changed direction slowly. Did he have that much trouble seeing?

God help her, she *had* disfigured him. His face was bright red. Blood and clear fluid seeped from the surface of his skin. There was a horrible odor in the room. Like the smell of burning flesh. Like the smell of the eight horses burned in the barn fire.

"Mel!" Cory held up a key. It had been there on the table all along.

"Good girl!" Mel jumped out of Lenny's way and joined Cory by the door.

Her fingers were clumsy like they were encased in gloves. She fumbled with the key, finally inserting it into the lock and giving it a quick turn.

"Get into the Jeep."

Cory needed no urging. Together they ran. Mel flung open the passenger-side door and helped Cory climb in.

"Mel, look!"

Mel turned to see Lenny framed in the doorway once more. Staggering like a drunk, he stood with his gun in his right hand. Blind fear overcame her. She slammed the passenger-side door and ran around the back of the Jeep to get into the driver's side.

She reached the door just as a sharp crack of a gunshot slit the darkness. Either Lenny was too incapacitated to hit her, or she was out of his range.

But Jake wouldn't know that. A sickening feel of terror caused her to gasp for air. *What if?*

The question barely surfaced before Jake emerged from the undergrowth beside the house, his own gun drawn.

"No, Jake!" she shouted, but it was too late.

In a surrealistic display like actors in a two-bit theater, Jake rushed forward. Stunned, Mel heard the pop pop of Jake's gun, and then Lenny's answering crack. Jake collapsed backward.

"Jake!" Cory's primal scream mirrored Mel's own.

In a wild move of desperation, Mel raced from the Jeep and flung herself at Lenny, hoping to catch him off guard. It didn't work. But somehow, she knocked the gun out of his hand. He grabbed her around the throat.

Lenny was so tall and strong. Vile. Evil. His crushing fingers cut off her air. Mel fought him, twisting and turning. Gurgling noises escaped from her open mouth. She couldn't breathe. She stared at his dreadfully scalded face. Lenny forced his eyes open a crack. Did he plan to enjoy her last moment?

That's when her final burst of adrenalin kicked in. With only one hope left and her remaining strength, Mel shoved her knee upward. She caught him in the groin.

In that split second, she saw the look of surprise on his mangled face and then he doubled over in pain. Cursing her as he fell to one knee, Lenny lost control at last. Mel sucked in a quick breath and with her booted foot shoved him hard in the chest. He crumpled onto the gravel.

Nothing mattered but Jake. She raced back to him where Cory cradled his head in her lap. His lifeblood from the wound in his head covered her clothes and hands.

"Oh, my God."

"Is he dead?"

"No, but he's bleeding bad." Cory's voice was tiny and afraid.

Nerves taut, heart pulsating, relief flooded over Mel. She stripped off her jacket and knelt beside him, using the jacket to bind up the wound.

"Then there's hope," she murmured. "Let's get him into the Jeep."

Somehow the two of them hauled Jake into the back seat. Cory let his head rest once more on her lap and held him in her little arms.

Mel looked at them, her hand on the door. "It will be okay." How often had she said that since she'd return to Royalty Farm?

Cory nodded, her eyes frightened but determined. Mel shut the door, and then climbed into the driver's side. She backed the Jeep out of the driveway, and the headlights skimmed the crumpled form of Lenny. She turned the vehicle around and gunned it.

Her only focus was to reach a hospital and medical help. All she heard was the hammering in her ears of her own heart, and Jake's earlier words—*I never stopped loving you.*

* * *

The August sun beat down with unrelenting force. It scorched Mel's face like an angry god. Perched on the paddock fence, her hands gripping the railing, Mel concentrated on the grazing horses and tried to forget the commotion going on behind her back.

A giant horse trailer had rambled onto Royalty Farm property an hour earlier. Bound for California after the show in Louisville, it had one more passenger to pick up—Royalty's Dreamer. The Five-Gaited World's Grand Champion had been sold to pay a sizable debt. But customers had already sent horses to them to be trained, and Dreamchaser had stallion bookings for the upcoming breeding season. Pop's plan had worked like a dream. Royalty Farm had been saved.

For Mel, her win at Louisville was bittersweet. She'd done what she'd set out to do—save the farm for Cory. Once again, she had put her daughter first. Ahead of Jake.

As the pattern of her life played out in her mind, she swallowed the tears of regret when she heard the engine of the big rig start up.

"She's gone." Jake came up by her side to lean his tanned arms on the railing.

Mel had said her goodbyes to Royalty earlier, but the finality of the horse's leaving hit her hard. The tears she had tried to suppress suddenly blurred her vision, and she backhanded her eyes. "She loaded well?"

"Like a champion," Jake said with a nod.

257

"She's such a good girl."

Mel knew her comment sounded silly, but she loved that horse. Royalty was the last one saved from the fire. Her leaving was another loss in a lifetime of losses. Anguish clogged Mel's throat. She swiped her hand over her eyes again fighting valiantly to hide her sorrow.

At least, she hadn't lost Jake.

She glanced down at him. His head was still bandaged from the scalp wound that had bled like crazy. He'd spent a few days in the hospital, mending fast. The police had found Lenny wandering down the dirt road. The murderer was now sitting in jail where Mel hoped he would rot.

Jake clasped his hands together and continued to lean into the railing as if he needed the support. "Cory is a bright girl. She beats us all at Clue," he said. "We're either going to have to tell her the truth or leave the farm."

"I know." The reality was like a weighted ball, pulling Mel down. "But if we leave, Vanessa won't have trainers for her new customers."

"Seems as if we've been in this place before. Damned if we do and damned if we don't."

Mel's world seemed to slow down. This wasn't easy for Jake either. She bit her lip as silence lingered between them.

"Perhaps it's not our decision to make," she offered.

He cocked his head, his gaze caressing hers. "What do you mean?"

"It's not our place to tell Cory because we aren't her legal guardian."

"What are you suggesting?"

"We need to tell Vanessa. Cory is her responsibility."

Jake frowned. "Isn't that a cop-out?"

"It may be," Mel said with a shrug. She climbed down from the fence. "But maybe we can't make a happy ending out of this."

Looking thoughtful, Jake put a fingertip under her chin and lifted it. "I don't know about that. I'm all for happy endings, remember? Dreams do come true."

"If you make them come true," Mel finished for him and walked away from him toward the barn.

He hurried to catch up. "I think we can begin to make this turn into a happy ending if you'll say you'll marry me."

She stopped and turned to face him. "This is not time for one of your jokes, Mr. Hendricks."

"I'm not joking."

"You can't say that to me in the middle of the driveway."

"I can ask you to marry me anywhere I please. Remember, I love you." Jake laughed and cupped her face into his hands. His lips descended upon hers in a liquefying kiss. "I love you, you stubborn woman."

"Oh," Mel sputtered, hardly able to think.

Jake lifted his head. "I'm assuming you love me too."

Mel's response was breathless. "Of course."

"And I'm assuming you'll finally marry me."

Mel threw her arms around his neck. "Of course, I will."

"Terrific!" Laughing, Jake scooped her off her feet in a powerful embrace and performed an awkward pirouette.

Her blood rushing in her ears, Mel savored his exhilaration, the safety of his arms, the very thrill of the moment. When she came down to earth, she pushed away ever so slightly and turned her gaze up to touch his face.

"We still haven't solved our problem," she told him seriously.

Jake took a deep breath. "Yes, I know. You're right about talking with Vanessa first, but I think someday Cory has to be told the truth. Besides, whatever happens from now on is *our* problem, one we work on together." He hugged her. "Bargain?"

Mel nodded her head. "Bargain."

With his arm around her shoulder, Jake drew Mel toward the wide entrance of the barn only for them both to be brought up short. High above them in the hay loft with her legs dangling over the side of the opening and an irrepressible smile on her face sat Cory. Had she heard them talking?

Jake squeezed her shoulder and grinned up at Cory. "What are you doing up there, kiddo?"

"Watching you guys."

Mel's breathing quickened. "Did you hear what we said?"

Cory's face fell. "No. You all were too far away. But I saw you kissing." She brightened. "Are you going to get married?"

Mel and Jake exchanged guilty glances. "Yes."

"It's about time," Cory said with a matter-of-fact little nod.

Mel's shoulders sagged with relief. "So, why would do you want us to get married?"

"Because you're my family," she told them.

Mel's mouth went dry, and she really thought her heart would crumble. Once more Jake squeezed her shoulder for support.

"How do you figure that?"

"You're part of my barn family. You know, Vanessa and Pop and Major."

"I see." Jake nodded his head.

Her blue eyes were serious. "Besides, if you get married, you'll stick around."

"You'd like that?"

"Yep."

His gaze rested on Mel like a blessing. "We'd like that too, wouldn't we, Mel?"

She looked up at him. "Yes, we would."

Jake turned back to Cory. "Well, kiddo, if you plan to show in Kansas City this November, you've got a lot of work to do. Hop down and the two of us will give you a riding lesson."

As Cory scrambled down from the hayloft, Jake kissed the top of Mel's hair. "It's going to work out," he said in a hushed voice, so Cory wouldn't hear. "Thank you so much for giving me my daughter."

Tears clouded Mel's eyes and joy caressed her heart. Whispering close to his ear, her response was like a kiss. "You were right. Sometimes dreams do come true."

The End

Also by Jan Scarbrough

If you enjoyed Kentucky Flame, please consider reviewing it, and check out the next book in the series.

Kentucky Groom

Can a marriage of convenience prove that a California millionaire can be the perfect Kentucky groom?

Sign up for my monthly newsletter mailing list at *www.janscarbrough.com/contact/* and be the first to know about new books and giveaways just for newsletter subscribers. I promise your email address will never be shared.

Follow me on BookBub at *www.bookbub.com/authors/jan-scarbrough.*

Visit me online any time at *www.janscarbrough.com* and my blog at *www.janscarbrough.com/blog/*

About Jan

Whether it is the Bluegrass of Kentucky, the mountains of Montana, or Medieval England, Jan Scarbrough brings you home with romances from the heart.

Jan is the author of two popular series set in the Bluegrass, writing heartwarming contemporary romances about home and family, single moms and children, and if the plot allows, about another passion— horses. Living in the horse country of Kentucky makes it easy for Jan to add small town, Southern charm to her books and the excitement of a Bluegrass horse race or a competitive horse show.

With author Maddie James, Jan has written the Montana McKenna series, the story of the family of James McKenna, a Montana rancher whose death changes the lives of his wife and children.

Leaving her contemporary voice behind, Jan has written paranormal gothic romances: Tangled Memories, a Romance Writers of America (RWA) Golden Heart finalist, and Timeless. Her medieval romance, My Lord Raven is a story of honor and betrayal.

A member of Novelist, Inc., Jan has published with Kensington, Five Star, ImaJinn Books, Resplendence Publishing and Turquoise Morning Press. Today she self-publishes her books with the help of her husband. She has published 23 romances.

Jan lives in Louisville, Kentucky, with two rescued dogs, one rescued cat, and a husband she rescued eighteen years ago. When she isn't writing, she loves to ride American Saddlebred horses, drive grandchildren to activities, and volunteer with Alley Cat Advocates. There is nothing she enjoys more than curling up with a good book.

Join Jan's mailing list at www.janscarbrough.com/ for news about new books and giveaways to only newsletter subscribers. Follow Jan on Twitter @romancerider

The Bluegrass Reunion Series Returns!

Kentucky Woman

What is Jack willing to do to win the heart of this spirited Kentucky woman?

Kentucky Blue Bloods

When Kentucky blue blood tangles with British blue blood, are they willing to take a gamble on love?

Kentucky Bride / Kentucky Heat

Two novellas in one book

How far is Cam willing to go for his business? Can he turn a skittish Kentucky horse trainer into his Kentucky bride?

Is Reggie crazy to think she can convince Hank he's more than just his daddy's name and fortune, without getting tangled up in his alluring Kentucky heat?

Kentucky Flame

Is there enough of an ember in the ashes of their past to reignite the flames of love?

Kentucky Groom

Can a marriage of convenience prove that a California millionaire can be the perfect Kentucky groom?

Kentucky Cowboy

Will Mandy take a second chance with her Kentucky
cowboy and risk her heart this time?

Kentucky Rain

Carrying a torch is ridiculous. There's no time like the
present to move on. But does Scott really want to?

*Contemporary romances about second chances set in the Bluegrass of
Kentucky that can be read as standalone novels with happily ever after
endings and no cliffhangers.*

Chapter One - Kentucky Groom

Villa Montalvo
Near Silicon Valley, California

"Aren't you going to kiss the bride?"

Jay Preston turned to find himself eye-to-eye with his father's new wife. Tall and willowy, his stepmother was swathed in white satin, lace, and diamonds. A froth of tulle circled her upswept blond hair like a halo. She smelled of Giorgio perfume and carried a crystal goblet of champagne.

He shrugged his shoulders. "Sure." Jay had always been a peacekeeper.

The woman's ruby lips, tasting of wine, were warm and inviting, assailing him with inappropriate demands. She was his stepmother, only three years his senior, and young enough to be his sister. As the kiss lengthened and his belly twisted with disgust, Jay realized this woman was nothing but trouble. And trouble he didn't want.

"Easy, son." Carter Preston grasped Jay's shoulder, breaking the unseemly contact much to Jay's relief.

Shrugging off his father's hand, Jay stepped back. With a paunch protruding over his red cummerbund, Jay's father looked silly in his white tuxedo, starched white shirt, and red bow tie. His reddish-gray hair was thinning, and he looked every bit in his late fifties. Nevertheless, the older man looked happy, turning his smiling gaze on his only son.

"Find your own woman," he said with a rude wink as if not fazed by his new wife laying an inappropriate lip lock on her young stepson. He turned his back, sweeping his new wife away as the orchestra played a Strauss waltz.

Jay watched them, knowing from experience that his father's apparent happiness was transient.

The tinkle of the new Mrs. Preston's laughter grated like fingernails on a chalkboard. He turned away. Why had he allowed Carter to talk him into coming to the reception? Was Jay as much caught up in the corporate game as Carter's other executives who were also in attendance?

Declining champagne offered by a white-coated waiter, Jay slipped into a vacant corner of the room. Sitting down, he raked his fingers through his hair and allowed the laughter and music of the wedding reception to settle around him.

How many was it now? Five? The new Mrs. Preston was the fifth bride, all blonds. Jay pondered how she could trust a man like his father, a man who had gone from woman to woman, seeking some form of happiness he'd never found.

The newlyweds twirled around and around to the lyrical strains of music and the approving applause of guests. Jay recognized the look in his stepmother's eyes. He had seen it before. Greed. The hunger for money and the power it provided, all satisfied by his father's wealth. Was that the real reason she'd married the elder Preston?

As the music ended, the smiling couple separated. A business acquaintance joined his father, clapping the white clad back and pulling his old man away possessively. Always time to discuss business. It was a Preston trait that had haunted Jay all of his life.

Now that he was deeply involved in Carter's company, Jay realized he hadn't inherited the same characteristic. Business was beginning to irritate him like the sound of the new Mrs. Preston's laughter.

Drawing his lips together into a straight line, he observed his stepmother gliding through the guests as if she hardly touched the floor. The superiority in her step was evident. The arrogant lift of her chin and her condescending glances, looking down her nose at her guests, told Jay so much. The French had a term for it. *Nouveau riche.* It made him nauseous. Like a revolving door, women had paraded through his father's life—except for his mother Martha, who had been Carter's first wife.

"Hello, Jay," a tiny voice said.

Jay dragged his gaze away from the party and looked down into the huge hazel eyes of his little sister. Her bronze-red hair and fair complexion reflected his coloring. Her straight nose, a mirror of his own, was dusted with freckles. Jay grinned at her, glad again he didn't have freckles, for although they looked cute on a girl, they would look silly on a man of twenty-five.

He opened his arms. "Hi, Glory."

"My name is Gloria Alison Preston," she said with her pert mouth pulled down into an indignant pout, but she climbed into his lap anyway.

Jay encircled her in his arms. She smelled of baby shampoo and chocolate cake.

"How old are you now, Miss Preston?" He rested his chin on the top of her head.

"Eight, and you know it."

"I forgot," he said in his defense.

She snuggled closer to him, and he tightened his hug.

"I rode my pony today," Gloria told him.

"Hmmm," he murmured into her hair. "Did you have a good riding lesson?"

She nodded. "Daddy said he would get me a five-gaited pony or an equitation horse when I learn to ride well enough. You know, like the one you used to have. And he said I could go to real horse shows, not just academy shows."

271

Jay gave her a squeeze. "Good for you." Both he and Gloria rode American Saddlebred horses at a local show barn. Today Jay's time was limited, but he grew up loving the sport. It had given him a sense of accomplishment at a young age when he greatly needed the self-confidence.

"They're cutting the cake," Gloria said matter-of-factly.

"I see that."

Which wife was Gloria's mother? Number three? Jay had tried to forget that fact too. But he remembered he had liked Gloria's mom. She was sweet. Not like wives two and four.

Crap. How sickening that sounded. Ticking off his father's wives as if he were counting sheep. He felt sorry for little Gloria, growing up without really knowing her father. Hell. He felt sorry for the fatherless child he had once been, even though he would never admit that to anyone.

His sister appeared to be without a babysitter. "How did you get here?" he asked.

"Daddy sent his limo," Gloria replied with a happy wiggle. "I gotta leave at nine 'cuz it's my bedtime."

What was his father thinking anyway? Dragging the little girl to his wedding reception without someone to watch over her? Carter's irresponsibility disgusted but didn't surprise him.

"Ladies and gentlemen, family and friends," the new bride cooed into the orchestra's microphone. "We are so glad you could share with us the happiest day of our lives."

Gloria turned her big eyes up at Jay. "What's her name?"

"Lori, I think."

She looked away. "She's pretty. I hope I'm pretty like that when I get married."

Gloria's innocence turned Jay's heart. "You're pretty right now, sweetheart." He kissed the top of her head.

The bride giggled into the microphone as a crowd gathered around the newlyweds, making it impossible for him to see them. It didn't matter. He knew the routine.

"Do you want a piece of cake?" Jay asked his sister.

"I had some already," she admitted. "The caterer gave me some. He made extra. It's chocolate."

"Oh."

His sister was certainly self-reliant. She might appear timid, but she got her way most of the time. She did with him anyway.

A smattering of laughter and applause resounded through the reception area. The deed was done. The old queen was dead. A new queen crowned. Long live the queen!

How cynical he had become.

"Friends, come and enjoy." His father winced as the microphone squealed. "And then join us on the dance floor."

The orchestra struck up a very poor rendition of "She Loves You." Somehow the orchestra and soloist just couldn't replicate the throbbing sound of guitar chords or the Beatles' strident singing. Holding hands, Carter and Lori tripped onto the dance floor like a couple of kids. They began to fast dance, throwing their arms into the air, laughing, and gazing into each other's eyes. What was the dance? The Watusi? The Jerk? Hell. His father was stuck in a nineteen sixties time warp and wife number five went along with it.

Jay gave his sister another small squeeze. "Want to dance?"

"Sure." Gloria jumped from his lap, took his hand, and together they navigated through the guests to reach the dance floor.

With her dainty steps, she was a good little dancer. Jay felt like a klutz, but he gave it his best.

"They don't have any good music," Gloria complained.

"Yeah." He nodded in agreement and unexpectedly plowed into the back of another dancer.

"Excuse me!" Jay looked around to see a stately, silver-haired woman beaming at him. "Mrs. Chapman, I was born with two left feet. I'm sorry."

The woman smiled in response and touched his arm with a bejeweled hand. "That's quite excusable, Jay dear. You have other talents."

"Yes, ma'am." She was making light of his clumsiness. For that he was grateful.

Squeezing his arm once, the woman turned back to her partner, her words loud enough to be heard over the music. "That's Carter's son, the computer prodigy. He created Sampson."

Carter's son—the boy genius who had bypassed college, going right into his father's company after high school, the kid who would eventually own the multimillion-dollar Preston Global Technologies in San Jose, California.

The pit of Jay's stomach twisted just as he twisted his body to the rhythm of the music. Skipping college had worked out better than he could have foreseen. Developing computer systems had come naturally to him, just as horseback riding had been easy years earlier. By putting him to work, Carter had forced Jay to prove himself. And he had done just that by creating Sampson, the wonder security software that now resided in every piece of Preston technology on the market.

Part of Jay was proud of his success, but another part, the emotional part, wished his father could accept him for himself. It was almost as if Carter expected him to demonstrate time and time again that he was worthy of the Preston name.

Glancing at the newlyweds who danced nearby, Jay wondered if the family name was anything to be proud of.

The music ended. Sweat had broken out along his brow. He grinned down at Gloria.

"Care for some punch?" he asked with a sweeping flourish of his hand toward the refreshment table.

"Sure."

As the strains of another waltz began, Lori and Carter blocked their path.

"May we exchange partners?" Lori queried, casting a coy glance at Jay.

Carter inclined his head and held out his hand. "Gloria?"

Eyes sparkling, the little girl smiled up at her father. "Sure."

It hurt Jay to watch the excitement in Gloria's face. He remembered how, at that age, he had also relished the crumbs of attention his father threw his way.

Father and daughter stepped away in the awkward imitation of a waltz. Jay found himself face-to-face with his new stepmother.

"Well?" She lifted an elegant eyebrow in challenge.

Jay held out his arms, and she came into them as if she thought she belonged.

"Quite a nice step up from the travel agency," Jay remarked, as he swept her around the room. He didn't try to erase the sarcasm from his voice.

She seemed to take stock of him, glancing up at him through narrowed eyes. "Yes, and Carter is such a dear." Her response was guarded.

"Isn't he, though?" Jay mocked her sweet tone of voice.

Her fingers tightened on his shoulders like a snake coiling around its prey. "Don't mess this up for me, Jay."

Jay laughed at her threat. "You're assuming a power that I don't have."

Her lips thinned. They twirled around the room.

"Let me explain something to you," he continued. "I've seen women like you come and go. You think you have a hold on him because the sex is good right now, but don't count on it. I hope you signed a good prenuptial agreement."

"It's different this time," Lori said with a smug glance.

"That's what number four said if I remember correctly."

"You're his only son. Carter values your judgment."

"Carter values my judgment when it's about the newest piece of software I'm working on, one that he hopes will make him another million. He certainly never consults me about his sex life or his choice of wives." The very thought made him smile.

"You're disgusting." Lori's voice was brittle.

"My sentiments exactly." Jay inclined his head toward her. "I've never liked golddiggers."

Almost on cue, the orchestra completed its song. Jay dropped his arms while Lori shot him a menacing look and then turned a sugary smile toward the approaching groom.

"Here we are, dear." Carter gave Gloria back to Jay.

He felt Gloria slip her hand into his and watched as Carter favored them with a smile that never quite reached his eyes. Lori took Carter's offered arm, and tipping up her chin, she looked down her nose at Jay, as if to say, *I'll show you.* Jay looked back blandly as the bride whisked away in a whoosh of satin.

Gloria tugged on his sleeve. "What time is it?"

Jay glanced at his Rolex. "Nine o'clock. I'll take you to the limo."

Holding hands, Jay walked his sister through the historic villa and down the wide steps to the driveway. They waited, drinking in the cool May air, the California sun already shut down for the night. When the limousine arrived, Jay helped Gloria inside and gave her a kiss. All too soon his little sister drove out of his life one more time. He climbed the steps to the Mediterranean mansion, feeling the loss of her small, warm hand in his.

Jay almost turned away from the lighted doorway, his mood bleak, but he shrugged his shoulders and strolled back inside to take a seat near the windows.

Somehow the music now seemed louder, the laughter more discordant. Jay crossed his leg over his knee and leaned back. What was the matter with his father? Why had he been unsatisfied with his mother's love and loyalty? Martha had put Carter through college, for God's sake, sacrificing her own education for his. And she'd loved him silently all through the years, never giving Jay any reason to hate his father. Carter had done that himself.

Sweeping a hand through his hair, Jay narrowed his eyes. For some time now, he had longed for that kind of devotion from a woman, the kind of devotion Martha had for Carter, even until her death. How he would ever know for sure he had inspired that kind of devotion?

The thought hit him like a poorly-pitched baseball. He was Carter Preston's son. Heir to the throne. A rich boy, and all the women he dated knew it.

Jay rubbed his ankle against his knee. He was fair-minded enough to concede being Carter's son had helped pave his way into the software development business. Granted, his father's company paid his large salary and gave him a bunch of perks, but it had been a fair trade. In return Jay had come up with the idea for Sampson, and he'd made himself indispensable to Carter and the growing business.

Jay expelled a deep breath. Who was he kidding? As much as he wanted to deny it, he was still Carter Preston's son. His reputation always preceded him. Women knew about his father's millions. And his own. That knowledge always colored their view of him.

Like the slap of cold air on a frosty morning, Jay realized he might never know the love of a good woman. A woman who would love him for himself. Too many of the women he had dated had resembled his new stepmother. They were after the Preston money, not the Preston man. Jay smiled at the irony. He and his father had more in common than he cared to admit.

Yet, Jay rejected the comparison once more. He refused to believe he was like Carter Preston, chasing the phantom of happiness. Sadly, he would never find his true love as long as he was Carter Preston's son. The realization deepened his foul mood.

"There you are." Carter's booming voice startled him. Jay climbed to his feet. "What are you doing?"

"Thinking."

Carter placed a forceful hand on Jay's shoulder. "Are you ready for the Ballard meeting on Monday? It's your first time to meet with a client alone. I'm sorry I won't be there." His father winked. "I'll be on my honeymoon, you know."

"Obviously." Jay held his gaze steady.

Carter slightly shook his son's shoulder. "You know this is a wonderful opportunity for us."

What was he driving at? "Maybe the meeting is too important for you to miss," Jay suggested.

Carter winked. "And miss my honeymoon?"

"I could use a break too."

"A break?"

"Yes, a vacation. I'm burned out."

"I didn't get a break when I was your age. Worked day and night to put myself through school and then went right into the business," Carter said, his voice intensifying.

Jay broke away from his father's grip and turned to confront him. "And right into the bed of another woman."

Carter frowned. "What kind of crap has your mother fed you?"

"My mother is dead, remember? And she never fed me anything. I've always had two eyes." Jay stood his ground, flexing his fingers.

Carter's eyes narrowed, and his voice lowered. "Have you got something to say to me, boy? What is it?"

"You make me sick," Jay spat. "You run around like some horny tom cat, bedding women, and leaving them when your fancy turns. Furthermore, you don't care about the two children you fathered, or the other lives you hurt."

"Is that all?"

"No." Jay heard the warning in his father's voice, but he couldn't stop himself. "I'm not even sure I like computers, let alone want to spend my whole life developing software systems for your stupid company."

"You ungrateful little bastard," Carter said through clenched teeth.

"Bastard? No. I was born three years after you married my mother. I seriously doubt that I'm the bastard." The audacity of his words shocked even Jay. Yet, a strange exhilaration surged up his spine, and he lifted his chin in defiance.

That's when Carter slugged him. A sudden pain propelled Jay backward. It took less than a second to realize what his father had done, and even less time to maintain his balance and right himself. He glared at the man who had sired him but who had never been a father. Heart in his throat, Jay balled his fist, wanting to strike back. He squared his shoulders.

"I guess the truth hurts," he said quietly.

Lori rushed to her husband's side and now clutched his arm. "Carter, what's wrong?"

Carter stood like stone. The only movement was the flex and release of the hand that had hit his son. There was something in his eyes akin to regret, but whatever it was, he didn't act upon it. Instead, Carter turned to his wife.

"It appears that my son doesn't appreciate the opportunities I have given him." He did not look at Jay. "Since that's the case, I wash my hands of the ungrateful son of a bitch. He'll get no more money from me."

Lori's look of triumph was obvious. Carter turned and drew her away—never looking back.

"He can find out what it's like to make it on his own," Carter said to his new wife loud enough for all to hear.

"If that's the way you want it then build your kingdom without the prince," Jay shouted at the retreating back.

His father's words left him reeling more than the blow to his chin. Had Carter disowned him? A sluggish, fearful pain crawled through his stomach. Jay slowly opened his fist, splaying his fingers out wide.

As suddenly as the fear came to him, Jay experienced a great surge of relief. The protection of the Preston fortune was gone. He had a chance to discover for himself if he could make it on his own merit in a field far away from computers.

Somewhere in the crowd, the bride threw her bouquet. His father didn't know it, but he had just thrown his son a symbolic bouquet. Maybe he could find someone who would love him for himself alone.

For the first time in his life, Jay Preston was free.

Thank You

For purchasing this book from
Saddle Horse Press